All the Luck

by

Kimberly Nee

All the Luck

Cover Art by *The Wild Rose Press, Inc.*

The Wild Rose Press, Inc.
PO Box 708
Adams Basin, NY 14410-0708
Visit us at www.thewildrosepress.com

Publishing History
First Edition, 2023
Trade Paperback ISBN 978-1-5092-5089-9
Digital ISBN 978-1-5092-5088-2

Published in the United States of America

"Told you I saw a coach," the shorter man said, his voice clipped and smooth. Then, he bobbed his head. "Duchess Mary," he said with a smile. "Forgive me my interruption, of course."

"Of course. After all, I'm rather used to them. However," the dowager didn't smile as her blue-gray eyes slid from him to the darker man, "perhaps you might wish to remember your manners, Ioan?"

"Of course. How terribly rude of me." He swung down from his mount, tossing the reins to his friend. "Hold Jupe for me."

"It would be my pleasure."

Sophie's heart hammered against her ribs. No. Her luck was never so good. This man was to be her husband? This tall, broad-shouldered, Greek god of a man? How on earth was he not already married? Surely some well-blooded English miss would have suited him.

The Greek god stood before her now, and up close, she realized his eyes weren't dark at all. No, they were green, actually. A perfectly beautiful shade of green, in fact. A wayward curl spilled over his forehead, right between those thick brows, and he didn't smile as he said, "You must be Miss Montgomery. Welcome to Blackthorne Hall."

She managed to pry her tongue from the roof of her mouth. "Y-yes. Yes, I am."

He caught her hand in his, then lifted that hand to brush the back of it with his lips. "It's a pleasure to meet you. I'm Ioan St. John."

CHAPTER ONE

Blackthorne Hall, Berkshire, England
Autumn, 1892

Ioan St. John studied the paper as the flames devoured it. Ever since he was a boy, fire had fascinated him. Even now, with boyhood far behind him, he was mesmerized by the way the flames blackened the missive's edges, the way those edges curled under, until nothing remained but ash and soot. How unfortunate that his problem wouldn't vanish as easily. How much simpler life would be if it could.

"I've not changed the way I feel about this, Mother." He didn't turn away from the fire crackling merrily on the hearth, satisfied it had done its job. "And I resent that I have no choice, no say, in this matter at all. After all"—now he turned to the woman perched on the settee as if she were the Queen herself—"it is *my* life."

"Stop being so dramatic." The dowager duchess scowled, rapping her walking stick against the Persian carpet beneath her feet. "It certainly doesn't suit."

"Doesn't suit?" He turned away from the fireplace, holding his mother's stare easily as he folded his arms. "No, none of this suits. And yet, here we are."

"And you know why we are here. The estate is failing. Do you truly wish to be remembered as the careless duke who lost everything his family held dear?"

His chest tightened at the accusation in her voice. "I

hadn't realized our financial troubles fell squarely on my shoulders, that it was all *my* fault. Seems to me, it took more than the year that's passed since the title became mine. And really, am *I* to blame for the country's failings? Or because America has found a way to outpace us? Or for my father's shortcomings?"

The dowager's thin lips disappeared as her scowl tightened. "Of course not. Don't be foolish. However"—the black ash cane rapped smartly against the carpet once more—"the responsibility of saving it *does* rest upon your shoulders. And that is why we are where we are today."

"Wonderful." He rubbed his jaw slowly. "And if I cannot tolerate this woman?"

"That hardly matters." With a low groan, the dowager rose from the settee. Although she used the cane mostly for effect, there were times when he thought she needed it more than she preferred to admit, and this was one of those times. It seemed to him she now leaned more heavily on her walking stick. Some of his anger drained as she came up to lay a somewhat gnarled hand on his shoulder. "You don't have to love her, Ioan. You don't even have to like her, if she is truly as insufferable as that. And no one would fault you, should you choose to… to seek comfort elsewhere."

He glanced down at her. The Dowager Duchess of Blackthorne had never been a tall woman, but at one point, the top of her head reached his shoulder. Now, it no longer did. Still, tiny and frail as she might be, she wasn't known as the Iron Duchess for naught, and even as a grown man, he knew to back down when she had her mind set. This was one of those times. He would marry the American woman due any day. He had no choice.

2

Too many people depended on him. His mother would never allow him to back out of this, not when Sophie Montgomery's wealth would save the St. John name and estates.

"Seek comfort elsewhere." He couldn't hold back his bitter laugh. "If Father had done that, you'd have skewered him to the wall with that cane."

"What has you so convinced he didn't?"

"What?"

"Your father and I were fond of one another." The dowager turned to stump back to the settee. "But he was… *insatiable*, as I expect most men are. I gave him his heir. My duty was fulfilled. Our arrangement was mutually beneficial. All I asked was that he be discreet, and he was."

He bit back a groan. This conversation was already awkward, and one he never thought—not in his worst nightmares, actually—he'd have with his *mother* of all people, so he moved around behind the settee. On the piecrust table stood an array of decanters filled with liquors of varying shades of gold from pale honey to rich amber, and this subject matter called for a drink of some sort. Crystal clinked as he tugged the stopper free, then clinked again when the decanter met his glass. "I don't exactly know how to respond to that."

"There is no need to respond at all. I had a boy. He had his heir. I was happy to sleep alone, and he was happy to sleep in London." Her thin shoulders rose in a quick shrug. "I highly doubt he slept alone."

"I'd really rather not know, if it's all the same to you."

"Oh, stop. You are no longer a child, Ioan. You know what is expected of you. You need an heir, and

3

with any luck, you will sire a son and then be allowed to go on your merry way."

"Go on my merry way." The bourbon went down smoothly, so he poured himself another. "And if she doesn't give me a son?"

"Don't be stupid," she admonished sharply. "You will try until you do have one."

"And if we have nothing but girls? Then what?"

"Then, your cousin Charles will inherit, and I'd rather that buffoon not set one foot inside the walls of Blackthorne Hall, if we can possibly avoid it."

He agreed with her. Charles was more of a wastrel than he could ever hope to be, and if he should inherit the dukedom, Ioan had no doubt the Montgomery fortunes would be pissed away in no time and their marriage would be all for naught in the end.

He needed a third drink.

But his mother's frown stopped him. He set the glass back on the silver tray stepping back as Marmaduke stepped up to take the glass away. With a sigh, Ioan moved around the settee once more, this time to sink into his favorite armchair, the one closest to the fire.

Most days, the library was his favorite of Blackthorne Hall's three-hundred-plus rooms. Warm and welcoming, the walls lined with books from floor to ceiling, he spent many a pleasant hour in there, reading, sometimes dozing on one of the comfortable sofas. It was quiet. For the most part, the servants left him in peace, only appearing when needed, disappearing just as quickly.

He could only hope his wife didn't read and wouldn't be comfortable in the library. Did American women even learn to read? He had no idea. He knew very little about Americans as a whole and even less about his soon-to-be fiancée, only that her name was Sophie Montgomery, her family made their vast fortunes in railroads, and their money was too new for New York society's liking. Too new for New York, perfectly acceptable for the Blackthorne coffers. After all, money was money when one looked poverty in the eye.

"Your Grace?" Marmaduke came back into the library. "Lord Pennington to see you."

Thank the Maker. A distraction from the inevitable. "If you will excuse me, Mother."

She waved him off. "Of course. Go." She looked up at Marmaduke. "I will, of course, be staying for dinner."

Ioan turned away before she could see him roll his eyes. Of course she was staying. He had the feeling she would stay in house until the unknown Miss Montgomery arrived and met her approval. And if she didn't approve of the American who was to be her daughter by marriage?

Ioan didn't want to think about it.

So, he resolved not to as he left the library and made his way toward the drawing room, where Stephen Rutledge, the Marquis of Pennington, greeted him with a smile and a boisterous, "Has the future duchess arrived yet?"

"Don't start," he replied. "I'm not in the mood."

"Oh, sweet Jesus." Pennington grimaced. "Is she *that* much of a beast?"

"No! That is…" He gestured to the doors leading from the drawing room to the side entrance, which was the closest point of entry to the stables. "I don't know. She hasn't arrived yet, so I haven't a clue if she is a beast at all. I've not met her yet."

"Come now, old man." Pennington clapped him on the shoulder. "How hideous could she possibly be?"

"She is nearly twenty-five and unmarried. That alone should speak volumes as to how hideous she could be, and it's probably best that I don't keep wondering. I'll know soon enough as it is."

Pennington's grin faded. "True. But then again, you need only make sure the lights are out."

Much as he would have loved to laugh at that, the idea that Pennington might not be far off the mark was enough to squash any bit of humor. He had no idea what this woman looked like, what she sounded like, what she was like at all. All he knew was that her family wanted the title he would give her, and his family needed the money the Montgomerys would pump into his coffers.

Even so, he still didn't want to think about it. He just wanted to lose himself on horseback, preferably relieving Pennington of a few hundred pounds on a wager or two in the process. There would be time enough for ruing the fortune—or lack thereof—bestowed upon him, forcing him into what would most likely be a farce of a marriage. For now, he'd much rather forget it was inevitable.

****

Sophie Montgomery had never shivered as much as she did when the coach rocked along the rutted road that seemed to be leading them into the middle of nowhere. The Berkshire countryside was nothing like back home. It was damp and foreboding, no crowds, no shops, no hustle and bustle of daily life. Nothing at all familiar. And although her family was right there with her, she felt utterly alone. An entirely uncomfortable feeling altogether.

Hot tears poked the backs of her eyes, so she squeezed them shut and turned stubbornly toward the window once more. She didn't want her mother or Edith to see her tears. It would mean another lecture on how wonderful an opportunity this was, how fortunate she was, and how even Joy was so very jealous of the circumstances surrounding their trip to England. *Marriage to a duke*, Joy had said. *Some girls have all the luck.*

Marriage to a duke or confined to spinsterhood. Those were her options, and neither one thrilled her. Ever since her debut, Sophie knew—she just *knew*—one of New York's wealthy bachelors would show interest in her. She need only be patient. In time, it would happen.

But it didn't. As the time went by, and the years passed, the cold, hard truth stared her down with frigid eyes. Not a one of them planned to ask for her hand. At first, she didn't understand it. She might not be a striking beauty, but she certainly wouldn't make anyone's eyes bleed. Plain wasn't ugly. Nor was she uncultured. Her parents exposed her to the opera, to the theatre; they brought in the best tutors to make the finest lady of their only child. She didn't slurp her soup or use the wrong fork, and champagne only went to her head that one time, which surely everyone had forgotten by now.

So, why did she remain unmarried? Why did she spend every party, every cotillion, every social gathering sitting on the side to watch all the other eligible misses get asked to dance, to stroll through a garden, to take a jaunt to Central Park? Why was she always the one left out of everything?

Nouveau Riche. In the eyes of the storied, established members of New York society, the

Montgomery family was new money and therefore not worthy of a second look. They would never be Astors or Vanderbilts. Would never be able to claim illustrious roots or romantic history. There were no alliances with powerful political families, no ties to senators or presidents or royalty in other countries. There was nothing special about her family other than they had become fabulously wealthy thanks to railroads. That was it, and that was *not* enough. They would always be newcomers, their money having come from railroads instead of fur trapping or banking. As new money, there was no possible possible Sophie Montgomery could be acceptable as a daughter-in-law. At least, not as long as other, more suitable women were available.

Coming to England had been her mother, Emily's idea. She'd heard of other young ladies who'd made successful marriages with the sons of England's nobility. And when she'd found the Duke of Blackthorne listed in *Titled Americans*, she was almost giddy at the thought of having a nobleman for a son-in-law. Especially a duke. Why settle for an earl or a marquis—whatever *that* was—when she could have a duke in her family? It had taken months of negotiations between Sophie's father, Randolph, and the duke himself to finalize the arrangements, and Sophie had no idea how much of a dowry her father offered, but whatever the amount, it was obviously enough, as they disembarked in London that morning and now headed toward some place called Blackthorne Hall.

She tried not to shiver at the ominous-sounding name. Perhaps it was nowhere near as dark and foreboding as it sounded. Perhaps it was the opposite, airy and welcoming, surrounded by lush lawns and beautiful gardens. It certainly had to have more foliage around it than her family's house in New York City, with its small gardens and manicured lawns. England already looked so much more open, more like her family's estate outside of the city.

Don't think about that, she chided herself.

She swallowed hard as they made a sharp turn onto a rocky drive. In the distance, a gray blur took shape. A house. As they drew nearer and the house grew larger, it loomed over them as if to warn her just how dark and gloomy life could be.

It was far grander and more imposing than any house she'd seen, and to even call it a house seemed to do it an injustice. But what else should one call the place? So, house it was, and it was immense—four stories and all dark, mossy stone. It would block out the sun, if the sun chose to come out from beneath its blanket of iron-gray clouds. As the coach rolled closer to the entrance, Sophie swore the air grew chillier, and when they finally stopped, she peered up at the rows of windows. How many rooms did it have? It looked more like one of the fine hotels in New York than someone's home.

The door opened, and her father, Randolph, said, "Here we go." He reached across the coach to pat her hand. "Try not to look so frightened, Soph. I'm sure the duke is nowhere near as austere as this building. He came across as fairly personable in his correspondence."

She managed a smile. "I hope not. This looks more like a museum. I do hope they give me a sack of colored rocks or breadcrumbs or something; otherwise I might never find my way from one room to the next."

He chuckled, which earned him a glower from his wife, to which he said, "Smile, Emily. I promise, your face will not crack."

"This is hardly a joking matter," she replied crisply, gesturing to the window. "The entire staff is waiting for us. See for yourself."

Sophie leaned forward, and her stomach twisted at the sight of all the men and women in livery, lined up silently along the edge of the drive. That twist worsened as a frail-looking old woman, dressed in exquisitely beautiful aubergine silk, stepped out as well, leaning heavily on a walking stick. No one smiled. They all appeared stiff and stoic.

"Is one of those men the duke?" Sophie asked as a footman came over and pulled open the door.

Neither her mother nor her father replied, and she didn't get the chance to repeat her question as her father said, "Out you get, Soph."

She did just that, resisting the urge to shiver as she stepped out into the damp chill of an English autumn afternoon. An older woman, dressed in staid gray linen, came around. "Good afternoon, Miss Montgomery. I am Mrs. Hopkins, the housekeeper." She turned a kind smile to Sophie's parents. "Mr. and Mrs. Montgomery, welcome to Blackthorne Hall."

Sophie managed to return the smile even as her gut churned and bubbled. "It's a pleasure to meet you, Mrs. Hopkins."

"Come and allow me to introduce you to Her Grace, the Dowager Duchess of Blackthorne."

Sophie's mouth went dry as she glanced back at her mother, who gestured for her to follow the housekeeper. Without thinking, Sophie blurted, "What exactly *is* a dowager duchess, anyway? Is she the duke's sister?"

She hoped not. No one told her much about the

duke, but she'd assumed he was closer in age to her than to her parents. Her belly flipped. She'd never given any thought that her parents might be marrying her off to an old man.

The very idea made her queasy, even as the housekeeper offered up a patient smile. "It's quite simple. She was the duchess until her son inherited. As his mother, she is now the dowager." Mrs. Hopkins's blue eyes were friendly as she looked back once more. "And once you and His Grace are married, *you* will become the duchess."

That sounded so formal, not to mention odd, to her American ears. "I will?"

"Yes, Miss Montgomery. After all," she added with a hint of patronizing, "you *will* be married to a duke."

"So many things to remember," Sophie mumbled, forcing a smile to her face as they drew near the old woman. With a sudden chill, Sophie realized she had no idea how to address a duchess, never mind a dowager duchess. What if she somehow inadvertently insulted her?

Mrs. Hopkins smiled. "Your Grace, this is Miss Montgomery. Miss Montgomery, Her Grace, the Dowager Duchess of Blackthorne."

Sophie managed to smile. "It is a pleasure to meet you, Your Grace."

The dowager bobbed her head ever so slightly. "And it is a pleasure to meet you as well, Miss Montgomery. Allow me to apologize for my son. He—"

With that, two men on horseback came thundering up the drive and Sophie didn't miss how the dowager's lips disappeared into a thin, white line for a moment. She turned back as the riders stopped and at that moment, her mind went entirely blank and she forgot how to speak.

Since she'd yet to actually *meet* the duke, she didn't know which man *was* the duke. But, she wasn't so certain it would matter much, as both men were a sight to behold. Both were strikingly handsome, reminding her of the Greek gods she'd read about on rainy afternoons at Willow Point. From a distance, they resembled one another and her first thought was that they were brothers.

But as they neared, it was easy to see they were most likely *not* related. Both were dark haired. Both were handsome, but their features weren't the same at all. One had an easy smile and blue eyes that even now danced with mischief. He smiled, not at all embarrassed by their loud entrance. It was easy to see he was the more jovial of the two and a slightly shorter than his compatriot.

Oh, but the taller one! He was darker than his compatriot, with a windblown mop of curly dark hair, and smoldering dark eyes beneath thick dark brows. His face wasn't as angular as his companions, but far bolder and infinitely more perfect.

"Told you I saw a coach," the shorter man said, his voice clipped and smooth. Then, he bobbed his head. "Duchess Mary," he said with a smile. "Forgive me my interruption, of course."

"Of course. After all, I'm rather used to them. However," the dowager didn't smile as her blue-gray eyes slid from him to the darker man, "perhaps you might wish to remember your manners, Ioan?"

"Of course. How terribly rude of me." He swung down from his mount, tossing the reins to his friend. "Hold Jupe for me."

"It would be my pleasure."

Sophie's heart hammered against her ribs. No. Her

luck was never so good. *This* man was to be her husband? This tall, broad-shouldered, Greek god of a man? How on earth was he not already married? Surely some well-blooded English miss would have suited him.

The Greek god stood before her now, and up close, she realized his eyes weren't dark at all. No, they were green, actually. A perfectly beautiful shade of green, in fact. A wayward curl spilled over his forehead, right between those thick brows, and he didn't smile as he said, "You must be Miss Montgomery. Welcome to Blackthorne Hall."

She managed to pry her tongue from the roof of her mouth. "Y-yes. Yes, I am."

He caught her hand in his, then lifted that hand to brush the back of it with his lips. "It's a pleasure to meet you. I'm Ioan St. John."

"It's a pleasure to meet you, Your Grace." Pride surged through her. She didn't stammer. At least, she didn't stammer much. She was also confident she didn't blush, either. There was still hope for her. Thank heavens for small favors.

He straightened up, still unsmiling, and looked over at her father. "Mr. Montgomery, Mrs. Montgomery, I am pleased to meet you as well, and welcome to Blackthorne Hall. I trust you will be made to feel at home."

Sophie bit the inside of her cheek as her mother went scarlet at the duke's warm welcome. "I—thank you, Your Grace. It is a pleasure to meet you as well." She looked over at Sophie's father. "Isn't it?"

Her father bobbed his head. "Absolutely it is, yes."

Ioan offered up a slight smile at that, then turned to his mother. "Perhaps we might go inside, where it's warmer." As he spoke, a soft rain began pattering down, so he added, "And dryer. Pennington, you are welcome to join us as well."

Two of the footmen stepped up to take the horses' reins as the other man climbed down, offering a pleasant, "Good day," to Sophie's mother and father as they brought up the rear.

The inside of Blackthorne Hall was no warmer or more welcoming than the exterior. Sophie's boot heels echoed against the marble beneath them, and when she looked down, her heart sank at how chipped the dingy white marble appeared. At least, she thought it was supposed to be white. It was really quite difficult to tell, seeing as how yellowed it had become.

The air felt even heavier, damper, than it had outside, and she drew her traveling cloak tighter about her shoulders as she trailed along behind the duke, who had fallen into step with his mother ahead of them all. She couldn't help but notice how he towered over the dowager, all broad shoulders and wide back, and as her gaze wandered lower, her cheeks grew warm. His buff-colored trousers fit him perfectly.

Oh, my...

Her thought made her cheeks warmer still and she held her breath, waiting for God to smite her for her lustful thoughts.

But no lightning sliced through Blackthorne Hall, of course. Even so, she couldn't quite make herself look away just yet.

"Wouldn't you say?"

The duke's voice caught her and she jerked her head up to find him staring over his shoulder, one brow slightly raised, and heat flooded her. "I—I beg your pardon?"

"I was just asking how travel across the Atlantic was. I haven't been abroad since I was a boy myself, but I do remember it being quite tedious. Was it for you?"

If he knew why she stared, he gave no indication of it. Still, he awaited her answer, so she nodded. "Yes, actually. I found it to be very tedious. Although," she glanced at her mother and father, who followed her side by side, "it was a lovely ship."

"Good." The duke smiled and at that moment, Sophie agreed with Joy.

Some girls did have all the luck.

CHAPTER TWO

Sophie had never seen anything at all like Blackthorne Hall. If she'd thought the exterior imposing, that was nothing compared to its interior. The entry led to an immense, open hallway, with a ceiling that gave new meaning to the word *vaulted*. Everywhere she looked, she saw history—from the artwork on the walls, to the furnishings, to the beautiful Persian carpeting beneath her feet. It was all dark wood and pale frescoes, no gilt or stained glass like in her family's home in New York. It seemed everything at Willow Point was designed by Tiffany, sparkling and gilded, while here, everything was dark and quietly proud in its heritage.

"Isn't this lovely!" Her mother elbowed her sharply in the ribs.

Sophie nodded. "It's quite lovely, Mother."

"I mean, it isn't quite as… brilliant… as back home, but it's still very nice."

"Mother!" Sophie rolled her eyes as both the duke and the dowager duchess looked back at them.

The dowager sniffed. "The Blackthorne Dukedom was created in the sixteenth century, under Queen Elizabeth. A good deal of the furnishings date back to that first duke."

Heat crept into Sophie's cheeks. "I beg your pardon, Your Grace. She meant no harm, of course," she replied, glaring at her mother, who shrugged. "It is simply a matter of differing tastes."

The duke slowed his pace, falling into step alongside her. "It would seem your mother prefers shiny to serene."

The heat in Sophie's cheeks worsened. "I think it probably is simply a matter of what she is accustomed to seeing. Wealth is measured differently in the States."

"So I've heard," he replied easily. "Americans are far more enthralled by shiny and sparkling than by anything of historical substance. Wealth is measured by gilt and not by heritage."

"Now, that isn't entirely fair, Your Grace," she replied evenly, trying not to let her irritation get the best of her. "You know nothing about our heritage at all."

"I know enough." He shot her a long look. "Such as all the gilt in the world cannot buy manners or grace."

Sophie stopped dead in her tracks. "I beg your pardon?"

"Was I not clear?" he asked, his eyes wide with innocence she was certain was feigned. "I beg your pardon. I thought I was."

"You were perfectly clear, and quite hypocritical, I might add. Mocking a lack of perceived manners is hardly gracious at all."

He winked and resumed his stride, calling, "Touché, Miss Montgomery. Touché."

She glared at his back as he fell into step alongside his mother. Was he simply making sport of her, or was he truly offended by her mother's words? It was so damn difficult to tell and she didn't know him well enough to guess. Good heavens, all of her mother's talk about good impressions and then *she's* the one to insult the duke *and* his mother *and* their history, practically in one sentence.

Wonderful.

"I do believe His Grace has met his match."

The low voice came from her right and she stared up at the dark-haired man beside her now. "I beg your pardon, Mr. Pennington?"

His blue eyes danced as he shook his head. "No need to beg my pardon, Miss Montgomery. I think it grand that the old boy has met his match in you. You will be good for him. Just promise me you won't throttle him *before* the wedding night." He winked. "I'd hate to see him die before... well... I should hate to see him die, period, actually."

"I assure you," she replied in the sweetest voice she could muster, "His Grace is in no danger of a premature demise at *my* hands."

"Oh, good. And promise me something else?"

She bit back a sigh. It was so difficult to tell if any of the English were mocking her, making sport of her, or were genuinely interested in anything she had to say. "And what might that something be?"

"When the time comes, don't make him beg, no matter how much he might deserve it."

"Beg?" She narrowed her eyes at him. "Beg for what?"

"Any part of you. You should, of course, make it difficult at first. After all, one cannot enjoy something if it is merely *given* to him. And on your wedding night... well... make him work for your attentions. I promise you," he winked "he will."

Heat swept through her to leave her feeling bright red. Part of her was horrified by his words, and the other part was thoroughly embarrassed. Perhaps it was that they were men, or that they were Englishmen in particular, but this hardly seemed an appropriate conversation to have with any woman, let alone the woman the duke was to marry eventually, the first time you've met her.

But before she could scold Pennington for his cheek, he let out a chuckle and sped up to join the duke and dowager once more.

"Miss Montgomery, what was *that* all about?"

Sophie looked over at her maid, Edith, and shook her head. "I haven't the foggiest. The English are a strange lot at times, it would seem."

"I'd watch out for that one, if I were you," the maid replied, glowering at Pennington's back. "I don't trust him one whit."

"Well, neither do I and fortunately, I'm not expected to spend much time in his company, I'll wager."

"Good. He looks like trouble." Edith reached out to smooth her hand down Sophie's right arm. "Of course, your duke looks as if he could stir up some trouble as well."

"He does, but in a good way."

"Miss Montgomery!"

"What?" Sophie couldn't hold back her smile. "He's a bit blunt, perhaps, a bit rude, but he *is* handsome, don't you think?"

"I do. And he knows he is and that women think so as well."

Yes, Sophie thought with an inward sigh. He probably *did* know it. She wasn't sure if that was good or bad. At the moment, she just wanted to stop feeling like an unwelcome house guest, as if she was an intruder who should just go away and leave them all in peace.

The duke and dowager led them down the long corridor, and into what had to be the largest library

Sophie had ever seen. Floor to ceiling windows along the eastern wall let in the graying light of the drizzly afternoon, and the fires crackling on the two hearths offered up a cozy welcome.

Bookshelves stretched to the ceiling, each lined with more leather-bound books than she'd ever seen in her life. Sofas covered in elegant burgundy velvet were tucked here and there, as were leather-upholstered wing chairs, and near each stood a table of cherry wood, each table holding a spray of beautiful flowers.

"This is the family library," the dowager said, gesturing broadly with both hands. "Miss Montgomery, you are, of course, welcome to peruse at your leisure. However, if you do choose to take out a book, there is a register over there," she pointed toward the corner nearest the windows, almost directly in line with the doorway, "in which we catalog the titles as they come and go."

"Of course, Your Grace." Sophie smiled as she moved to the shelves just behind the stand holding the register. "These are all so lovely," she breathed, her eyes wandering over the gold-stamped titles. Most were books she'd never heard of, some looked downright boring, but then one author caught her eye. "Charles Dickens… I adore Dickens."

"Do you?" The dowager's voice rang with approval. "Have you a favorite?"

She turned back to find the duke, the dowager, and Pennington all seated on two of the damask sofas, while her mother and father perched on the other. "I do, actually. *A Christmas Carol*."

The dowager looked as if she was about to smile, but it never quite materialized. "I prefer *Oliver Twist*, myself."

"I quite enjoyed that as well." Sophie looked from the dowager to the duke. "Do you read Dickens, Your Grace?"

He looked up. "I beg your pardon?"

"I asked if you like Dickens."

Pennington snorted. "I'm not so certain he can even read, Miss Montgomery."

"Don't be a dolt," Ioan snapped, then turned to her with a smile. "I don't *dis*like Dickens, but I'm much more an outdoorsman, if you will."

"He likes to ride horses and to discuss riding horses and read about horses. But, don't even *think* to suggest a hunt, Miss Montgomery. He will lecture you until your ears blister," Pennington supplied.

"Thank you for that sterling summation, Pennington," the dowager broke in dryly. "If you've nothing constructive to add, I suggest you keep your observations silent."

Pennington had the good grace to blush at that, much to Sophie's surprise. His pale cheeks flushed a dull dark red, the color stretching up to disappear into his hairline. "I beg your pardon, Your Grace."

"Now," the dowager turned back to Sophie, "what else do you read?"

"Sophie reads anything and everything she might get her hands on!" Emily's voice boomed all throughout the library, much to Sophie's horror. "Why, back home, we have to hide her brother's law books, or else she'd read those as well."

To her chagrin, Sophie's grew hot as everyone in the room stared at her. Her mother meant well, but Sophie wished the elegant Persian carpet beneath them would simply open up and swallow her whole. That feeling intensified when the dowager asked, "Law books?" with no little surprise.

Her cheeks burned as she slowly nodded. "I was curious about something and wanted to look it up."

"So, your son," the dowager turned back to Emily, "is a solicitor?"

"He is and he is employed by one of the finest law firms in New York!" Randolph boomed. "Blatchford, Seward, and Griswold, to be precise."

Both the duke and dowager smiled politely but were clearly unimpressed by this. Pennington hid a grin behind his hand, but not before Sophie saw it, and the urge to kick him as hard as possible in the shin surged through her. Clearing her throat, she said, "It is a very well-respected law firm in New York. Mr. Seward was Secretary of State, and Mr. Blatchford became a Supreme Court justice, so it was a great accomplishment for Samuel to be offered a position with them."

The duke sat forward. "It certainly sounds it." He glanced from his mother to her mother, then added, "Would you care to take a tour of the grounds, Miss Montgomery? It looks as if we've a break in the weather."

He most likely offered as a way to keep an already uncomfortable situation from growing worse. Or perhaps he needed some fresh air. Whatever the reason, Sophie was grateful for the excuse to get away from the now-too-warm library and so she smiled. "I would, Your Grace. Thank you."

"Are you so certain that is wise?" Emily asked, her forehead creasing. She looked first at Randolph and then at the dowager. "Does Sophie need a chaperone?"

"I don't think you need worry about such things," the dowager replied. "There are no prying eyes at Blackthorne Hall, and they will, after all, be married, so it's rather a moot point."

"I understand, but still—"

"Everything will be fine, Mother," Sophie broke in as she got to her feet.

Pennington also made to rise. "I will make certain they keep out of trouble, Your Grace."

The dowager rolled her eyes. "You stay where you are, Pennington," she told him with a firm rap of her walking stick against the carpet. "I can assure you, Ioan needs no assistance escorting Miss Montgomery about the grounds."

The duke gestured toward the far end of the library. "This way leads to the gardens. Not much is blooming, I'm afraid, but the view is still a lovely one."

Sophie shook her head as she followed him. "I don't think I'll mind. I love how the leaves look when they change colors this time of year."

"Then come with me, Miss Montgomery. You'll see England is not necessarily so very different from New York."

CHAPTER THREE

Fortunately, the rain had abated, for the most part, but it was still so chilly. Sophie tugged her cloak tighter, which did not go unnoticed by the duke.

"We don't have to remain out here, if you're uncomfortable," he said, glancing down at her.

"It's no trouble, Your Grace." She managed to smile even as a shiver tickled along her spine. He seemed friendlier now, looked a bit more at ease out from beneath his mother's watchful, steely-eyed gaze and her mother's blunt tongue. Their breaths puffed out in white clouds of vapor, and the duke's pale cheeks grew ruddy in only a few minutes. "Weren't you cold while you were riding?" she asked.

"Cold?" He shook his head. "No, not at all. I tend to forget about the weather, be it good or bad, when I'm on horseback. It's a bit of freedom for me, to be able to venture where no one can find me for a while."

"Except"—she glanced back at Blackthorne Hall, where she could just make out Mr. Pennington in the doorway—"for your friend." She looked up. "He seems put out that he wasn't invited."

The duke's shoulders rose in a lazy shrug. "He'll get over it."

"The two of you are close?"

"We are. We've known each other since we were children, and he's like a brother to me." The duke gestured toward the western line of trees. "Pennington House is just beyond those woods."

The leaves had begun their transformation, red and gold dotted the horizon. In the distance, she could just make out the black shape she assumed was Pennington House. It looked so small, but she had the feeling it was probably just as grand as Blackthorne Hall up close. "Are they your closest neighbors?"

He nodded. "They are. Come." He guided her around the skeleton of what would most likely be a lovely rose bush come spring. "This path heads toward the orangery."

"Orangery?"

"You'll see. You'll like it. It's warmer in there than it is out here."

"Then yes, I probably will like it." Her hands, clasped inside the fox muff she carried, were warm and cozy. Overhead, leaden gray skies threatened to open up on them once more, and the wind bared its teeth to nip at them as they wound their way along the garden path. "Have you neighbors to the east as well?"

"We do, but they are seldom there. The countess prefers London, so that's where they live mostly." He glanced down at her hands, buried inside the muff. "Are you so terribly cold?"

"It's the dampness, really. Back home, it's cold this time of the year, but far drier."

"We can return to the house, if you wish."

She shook her head. "You promised me colorful trees, Your Grace. And I'm still so very curious about the orangery."

"Please, I do wish you would call me Ioan."

Sophie glanced up at him. "I could never be so

informal."

"Of course you could," he replied, pausing to turn toward her. "I promise you, I won't mind and I won't scold you about it in front of anyone."

"I just don't think I could." She shook her head. "Although, I must confess, it's lovely, if a bit unusual."

"It's Welsh," he replied. "My grandfather was from Wales."

"Was he the duke before your father?"

The duke shook his head. "No, this is my mother's father. She's the Welsh arm of the family, although she doesn't like to admit it. She'd much rather be fully English."

"She sounds like my father. He has a French ancestor, and it drives him mad, though I don't know why. It isn't as if France is our enemy or anything, but he doesn't like to think about it."

"The English and the French have a bit of a colorful history between them, so perhaps that's why."

"I know, but in recent times, things have been peaceful. I think he feels we'd be more... acceptable... back home if he didn't have French blood. It makes me think someone has said something to that effect to him, but I don't know." She sighed softly, rubbing her left thumb against her right. "The funny thing is, I never cared whether we were considered equals with those in society back home. It's only their opinion, and they aren't happy unless they have someone to look down upon."

"And that is how you ended up here, isn't it?"

She looked up at him once more. His cheeks were ruddier still, and dark curls spilled over his forehead. "I know why you wish to marry me, Your Grace, if that's what you mean."

The winds kicked up, sending those curls fluttering up before they came to rest over his forehead once more. "Was it kept secret from you? I mean, until you arrived?"

"No." She fought down the urge to sigh. "I've known since Papa returned to New York with your proposal in hand. I know this is no love match, and I know why you're settling for an American girl instead of taking an English bride."

"It isn't personal, Miss Montgomery," he replied softly. "And I don't dislike you or resent your being here. I hope you know that."

She peered up at him, her heart beating faster as the questions took shape in her mind. "But, you aren't happy about the circumstances, are you? That's the feeling I get from you."

Although she phrased it as a question, she knew the answer before she even asked it. Even so, her spirits sank as his eyes widened briefly and then he shook his head. "I'd be lying if I said otherwise, I'm afraid."

Sophie turned her gaze down, to the small stones beneath her shoes. His answer was expected, but that didn't mean it didn't sting to hear out loud. "Thank you, Your Grace, for being honest with me." She managed to meet his eyes and forced a smile to her lips. "I appreciate that."

He sighed softly. "I apologize if I've said something I shouldn't, but I have no desire to see you hurt because you've been led to believe something that simply isn't true. I would have preferred to remain a bachelor, truth be told, but since that isn't possible—"

"Please." She tugged one hand from the muff to hold up. Anything to halt his speech. Each word stung more than the last. "Don't. I appreciate honesty, but—"

"I've done it again." He turned away and raked one hand through his hair, then let it come down to slap against his thigh. His expression grew pained, a hint of rising red along his cheekbones. "Miss Montgomery, I see no reason for us to be enemies, not when this marriage is going to take place sooner rather than later.

"But at the same time, I cannot pretend there is anything more here than a business arrangement. One we will both benefit from. My family is saved from financial ruin, and you have a title and a place here, in our society. You will most likely find more doors opening to you in New York as well."

"We both benefit..." She couldn't get her voice above a whisper. Although she knew before they even left New York that this was no love match, Sophie had let herself dream that maybe—just maybe—the Duke of Blackthorne would take one look at her and fall madly in love with her, the way it happened in those silly novels Joy always hounded her to read.

But this was no silly novel, and this duke was not about to drop to his knees to pledge his undying love to her. He needed her family's money. That was all, and there was nothing wrong with that. She certainly wasn't the only young woman to travel to England for the same reason. Why, she and Joy knew at least two other women, wealthy beyond belief but not up to society's standards, who'd come to London as well. Both had married earls. She was no different.

Except she was. Completely different.

With a sigh, she looked up at him. A handsome duke out of a love story, and he wanted her only for her family's wealth. Nothing personal, mind you. But also, not something he wanted, either.

This was *not* how the story was supposed to go.

Tucking her free hand back into the muff, she said, "I do appreciate the honesty, Your Grace. It's a nice change from what I've become used to."

However, he didn't look at all mollified by her words. His forehead creased, his expression darkened. "Miss Montgomery, I…"

With a whisper of wind, rain fell once more, so she cleared her throat. "Perhaps it would be best if we went back inside. The orangery will keep for another time."

"Miss Montgomery—"

She didn't let him finish, but turned heel to make her way back inside Blackthorne Hall. The library felt only slightly warmer than the outdoors, but at least she could use the cold as an excuse for her red nose and watery eyes. As she slipped her hands free from the fox muff, she said, "Would anyone mind if I moved closer to the fire? The rain and wind have left me nearly frozen."

She didn't wait for a reply, but set the muff on the sofa, and moved closer to the hearth. The warmth felt wonderful against her outstretched hands. Her eyes watered again as she stared down at the dancing flames, but she managed to hold back the tears. Why the deuce was she crying? She cared no more for the duke than he cared for her, so it wasn't as if he'd broken her heart.

Perhaps it was because she hadn't expected him to be… well… *him*. She hadn't expected to find a veritable Greek god in soggy, cloudy England. Somehow, a marriage of convenience would be so much easier if the duke were plain or even homely.

But he wasn't. He was the sort of a man a girl fancied meeting—tall, dark, handsome. With broad shoulders. Beautiful green eyes. Lips that looked as if they knew their way around a kiss or two.

Her spine stiffened. *What*? Where the deuce had *that* come from as well?

She bit back a sigh as she flexed her fingers. Back home, her family was considered *nouveau riche,* and as new money, the old society families saw them as interlopers. Because of that, the older families didn't consider the Montgomery family as being one of their kind, as social equals, and that meant Sophie's marital prospects were somewhat dim. The scions of the high society families would never be given permission to marry her, and the men whose families *did* find her acceptable would never be acceptable as far as her own family was concerned. Which left her in a very precarious situation, indeed.

When her mother first broached the subject, Sophie had her hesitations. It seemed cold and calculating, marrying a man she'd never met, never mind a man she didn't even love, Somehow, she always thought she would be madly in love with the man she married. At the very least, she would know his name, if nothing else. Either way, this was not quite what she'd expected.

Pennington broke into her reverie. "Where is Blackthorne?" he asked, his forehead creasing as he turned to look toward the door. Without thinking, Sophie turned toward the doorway as well, just in time to see Blackthorne round the corner.

"He is right here," the duke replied, raking a hand through his hair once more as he strode to the far corner, nearest the windows. He tugged a thick braid of dark green cord that hung just beyond the draperies, and a few minutes later, the library doors opened and Mrs. Brewer bustled in.

"You rang, Your Grace?"

"I did," he replied. "Please have water heated for both Miss Montgomery and me." He brushed water from first his left sleeve, and then his right. "It's downright miserable out there, and I'm chilled to the bone. And I'd wager Miss Montgomery is as well."

To Sophie's surprise, the duke offered up a smile aimed at her as he said this and although it didn't change how his earlier words stung, it still did something odd to her insides, made them twist and dance in an unfamiliar step. Unfamiliar, but not entirely uncomfortable, either.

She managed to smile back. "A bath *would* be appreciated."

Mrs. Brewer nodded. "I will see to it at once, Your Grace." She turned to Sophie. "Please come with me, Miss Montgomery, and I will show you to your room."

Sophie's spirits sank as she followed the housekeeper out of the library and down the shadowy corridor to the elaborately carved main staircase. Everything about Blackthorne was beautiful and elegant, and with every step, she felt more and more out of place. For the first time in a long time, she was homesick and wanted more than anything to go back to New York.

****

30 October, 1892

Dearest Joy,

Remember when I first told you about Papa's plan to marry into the English aristocracy, and we joked about my becoming a princess? Well, here we are, and let me assure you, it isn't exactly *as we thought it would be. Not entirely, anyway.*

I've met the Duke of Blackthorne, who is perhaps

the handsomest man I've ever laid eyes upon. You would have to see him to believe him, Joy, for he is that *beautiful. He's tall, well over six feet, I'd imagine, with dark curly hair and the broadest shoulders I have ever seen. He makes Duncan Fellows look like Tiny Tim! His eyes are green—a strikingly beautiful shade of green, to boot, not that it matters, and he has a lovely smile. He looks so dark and foreboding, but he is really quite the gentleman. We went for a walk through the gardens— which was odd, seeing as how most everything is dead for the winter—and he took such great pride in everything having to do with Blackthorne Hall. I have much to learn about his history, and the history of both his dukedom and his country.*

I wish I could say it was all wonderful, Joy. Really, I do. But the truth of the matter is I feel so out of place, and as if I'm being made sport of to boot. Not by His Grace—he says I am to call him Ioan, but I cannot bring myself to be so informal. What will his mother think? What will Mother and Papa think??—but by a friend of his. Mr. Pennington. I know that isn't quite what his name is, but the English and their titles make so little sense to me, I'm afraid I'll never *get it right!*

Mr. Pennington is a marquis, and I have precious little idea what that even means, but his rank is below His Grace's (who himself is only just below royalty, if you might believe that!) but they are good friends, so they call each other Pennington *and* Blackthorne. *Now, to my face, Mr. Pennington is quite charming. But, at one point, I'd fallen behind His Grace and Mr. Pennington, but not so far behind that I didn't hear Mr. Pennington refer to me as a* quaint colonial. *As if I was a pet in a shop. His Grace told him to mind himself, but I cannot help but wonder if he feels that way as well.*

It's cold and rainy here. And this house, if one can even call it a house, is much more like a museum. The Metropolitan Museum of Art is far cozier and less imposing! But, for all its grandness, it's quite damp and drafty. As I write this, my fingers are numb from the cold, but if I move closer to the fire, I'm afraid I'll char.

I miss you, Joy, and look forward to hearing from you. Give everyone my best—and don't let Duncan know I think he's much like Tiny Tim.

Yours always,

Soph.

Sophie set down her pen and let out a soft sigh. Rain pattered the windowpanes, and every now and again, droplets sizzled on the hearth. The flames continued to dance merrily, but it was only too bad the heat didn't venture much past the hearthrug. Her fingers were, indeed, very cold.

To her dismay, there was no indoor heated running water. Instead, she had to wait while water heated on the fire and was then brought up to the small tub in the equally small bathing chamber. Not like back home, where heated running water was the standard in most homes along her street. She couldn't imagine her father having buckets of hot water brought up for his bath. It simply would never do. But here, it was practically the Stone Age, and she had never realized how long it took to heat water.

Despite the chill, her room was really rather lovely. Done in shades of pale blue and green, with moss green draperies and bed hangings. The bed was enormous, taking up what seemed like most of the room, and there was a cozy bench built into the windowsill overlooking the back lawns. Rain pattered softly against the mullioned panes and, every so often, hissed into the crackling fire. She might not like the primitive bathing methods, and the damp chill left much to be desired, but all in all, she found the accommodations lovely.

By the time her bath was ready, she was almost too tired to care. Yet, she found her way into the tub, and when she finished and crawled into bed, she was asleep before her head hit the pillow.

CHAPTER FOUR

The storm blew out during the night, and when Sophie opened her eyes, the sun took her by surprise, as it was the first time in days that the rain had stopped. It did much to lift her spirits as she swung her legs over the side of the bed and eased down. The marble beneath her feet was cold, and she couldn't hold back her yelp as the chill bit into the soles of her feet.

"Miss Montgomery?" Edith bustled into the room. "Is everything all right?"

"It's fine, Edith. I wasn't expecting it to be so cold." Sophie laughed at her own foolishness as she eased her feet into the slippers she'd left beside the bed. "I'm just so happy to see it's stopped raining."

Edith smiled as she moved to draw back the heavy midnight blue draperies. Sunlight splashed across the floor and drenched the foot of the bed, and Sophie's smile widened as she moved to stand at the windows. Her room overlooked the lush, sprawling rear grounds of Blackthorne Hall. In the distance, she spied a pond, or perhaps it was a lake; it was difficult to tell from her vantage point. Either way, it looked to be some distance away. The trees were almost bare by now, but she had the feeling that, come spring, they would create a lush canopy and provide lovely shade for an afternoon stroll.

The wardrobe doors squeaked behind her. The fabric rustled as Edith dug through the dresses Sophie had brought from home, but Sophie paid that little heed as she gazed down at the vast lawns. From her window, she saw the ballroom, almost as grand as Blackthorne Hall itself, running along the rear wall of the western wing. The ballroom's back wall was all glass, glinting even in the soft morning light. She could only imagine what it would be like at night, all softly lit and filled with festive partygoers. Although the society mothers would never allow one of their sons to marry her, they had no trouble inviting the Montgomery family to any and all events. It was almost as if they wanted to flaunt their wealth, their status, before her family, to make them wish—to yearn, actually—to be part of that world in its entirety. Well, perhaps she would never be in their world, but the time would come when they would all wish they could be even a spectator in *her* world.

"Duchess of Blackthorne," she murmured, tracing her fingertips along the rippled glass windowpane. "Edith? Will I be Lady Sophie St. John? Or perhaps Lady Blackthorne?" She frowned, turning away from the windows. "It's all very confusing."

All she saw of her maid was Edith's backside, and the maid's voice was muffled as she replied, "I haven't the foggiest, Miss Sophie. I could ask below at breakfast."

"You're dining with their servants?"

"Oh, yes." Edith backed out of the wardrobe, exhaling to blow a wayward coppery curl out of her eyes. "I have been since we arrived. Although I find it odd, how they address me as Montgomery. Apparently, that's the custom here, but it sounds so… jarring, to me. Still, they're lovely people, the lot of them. They think very highly of His Grace."

"I can see that. He seems a pleasant sort to work for."

"You don't sound as if that makes you happy."

"Why should it make me either happy or unhappy?" She turned back to the windows. Although the light grew brighter as it stretched across the lawns, her rising spirits felt deflated. "I won't be in his employ."

"Well, I took it to mean he is a nice man, and if he is decent to his employees, I would imagine—"

"He will be decent to his wife?" Sophie finished for her, shaking her head. "Edith, I know I'm supposed to be happy with that, but the truth of the matter is that I would rather my husband *not* be merely decent to me."

"Decent is a place to start, Miss Sophie," Edith replied softly, closing the wardrobe door with a resolute bang. "If you were expecting him to topple head over heels in love upon seeing you for the first time, I could have told you that you'd be disappointed. He doesn't even know you, how could he possibly love you already?"

Edith was right, but that didn't stop Sophie from scowling at her. "Thank you very much, Edith. That is just what I needed to hear."

"Miss Sophie, all I meant was—"

"I know what you meant." Sophie turned back to the windows. "You may go now. I'll have my breakfast up here, if you would fetch it for me."

"Of course, Miss Sophie."

Sophie ignored the hints of hurt along the bottom of Edith's words as she moved to slip back beneath the velvet coverlet once more. As she sank into the pillows, a heavy sigh bubbled to her lips. Now she owed Edith an apology on top of everything. Not to mention, Sophie felt stupid, and no one liked feeling stupid. Yes, she supposed on some level she *had* hoped the duke would take one look at her and swoon. How romantic would that be? It would make the entire marriage of convenience so much more palatable to her.

On the voyage across the Atlantic, she entertained herself by imagining the scene—he would look at her, and a slow smile would creep across his face. Adoration would glint in his eyes. He would hang on every word she spoke. Then he would swoon.

Not that she was the sort of woman men swooned over. No, she was far too plain, too soft-spoken to ever be the sort that gentlemen flocked to, elbowing one another out of their way so they could be the man fortunate enough to be nearest her. Joy was that sort, of course, and that was why she remained in New York instead of coming to England as well. If she'd come with them, Sophie would never stand a chance. No doubt the duke would take one look at Joy, with her deep blue eyes and glossy, blue-black hair, and would forget his own name. She was most definitely the sort men swooned over.

She frowned, punching the pillow to soften it. Yes, she was happy that the duke seemed to be a nice man, and that he was a decent employer spoke volumes as well. Servants knew everything that went on in a household, and they were very protective of their families, so even if the duke was an ogre, she didn't think his servants would say anything to outsiders.

The door opened, and Edith returned bearing an elegant wooden tray laden with more food than Sophie could ever possibly eat. It was the same thing every meal. Where she would have a pastry and perhaps a cup of tea or coffee back home, English breakfasts were served as if one might never eat again. There was toast, jams of three different flavors, sweet butter, ham, a sort of scrambled eggs that were a bit runny for her liking but oddly delicious just the same, bacon, an assortment of pastries, and a pot of tea. How Edith managed, Sophie would never understand.

Sophie sat up. "Edith," she said, smoothing the coverlet to keep her hands busy, "I owe you an apology. I shouldn't have snapped at you the way I did. It isn't your fault I harbored such a silly notion. You were correct in pointing out the fallacy in my logic."

"There's no need to apologize, Miss Sophie." Edith set the tray carefully over Sophie's lap and flicked open a snowy white linen napkin to hand to her. "Having seen the duke, I'd wager you aren't the only lady to wish to turn his head."

"I doubt I am." Sophie plucked a piece of toast from the plate bearing a small stack. "Is that raspberry jam?"

"I believe so."

"Delightful." Sophie first spread butter, then scooped a dollop of jam onto her toast. "Still, I should have known better. Things such as love upon first look only ever happen in novels, anyhow. Especially when you've a man who looks like the duke and a lady who looks… well… like me."

"Bite your tongue, Miss Sophie." Edith frowned at her. "There is nothing wrong with the way you look a'tall." She took the knife to set on the small plate. "Did the duke say something derogatory about you? Did his friend? Has anyone?"

Sophie shook her head. "No, not at all." She took a bite of her toast and chewed it slowly, then swallowed before adding, "No, but let's not fool ourselves, Edith. I'm rather plain and boring."

"You are hardly either and you know it."

Sophie took another bite as the maid tidied up the room, gathering the clothing that needed laundering into the small basket tucked in the shadows of the wardrobe. She bustled out of the room with the basket, Sophie worked her way through her breakfast. The jam was only a bit tart, the raspberries most likely the last of the season, and it complemented the sweet butter perfectly. She finished the last of her toast before scooping some eggs. They weren't nearly as flavorful as the toast and jam, and although her tea was cool by the time she drank it, she enjoyed it just the same.

When Edith returned, Sophie picked up the conversation as if her maid had never left, which was something of a habit with her, and one with which Edith was very familiar.

"Of course I am. You've seen how men flock to Joy at cotillions. They have since we were children. They practically trip over their tongues whenever she walks by, and I'm amazed her back hasn't burst into flames from the heat of their stares."

Without blinking an eye, Edith shook her head as she replied, "Miss Sophie, because *you* do not see men react to you, does not mean they don't. And stop comparing yourself to anyone else. You are quite lovely in your own right and you know it. Now"—she stepped away from the wardrobe, a dress in each hand—"do you prefer the pale green or the pink?"

"The green." Sophie wiped her mouth then set the tray away from herself so she could climb out of bed once more. Padding toward her maid, she said, "Lovely in my own right is merely a euphemism for calling me homely, you know."

"Miss Sophie!" Edith's eyes went wide with horror. "I did no such thing."

"You don't have to. Others have already seen to it for you."

"What? Who has said such a thing to you?"

Sophie pretended not to hear her as she took the pale green day dress from Edith and strolled back to lay it out on the bed. The muslin was brand new, sewn especially for this trip, as was just about all of the clothing she'd brought with her. Her mother spared no expense and would take no chance. If this match fell through, they would return to New York in shame and be shunned even worse than before.

That thought left a tight knot in the pit of Sophie's stomach. The last thing she wanted was for this to not work out. Her mother simply would never forgive her if the duke changed his mind now.

CHAPTER FIVE

After breakfast, Sophie went below to find her mother and the dowager duchess in the library, both sitting by the fire, opposite one another on the brocade sofas. The immense room was so quiet, the only sound that of the fire crackling and popping on the hearth. If the dowager and her mother were conversing, it must have been in whispers, for as she came around into the library, Sophie heard no voices.

"Good morning, Mother," she said, then dipped into a curtsey. "Good morning, Your Grace."

"Please," the dowager held up one somewhat gnarled hand, "there is no need for that foolishness. If you wish, you may address me as *Mother*, as my son does. Or, if you wish, *Duchess,* or even Duchess Mary, as Pennington seems to favor, are also acceptable until the wedding takes place." Her already somewhat wrinkled face creased even more as she smiled. "I do hope you will feel more comfortable with *Mother* once *you* are the duchess."

The duchess. The enormity of those two words hit Sophie like a dash of cold water to the face. No more would she be Sophie Montgomery, of the upstart Montgomery family. No, she would be Her Grace, The Duchess of Blackthorne. She would be equal to the lords and ladies of England (with the exception of members of the royal family, of course,) and when she and her husband ventured to New York, the very families who thought her not good enough to join their ranks would slit one another's throats to wrangle invitations to gatherings *she* hosted.

It would almost make up for there being no love in her marriage.

Almost.

But Sophie's mother beamed brilliantly now. "The Duchess of Blackthorne. It sounds so elegant." She turned to the dowager. "And when would you like this wedding to take place?"

"I think we should give Miss Montgomery and the duke a bit more time to come to know one another," the dowager replied, turning back to Emily. "It might be awkward otherwise." She tapped her silver-headed cane against the parquet floor. "So, I thought perhaps a Christmas wedding would suffice."

"Christmas?" Emily glanced first at Sophie, then back at the dowager. "But, that's quite a ways off, isn't it? I thought, perhaps, Thanksgiving would be better."

Sophie wasn't the only one staring at her mother. Not only did the dowager stare, but there were more than hints of horror in that stare. "Thanksgiving? *American* Thanksgiving? Why ever would we do that?"

Nonplussed, Emily charged forward. "Because it would be a wonderful day for a new beginning and—"

"It makes no sense at all. And Ioan and Miss Montgomery have only just met one another. Surely, you'd rather the bride and groom know a little *something* about each another first, wouldn't you, Mrs. Montgomery? I mean, rather than be complete strangers to one another."

To her credit, Emily blushed. "Well, yes, of course

I would. But… my only concern is… well…" She glanced over at Sophie then back at the dowager. "I'm concerned the duke might meet someone else in the interim."

Sophie flinched at the dowager's look of utter disgust, as if she'd found a hair in her tea. The dowager stared at Emily, her mouth opening and closing several times before she settled on a haughty, "I beg your pardon?"

Nonplussed, Emily forged ahead. "The duke is a fine looking man, and there must be so many woman who would love to call him their husband, and well, Sophie…" She hesitated, but then finished with a lame, "I am merely concerned he might meet someone he feels more suited for him. That's all."

Heat climbed Sophie's cheeks and she wished the floor would open up and swallow her. Her own mother thought her too dull, too plain, to hold the duke's attention for too long. The horrified expression on the dowager's face made the heat in Sophie's cheeks even worse. She stared at Emily as if afraid the American woman had gone mad.

"Might meet someone else? Out *here*?" The cane rapped smartly against the floor once more and the dowager shook her head so hard, her iron-gray curls actually bounced. "If you've not noticed, Blackthorne Hall is quite removed from the hustle and bustle of London and we've yet to have any wayward travelers suddenly appear at our doorstep with the intentions of running off with the duke." She glanced over at Sophie. "Not to mention, a St. John keeps his or her word, even *if* something better happened along."

Although Sophie was rather sure the duchess meant

to be reassuring, her words only stung. Something better. It most likely translated into some*one* wealthier. After all, the duke and his mother didn't mince their words or hide the facts. The most desirable thing about her was her family's money. She knew it even if the dowager didn't know she knew.

Sophie wished that, just for once, her mother could keep quiet. It seemed every time she spoke, she inadvertently insulted the dowager. Or the duke. Or Blackthorne Hall. Or England in general. It was embarrassing enough that every time her mother spoke, Sophie saw her father wince.

If her parents' marriage had been a love match, she'd have been amazed, for they gave almost no indication that any love had ever been shared, or if it had, that any still remained between them. She couldn't even say for certain her parents even liked one another, for they didn't act as if they did. They rarely touched, almost never joked or teased one another. There were no special smiles or knowing looks. Not a single one. They acted more like casual acquaintances at best, with no warmth or regard shared between them at all. This was one thing Sophie feared. She didn't wish to spend the rest of her life feeling as if she was trapped, the way her father sometimes seemed to feel, judging by his words and actions.

She didn't want to be unhappy. Not for the rest of her life. That was a terribly long time to be miserable.

A hint of color came to Emily's cheeks, but she shrugged just the same. "I would still rather sooner over later, for everyone's sake."

"No, December is far better, but"—the dowager glanced back at Sophie and smiled—"perhaps the beginning of the month would be best."

Emily's smile became more smug. "I'm so glad you're so… reasonable." She tucked a wayward lock of dark hair behind her left ear. "Your Grace," she added.

She paused, as if expecting the dowager to insist on less formality between them as well. But when the older woman remained silent, Emily's smile faded. "I only want what is best for Sophie and the duke, of course."

"Of course you do."

Sophie winced at the sarcasm dripping from those words, but Emily didn't seem to notice as she plunged ahead. "No, I suppose I was simply caught up in the romance of the occasion."

The romance? Had she gone mad? Sophie jerked her head up at that and caught the dowager's eye. To her surprise, the dowager winked. "It will be just as romantic during the Christmas season, Mrs. Montgomery. I promise you that. Most likely even more so. Christmas has a way of adding its own magic to an occasion."

"Yes, of—of course it will." Emily cast a nervous glance at Sophie. "I just didn't want you to worry, Sophie."

Sophie fought down the urge to roll her eyes. Didn't want her to worry? With all of the other things she already worried about, what was one more, really? Still, it wouldn't do to bicker with her mother, so she managed to smile. "Which I appreciate, Mother."

Smiling, Emily reached over to pat her hand. "A Christmas wedding would be wonderful, wouldn't it?"

She nodded. Actually, the thought of a Christmas wedding made her inexplicably happy. She had always loved the season, despite the fact that she spent most of her time at the various Christmas parties and balls seated along the perimeter of the dance floor, wishing one of the eligible men would ask her to dance. It did happen from time to time, but each dance felt so stilted and uncomfortable. It seemed everyone knew one another, while she knew none of them, aside from Joy.

But to be married at Christmas? She could think of no better time. "It would, Mother. Indeed."

The dowager smiled. "I will arrange for a seamstress to pay us a call, unless you'd prefer to venture into London for several days?"

She directed this at Sophie, who thought it a splendid idea, but before she could say anything, Emily jumped in. "Oh, thank you, but no. Such a dirty city. You can *see* the air."

Sophie could only stare at her mother in disbelief, while the dowager offered up a wan smile. "So, I take it New York is cleaner, in your estimation?"

"Oh, yes."

"Really?" The dowager's left eyebrow crept up ever so slightly. "Because it certainly didn't seem so to me last time I was there."

"And when was that? Mayor Hewitt has done fine things."

"Is that so? I saw none of them last spring."

Emily shrugged. "Perhaps you simply didn't look hard enough."

Fortunately, the library door opened and dissolved the tension as Marmaduke came into the room. "Your Grace, a missive for you has arrived."

"Thank you, Marmaduke," she said, leaning heavily on her cane as she got to her feet. "If you will excuse me." She looked over at Sophie. "I will see you at luncheon, and perhaps we might go over some sketches for your wedding gown."

"I would like that, Your Gr—" Sophie caught herself at the dowager's pointed stare. "That is, er… *Mother*."

The dowager's smile was surprisingly warm. "It will feel less stilted as time passes, my dear. You will see."

Sophie stood when the dowager was finally upright, while Emily didn't, until she realized her mistake. Then she shot up from the sofa. The dowager rolled her eyes, but said nothing as she stumped from the room. Once the door closed, Sophie shot her a look. "Mother, really? You do realize you've insulted our hostess, don't you? More than once over the course of this conversation alone actually."

"I did nothing of the sort. She insulted New York."

"Not *that*!" Sophie moved closer to the fire, holding her hands to the heat. "Questioning when the wedding should be held by suggesting I'll be thrown over at any moment? The remarks about London simply added to the insult. If Papa were here, he'd look ready to die."

"I meant no insult." Her mother joined her at the hearth. "But, we both know the only reason the duke even agreed to meet you is because his family needs your dowry. They *need* us. We merely *want* them, and there are plenty of other wealthy, eligible, *titled* men left in this country should this arrangement fall through."

Yes, she knew that, but that didn't mean it didn't hurt to hear. Without taking her eyes from the dancing flames, Sophie said, "Thank you, Mother. That's *exactly* what I needed to hear."

"You need to be practical, Josephine. This man is powerful and handsome and everything a young lady would dream of, and you are *not* the only young lady in

England, you realize. It would do you well to at least *try* to impress him. I'd hate to see him playing about on you after you've married. If you don't take care, you will see how quickly he can betray you."

Sophie winced over the use of her hated Christian name *and* her mother's blunt words. "I *do* realize it and even if I didn't on my own, I have you to remind me at every turn." She turned to her mother. "I am painfully aware of what I need to be. And if I wasn't, again, I have you to remind me. And should he play about, as you so succinctly phrased it, you don't think I would tell you, do you?"

"Then you would do well to remember the wheres and whys, Josephine. You cannot allow this match to fall through."

"I can—" Sophie stared at her mother as if she'd never seen her before. And in some ways, she hadn't. True, her mother was always quite conscious of exactly where the Montgomery family stood when it came to New York society, but this was the first time Sophie ever felt the blame placed squarely upon her shoulders. How was that even possible? It certainly wasn't her fault her family was too *nouveau riche* for society's liking. She didn't cause New York society to look down its collective nose at them. She was two when her father struck his fortune in the railroads.

She bit back a sigh, the fight draining from her. Arguing with her mother was pointless. Even if Emily realized she was wrong, she'd never admit to it. A lifetime of living with her taught Sophie that much. It was easier all around if she simply agreed with her. "I know, Mother. I know."

"Good." Emily moved to stand in front of her,

catching Sophie's face between her palms. "You *will* make this match work, Josephine. I know you will."

She knew she would, too. Because of her father's bank account. Still, she nodded numbly. "Of course I will."

CHAPTER SIX

Early mornings were Ioan's favorite time to go riding. The hours before the world came awake were the most peaceful, and he found he did his best thinking when astride Jupiter, his massive black gelding. Since the Americans' arrival ten days earlier, he found himself seeking that solace more and more, but not quite for the reasons he'd envisioned.

He found himself pleasantly surprised by Sophie Montgomery. He hadn't expected his bride-to-be to be quite as charming as she was, or as pretty as she was, or any of the things that she actually was. When his mother first broached the subject of taking an American heiress as his bride, he could only imagine the worst of the worst. After all, there had to be *some* reason why an otherwise perfectly marriageable woman was not yet married by her twenty-fifth birthday, wasn't there?

Then he'd met Miss Montgomery and found himself at a loss as to why any sane American man had not yet snatched her up for himself. It made no sense. She was witty and warm, and from the few conversations of depth they'd had, he found her to be quite intelligent as well. It was true she was a bit rough about the edges, but that was to be expected from a colonial, wasn't it? America was still somewhat wild and untamed, and he certainly couldn't expect her to be as proper as an English miss. Besides, it wasn't as if she was some sort of harridan.

She was, as Pennington described her, quaint, and in time, he was certain she would adapt and fit in perfectly.

Jupiter picked his way around a fallen tree, knocked over by the previous night's storm, no doubt. He'd have to get Mr. Harrington out here to assess the storm's damage and remove any other fallen trees and branches.

They came to the clearing near the lake. Come warmer weather, he didn't doubt Sophie would want to come down to the lake and picnic, or perhaps even swim in the brackish water. He didn't know, but it seemed an American thing to want. He should probably talk to Harrington about that as well. The grass around the lake grew wild and unkempt, snakes most likely lurked there, and turtles as well. He couldn't remember. It'd been years since he'd last been anywhere near the lake, perhaps because he'd nearly drowned in there as a boy. In fact, he rarely went anywhere near the water, if at all possible. He preferred horseback to water and wasn't much one for swimming.

Jupiter's ears flicked, but he plodded on around the lake. Ducks quacked at one another, while others took off or splashed in the water. These were the sounds to which Ioan was most accustomed. An only child, he was quite used to being alone and in fact, preferred the solitude. Out here, at Blackthorne Hall, he had all the solitude he craved. He and London didn't suit. He'd had enough of London as a child, when his father insisted they live at the Blackthorne townhouse in Grosvenor Square. It was too big. Too noisy. Too crowded. Berkshire suited him so much better. Here he could ride and just be left alone. It had been idyllic once he'd come of age and no longer had to live where his father determined they should live. He'd bid London a blessed farewell, much to his father's dismay, and settled quite happily in Berkshire, where his mother lived as well.

A dull chill crept over him as he caught sight of the family chapel in the distance, and without thinking, guided Jupiter toward it. There, beyond the low stone wall, was the final resting place of the eighth Duke of Blackthorne. Last Christmas, with the family gathered at Blackthorne Hall, his father had taken ill. Two days later, he lay down for a nap and simply never woke from it. Just like that, he was gone and Ioan was the new duke.

And a whole new set of problems came with his new title. The first, and most pressing, one?

He needed to find a wife.

The second?

His family's finances were in ruin. Unbeknownst to him, and especially unbeknownst to his mother, Robert St. John had a fondness for gambling. For liquor. For women. He'd gone against the suggestions made by his advisors and made one poor investment after another. In short, he'd nearly bankrupted the family.

That was when his mother, already grieving to a certain degree and now learning just how dire their situation had become thanks to her husband's poor choices, came up with the idea of an American heiress. Everyone knew Lady Randolph Churchill had helped solidify her husband's family's coffers. And she was but the first of many wealthy American women to marry into the English aristocracy. The bride fortified her social standings on two continents, and aristocrat families padded their fortunes. It was a win-win for both parties.

He certainly wasn't completely averse to the idea. The thought of an American wife intrigued him. Most of the ladies in his social circles were interested in only his title, but if they knew the truth behind St. John family finances, they would run like hell in the opposite direction. The ones who weren't concerned by such things... well... their families would never give permission. Who would want their daughter to marry a titled pauper? No, the dowager's solution was the perfect one.

So why did he just want to travel to London and disappear?

No, that wasn't entirely true.

He swung down from the saddle, looped Jupiter's reins about a low branch, and stepped into the cemetery. Robert St. John had been buried in what would be the sunny patch once the sun broke through the clouds. As he stood there, looking at the tombstone without really seeing it, Ioan felt the familiar anger twisting deep in his gut. Because of his father's weaknesses, he, Ioan, had to right everything, and the only way to do that was to marry a woman simply for her money.

That was it. That's what stuck in his craw. He wasn't much of a dreamer, not much of the fanciful sort, but it seemed far too cold and calculating—something Pennington might do. In fact, he was rather surprised Pennington's own mother hadn't suggested such a thing. Everyone knew the Rutledge coffers hemorrhaged money these days. Even Pennington himself liked to joke about how they were but a stone's throw from being in the poorhouse. Yet, unlike Ioan, Pennington didn't seem at all fazed by it. In school, he'd gone for his degree in law, and seemed quite content being a virtually penniless marquis. One who practiced law, no less. Of course, Pennington would never find himself in the same situation. His family didn't seem to mind being dragged into the present, into the modern world. They almost seemed relieved by the change.

But for Ioan, he couldn't simply look the other way. Pennington could because he honestly didn't give a damn about the people employed at Pennington House, or in the village, or any of it. He seldom ventured out into Berkshire, preferred London and his life as a solicitor. It suited him in so many ways. He was here now as a show of solidarity for Ioan. Once the wedding came and went, Pennington would be on the first train back to London without so much as a backward glance.

The very thought of being cooped up in an office all the time, suing this fellow or that one, curdled Ioan's stomach. It wasn't that he didn't like work. He didn't like working indoors. Out of doors was where he belonged, with his horses and his livestock. Unlike his peers, he didn't hunt, abhorred blood sports of all sorts. He'd much rather mend a bird's broken wing or care for an injured fox than shoot and kill anything. He'd never fit into the world into which he'd been born, and now he had no choice but to somehow force himself to do so. His first step was marrying to secure the St. John fortune; the second one would be to produce the next duke. Once that was finished, no one would give a damn *what* he did.

"And this is because of you, you know," he muttered, scowling at the elaborate granite stone. "You were the wastrel and now *I* am responsible for cleaning up your mess. Thank you for that."

"Talking to yourself these days, Blackthorne?" Pennington's lilt floated on the damp air from behind him. "Careful or someone might think you've gone mad. Then you'll be the Mad Duke instead of the Most Eligible Duke."

"Let them," he replied without turning around, "and ask me if I care."

"Oh, come now, old man"—leather squeaked, then footsteps on damp earth squelched behind him and Pennington stood at his right shoulder—"surely it isn't as bad as that."

"You know it is and you know why." Ioan peered over at Pennington, whose face was ruddy from the damp chill and whose dark hair poked up at all angles. "Good God, man, you look as if you spent the night balled in a corner somewhere."

Pennington grinned as he made a halfhearted attempt to smooth down his wayward waves. "I wanted to see how fast I could get Maurice to run. Damn near lost my head to a low branch, so I have a few cross words for Harrington the next time I see him."

"Afraid you might ruin that pretty face?"

"Something of that sort." Pennington's hands went still. "So, why are you out here, anyway? I thought you wanted only to spit on the old man's grave, not talk to it."

"I haven't the foggiest why I'm here, as it wasn't my destination. I think Jupe was toying with me. Perhaps my father has come back and only Jupe can see him."

"I highly doubt that. Fairly certain one doesn't simply leave hell when one wishes."

Only Pennington could get away with such a statement. He knew the truth. Knew father and son barely tolerated the sight of one another, family by blood and that alone, and he had known it since he and Ioan were boys at Eton. They were so much alike, only children, not quite the same as the other boys. They became friends when Pennington thought to tease Ioan about his unusual given name. In a rare fit of temper, Ioan threw a punch, broke Pennington's nose, and while they both waited in the headmaster's office, a friendship was born.

"Be that as it may, I'm here and I have no idea why. I had nothing to say to him in life, even less to say now that he's gone." Leaves crunched beneath Ioan's boots as he turned away from the grave. "And even odder still, is why *you* are here. I thought you'd have gone back to London and stayed there."

"I was curious, man. So I returned last eve."

"Curious? About a graveyard?"

"Funny." Pennington elbowed him sharply in the ribs. "No, how things went with your little American. She seemed a bit upset when she returned to the library the other day." Another elbow jabbed him in the side. "Did you try to sneak a kiss or touch something you oughtn't?"

"Hardly." He tugged Jupe's reins free, gathering them in one hand. "I was honest. Painfully so, it would seem."

"And in the end, said something oafish?"

"Basically, yes."

Pennington rolled his eyes. "That is *not* how you win over a young lady, Blackthorne. You know that."

"I'm not trying to win over anyone."

"Perhaps you should be trying." Leather squeaked once more as Pennington shoved his foot into a stirrup, then hefted himself astride Maurice. "You might just surprise yourself and find you *like* this American of yours. She's really quite lovely, even if she is a quaint colonial."

"Then *you* court her."

Pennington threw back his head to let out a laugh loud enough it frightened the ravens in the branches overhead. They took off into the sky, chattering furiously as they flew from the treetops into the distance. Ioan scowled. "Well done, Pennington. You frightened the lot of them."

"Please," Pennington scoffed, giving an airy wave, "they are merely horrified by your suggestion that I should court the woman your mother, who terrifies me to my soul, I'll have you know, wants *you* to marry. It's not only stupid, but utterly daft."

Ioan looped the reins loosely about his left wrist. "Don't remind me. This whole matter is daft."

"I don't know, old man." Pennington nudged Maurice's sides. "It worked out rather well for the Churchills and the Alamains and the Creasleys."

"And I'm happy for the lot of them. But, you will forgive me if I wished I had another out."

"Why?" Pennington looked over at him as Jupiter fell into stride with Maurice. "Your bride is a pretty girl, Blackthorne. She's educated, which is more than I can say for most of the women who pant after you. She's a bit on the shy side, but that's to be expected, since your mother is terrifying and you know it."

"She is all of those things. And yet…"

"You don't like her?"

"I don't *know* her."

"So *get* to know her."

Ioan bit back a sigh. "I will. I just would prefer to do it *before* it's too late."

"Before it's too late? It's a wedding, old man, not a funeral."

"You know what I mean."

"Yes, I do and before you ask, yes, I think you're being melodramatic, which isn't like you." Pennington reached over to clap him lightly on the back. "Stop worrying and look forward to it. Especially the wedding night"—he wiggled his eyebrows—"as I will be expecting a full report when it's over."

Ioan snorted as he swung back into his saddle. "You'll be forever thirteen, won't you?"

"Always, my friend." Pennington jabbed his heels into Maurice's sides, and as the gelding broke into a gallop, he added, "Isn't it nice to know some things will never change?"

"Only somewhat comforting, Pennington," he called back, urging Jupiter into a run as well. "Only somewhat."

CHAPTER SEVEN

After she left the library, Sophie wasn't exactly sure what to do with herself. The dowager was nowhere to be found, and her parents were ensconced in their room, no doubt already planning the grand ball they'd host in New York when their daughter, the newly minted Duchess of Blackthorne, returned home with her duke in tow to make all of New York society pea green with envy. That left her to her own devices in a house in which she could easily become lost.

Blackthorne Hall was even grander on the inside than it had appeared on the outside, and while she wanted to explore, she hesitated. How embarrassing would it be to actually get lost in her future home? Or worse, find herself somewhere she oughtn't be and end up in trouble with the duke, or worse, her soon-to-be mother-in-law. With the way things had gone so far, it wasn't an impossibility.

With a soft sigh, she strolled the airy second floor mezzanine. It overlooked the main hall, and when she leaned against the fine marble rail to peer down at the equally fine marble floor, she smiled. Inlaid in black marble against the white marble, was the letter B, accented with elegant gold leaf.

From her perch, she watched the Blackthorne maids bustling below, the swishing skirts of their dark green dresses the only real sound they made. However, if she listened very carefully, Sophie made out a few words of the chatter between the women. Their voices were soft, their words softer still, but every now and again, one would laugh, and judging from the camaraderie she saw, the maids all liked one another and seemed happy to be there.

She'd always assumed all British people sounded alike, but as her time at Blackthorne passed, she realized that nothing could be further from the truth. Some women had soft, elegant accents, others a harder bite to their speech. One hailed from Scotland and rolled her *r*'s at every turn. An Irish lady had a brogue so thick, Sophie barely understood what she said. It was a melodic mix and a welcome change from Willow Point, where everyone sounded almost identical.

Little by little, the maids dispersed through the house to finish their tasks and silence fell once more. Sophie went below, this time via a different staircase, and found herself down by the ballroom.

Just before it, she came upon a music room, with black and white tiles on the floor and a rear wall of all glass. Sunlight poured in through those doors, drenching everything with its bright warmth. Closest to that glass wall stood a piano, and she crossed to sit at it.

Playing scales loosened her fingers and before long, scales became Mozart, soft and soothing. She didn't know how long she played, nor did she care. For the first time since arriving in England, she felt at peace.

As the last notes tinkled away, the hair along the back of her neck stood up and she slowly turned to see the duke standing in the doorway. He leaned against the doorjamb, arms folded, and smiled. "I do hope you aren't stopping on my account, Miss Montgomery."

Heat climbed into her cheeks. "N-no," she said, shaking her head. "That was the end of the piece."

"It was lovely. Mozart?"

She nodded. "Piano Sonata Number Fourteen. It took me ages to learn, and I like to play if every chance I can because I do *not* want to forget how to play it and let all of that work go to waste."

He crossed over to the piano and gestured to the bench. "May I?"

"Of course." She shifted to make room for him.

The wood groaned softly as he sank beside her. "My mother saw to it I took lessons, but I'm afraid I'm far too much the oaf to play anything more complicated than scales."

"You are hardly an oaf, Your Grace."

"I am when it comes to music." He held up his hands. "These are not the hands of a pianist by any stretch."

No, they truly weren't. They were certainly large enough, but instead of slender, elegant fingers, his were blunter, and calloused, as if he didn't trouble with gloves when riding. The ring finger of his left hand was crooked. "Did you break this?" she asked, gesturing to that finger.

"I broke the entire hand," he told her. "And no sooner had it healed, than I broke the finger."

"How did you manage that?"

He lowered his hands, then clenched and relaxed his left one. "Defending the honor of a friend."

The motion tightened the ropes of muscle along his forearm, which was exposed as his shirtsleeves had both been rolled back, to her surprise. She looked from his forearm, back up. It was easy to imagine him doing such a thing. He seemed to have an air of honor about him, of one who would think nothing of stepping up to defend a friend, lady or otherwise. "A woman?"

"No. Pennington, actually." He let that fist come to rest on his thigh.

"Really?"

"Really." He tapped one of the keys with his right forefinger. "What else can you play?"

"In its entirety? Only this one. I can play snippets of other pieces, but this one was always my favorite." She looked up at him once more. "May I ask you something?"

He shifted slightly toward her on the bench, his elbow coming to rest on the front of the lid. "Of course. You may ask me anything you wish."

"How does one break his hand, and *then* break a finger when it's all over? I should think you would have taken great pains to *not* risk breaking another bone."

To her relief, he grinned. "It wasn't intentional, I assure you. Nor was it welcomed, either." He glanced down at the hand on his left thigh. "I caught it in my horse's bridle just seconds before said horse decided to bolt."

She couldn't hold back her wince. "Oh, my… That sounds incredibly painful."

"It was. I don't recommend it."

"I'll make note of that."

His serious expression melted away, replaced by a smile. "Good. I should hate to see you lose one of these quite talented fingers."

"You really can't play more than scales?"

"I haven't in a long time, no."

She trailed her fingertips along the ivory keys, the

notes tinkling into the air. "Try, Your Grace. You might surprise yourself."

"I'd be astonished, to be honest."

Without thinking, she caught his left hand in both of hers to guide it to a key. His palm was slightly rough, very warm, and her hand vanished beneath his. His were far bigger than she'd originally thought. "You have nothing to lose by trying, then, do you?"

"You are persistent when you wish to be. Has anyone ever told you that?"

She glanced up at him. Neither anger nor irritation colored his words, but since she didn't know him all that well yet, she wanted to see if he gave any other indication of either emotion. However, to her relief, he smiled as he let her move his hand, and there seemed to be a hint of the devil in his green eyes. "I learned it from my teacher. I tried his patience to no end, I'm afraid."

His hand came to rest over the span of four keys. She eased her right one from beneath it. "Do your worst, Your Grace."

He let out a heavy sigh, one that would have sounded exasperated, were it not for the grin on his lips. "You will regret doing this, Miss Montgomery. I promise you that much."

Without thinking, she nudged him with her shoulder. "Just try."

To her surprise, he nudged her back. "Quiet, then, and let me concentrate."

"Oh, I beg your pardon, Your Grace." She nudged him once more. "Am I distracting you?"

He returned the favor again. "And if I said you are?"

"I'd say too bad. Play." She bumped him one last time.

With that, his fingers moved along the keys, slowly at first, but then he picked up speed and her urge to tease him died away as his smile melted into a more somber expression. The first notes were rough, but then, to her great surprise, he fell into one of the most beautiful pieces of music she'd ever heard. The notes were silvery and sweet, the melody as playful as he was serious, and when they faded into memory, she could only stare at him.

His hands came to rest on the keys and he smiled as he gazed down at her. "You look surprised, Miss Montgomery."

She stared first at his hands, then up at him, "You said you couldn't play."

He shrugged. "I lied."

"Your Grace!"

"What? I'd have rather surprised you with this than boasted about my years of lessons. How boring would that have been?" He turned back toward her. "I was the son of a duke, Miss Montgomery. Lessons were all I knew—Greek, Latin, riding, music. If my father had had his way, I would have been little more than a spoiled, pampered boy who pouted when he didn't get his way and who grew into an equally spoiled, pampered lord of the realm who did the same. And I'd have despised me. You most likely would have despised me as well."

She didn't quite know how to respond to that. At first glance, he was indeed that spoiled, pampered boy who wanted for nothing and felt entitled to anything he desired. But in the short time since her arrival at Blackthorne Hall, she didn't get that feeling from him at all. He was nothing like she imagined him to be. Nothing like she'd ever imagine any duke to be.

"So, what other secrets do you keep?" she asked.

"For all of the years I studied languages, I really don't speak any of them well. In fact, even English gives me trouble from time to time."

"I don't believe *that* for a moment."

"Try me." He winked. "I play piano far better than I speak Greek."

"I can't imagine you have a great use for Greek here."

"No greater than the use I had for piano lessons. This was the first time I've touched the keys in years."

"That is a shame. You play beautifully."

"Well, perhaps I will take it up once more." He gestured to the keys. "So, you cannot play anything else?"

"Not as well as that one, I'm afraid."

"Try."

"Do you wish to see me fall on my face?"

To her surprise, he shook his head. "Not at all. It's just I've a feeling you play much better than you give yourself credit for."

Heat crept into her cheeks once more, but this wasn't at all uncomfortable heat. Rather, it was unexpectedly pleasant, and the smile accompanying it made her belly twist into oddly pleasant knots. When he smiled, the skin at the outer corners of his eyes crinkled in a very lovely way she hadn't noticed before. "What makes you say that?"

"I don't know," he murmured, and the hand that had been resting on his thigh now came up to her cheek. With his forefinger, he caught a wayward wisp of her hair to draw it away from her face. "You seem the modest sort. Almost to a fault, really."

He repeated the motion with his forefinger, only this time she didn't think a strand of hair was the reason why. Not that it mattered. The gentle graze sent a rush of tingles along her cheekbone, made her eyelids heavy, made her almost sigh.

"This room suits you," he went on, his voice a low, rumbling whisper. "Here, like this, in the sunshine… you look… beautiful."

Her breath seemed far more difficult to catch than usual and his stare mesmerized her. His eyes were greener today. The sunlight played along his wayward dark curls, danced over the strands to offer up highlights of gold and russet. His hair looked as if he hadn't troubled with a comb or brush, but simply ran both hands through it in a halfhearted attempt at taming it. He looked as if he'd just galloped a mighty horse across the moors, (that was what the English called their open tracts of land, wasn't it?) windswept and roguish.

"Th-thank you," she managed to whisper back, her belly churning wildly.

His eyes grew heavy-lidded and sleepy, but he didn't look away as he leaned toward her. Her heart leaped up into her throat.

He was going to kiss her.

Her eyes closed on their own as his lips met hers. They were warm. Soft. Caressed hers as they covered them. They moved with a sensual slowness against hers, parted slightly.

She started when the tip of his tongue nudged against her lips, and without thinking, she parted them. Her toes actually curled at the silken heat of his tongue as it slid along hers. Oh, good heavens… no man had ever kissed her so thoroughly before. Or so teasingly. Or

67

so… wonderfully.

Because it truly was a wonderful kiss, one that started out slow and sweet, then deepened as the duke caught her face in his hands, then thoroughly explored her mouth. It was, without a doubt, the most sensual kiss she'd ever received, a caress if ever there was one, and she felt it clear through to the tips of her toes.

He broke the kiss, but his lips brushed hers as he whispered, "Sophie…"

That whisper was breathless and airy, and she forced her eyes open to find him gazing at her. His hands tightened against her cheeks, his eyes grew heavy-lidded once more, and this time, she lifted her lips as he bent toward her once more.

"There you are! Dun—oh, I beg your pardon!"

She and Ioan practically jumped away from one another, the duke shooting up from the bench so fast, he caught the rear leg with his boot and stumbled. Thankfully, he caught himself before he hit the floor, and she spun about to see Pennington in the doorway, looking aghast at what he'd interrupted.

Ioan cleared his throat. "Where is Marmaduke?"

"How the deuce should I know?" Pennington asked, his cheeks pink. "Am I interrupting something?"

Sophie looked from him to Ioan, whose cheeks also held a hint of color. His dark curls danced as he shook his head. "Not at all. What brings you here?"

"Excuse me." Her cheeks burning, Sophie somehow still managed to smile as she brushed by first the duke, then Pennington. She paused in the doorway long enough to peer at both men over her shoulder. "I am sorry if I've overstepped by coming in here, Your Grace. I won't do it again."

"Miss Montgomery, no," he said, finally meeting her eyes, "that isn't necessary. You are to feel free to come and play whenever the mood strikes."

Pennington's own eyes narrowed as he looked from her to Ioan and back. "Have I missed something? It looked as if the two of you were kissing and now, you're angry with one another?"

To her surprise, Ioan shook his head. "I'm hardly angry, Penn."

"Nor am I," she said, her gaze remaining firmly on Ioan. "But I do feel as if I'm intruding, so if anyone needs me, I will be in my room."

She didn't wait for either man to stop her, but hurried out of the music room, praying she didn't bump into her mother or the dowager along the way.

CHAPTER EIGHT

Pennington peered around the doorway and whistled softly. "If she turns any redder, I'm afraid she's going to melt."

Ioan swallowed the oath rising to his lips. "Your timing could use a bit of work, you know," he said, unable to keep the irritation from his voice as he moved to close the door.

"How the deuce was I supposed to know you'd try to seduce her on top of a piano?"

Ioan shot him a look. "I was hardly trying to seduce anyone, you oaf. And even if I was, it would *not* be in the music room in the middle of the day."

"But you don't deny you were kissing her."

Pennington's voice held more than a hint of laughter as he moved away from the door to the settee over in the corner by the harp. The velvet crinkled as he sank onto it, while Ioan moved back to the piano. He dropped onto the bench. "No. I don't deny it. Why would I? But, before you ask, I don't even know why I did it."

"Because she's cute?"

Ioan rolled his eyes. "That had nothing to do with it."

"You don't think she is?"

"I didn't say that, but it's neither here nor there."

Pennington leaned forward, his clasped hands dangling between his knees. "Why the deuce not?

You've got to make babies with this woman, you know. It will make it easier if you think she is cute."

He arched one brow. "Make babies with her?"

"Don't try to change the subject." Pennington shook his head. "You know exactly what I mean."

This time, Ioan didn't even try to hold back his sigh. "Yes, I do know what you mean and yes, she's very pleasing to the eye, but that really isn't the important thing, you know."

Velvet crinkled again as Pennington rose and moved to the harp. He plucked two strings before saying, "Pleasing to the eye. Damn, Duke, you truly are a poet, aren't you?" Another note floated from the harp. "You'd best be careful not to woo her into madness with that poetry."

"Enough," Ioan snapped, frowning down at the ivory keys. "What do you think I should be doing, Penn? Declaring undying love for her when I barely know more than her name?"

"Well, that didn't seem to matter much when you were shoving your tongue down her throat, did it?"

Ioan glowered at him, growling, "Go away."

"I won't." Pennington plucked the strings once more. "The trouble with you, Blackthorne, is that you are afraid you might actually like this young lady."

Ioan looked up from the keys then, to find Pennington innocently gazing at the harp. It was a tactic he knew well. Pennington loved to provoke, then sit back as innocent as a babe and wonder aloud why Ioan grew so irritated with him. And irritation was only the beginning. Before long, Ioan would want to throttle Pennington blue and would wonder just how he'd react, should Ioan order Marmaduke to toss Pennington bodily from Blackthorne Hall. "That just might be the most idiotic thing I've ever heard you say. And *that* would be saying something."

"Why? It makes perfect sense." Pennington forgot about the harp and its strings, his hands coming to rest on his thighs as he added, "You have to marry her. That's a forgone conclusion. So, why not just admit you like her and that you probably won't mind sharing a bed with her after all? That she will save your family's collective skin is just a gift."

Pennington was the only one outside of the family to know of Ioan's financial difficulties, and that was only because he was like a brother and always had been. Which was also the only reason why he was still talking. Had he been anyone else and said those things, he'd be an unconscious heap on the Persian carpet.

Of course, that didn't mean Ioan wouldn't be annoyed with him. Or let him know of said annoyance. "It's probably wise for you to stop talking now."

"Have I struck a nerve?"

"I am not joking, Penn. Quiet."

"So I *have* struck a nerve. Good." Pennington crossed over to lean an elbow on the piano's lid. "You are being a fool, Blackthorne, and you know it. It's no secret that you have to marry. And it's also no secret that your wife will be expected to produce a son, so we both know you and the lovely little American will be doing more than simply kissing in the coming days. And although it *is* a secret to the rest of the world—but not to me—that your family is in serious financial trouble, your lovely little American will alleviate that as well. She seems the likable sort. She isn't as colonial as I thought an American miss might be. So, why are you being such a jackass about her?"

"Because not only have I no real desire to get married as yet, *or* have children—no matter how lovely the lady in my bed might be—but the decision was not even left up to me. The choice of bride was not left up to me. None of it was left up to me, while all of it affects me. So, perhaps *that's* why I'm being such a jackass about her!"

Pennington stared at him for a long moment, his jaw somewhat slack. Then, he regained his composure and shook his head. "You are an idiot, do you know that?"

"Am I?" Ioan calmly folded his arms and leveled a look at Pennington. "Dare I ask why this time?"

"You're crying like a little boy who doesn't want to take a nap despite the obvious fact he really needs to."

Ioan drew in a slow breath to calm his bubbling temper. The last thing he wanted or needed was a row with Pennington. "And this is coming from a man who hasn't a clue as to what this is like from my end. Who has no one to worry about but himself."

"Oh, rubbish," Pennington snapped, slapping his hand against the lid.

"Rubbish? Really? So, have your parents selected a wife for you? Have they told you, without even asking your opinion, that you are going to marry some woman you've never even laid eyes upon before?"

"No." Pennington's voice dropped to a low growl. "And we both know why."

"Yes, we do. But even if that weren't so, you and I both know, this would *not* sit well with you, but would stick in your craw every moment of every day. So, perhaps," he said, rising, "you will forgive me, if I see this in a more somber light than you."

"A more somber—" Pennington stared at him as if he'd gone mad. "Do you even *hear* yourself? She will be a wife, not a warden and certainly not an executioner, so you'll have to forgive me if I fail to see what is so terrible about the whole mess."

How did he even begin to explain it when he didn't exactly understand it himself? No, it really wasn't quite so terrible. Sophie Montgomery was lovely, she was witty and warm, and she made him smile, made him comfortable. When she'd nudged him, he'd done it back without a second thought, without a moment's hesitation. And the look on her face when he played the Beethoven piece? Priceless. Her eyes were wide and luminous, her smile equal parts amazement and exasperation. That was when he noticed just how kissable her lips looked. He had to know if they were as delectable as they appeared.

They were.

But now, he combed a hand through his hair. "It isn't terrible at all, Penn. It just isn't what I wanted, either."

"Look." Pennington sank onto the bench beside him. "Life seldom works out the way we want or plan. You know this. Perhaps better than most."

Ioan nodded slowly. "Truer words have never been spoken."

"So, rather than fight it, why not embrace it?" Now it was Pennington's turn to nudge him gently in the ribs. "Your bride is a lovely woman, Blackthorne. And, this engagement means you are spared all of the devious little ladies around here who so covet becoming the Duchess of Blackthorne. Who care more for some fool title than they do the man who'll give it to them."

If ever there was a silver lining, this was it. He wouldn't have to contend with schemers and women hoping to be caught in a compromising position with him. Of course, if they knew the truth about the St. John family, they wouldn't be in such a great hurry to land him as a husband, but that was neither here nor there. Not only that, but he would never need worry or fret over his bride's motives. While Sophie hadn't chosen him specifically for his title, her parents certainly had. The fact that he'd chosen her for equally mercenary reasons made them even to a certain extent.

"Also true," he mused, looking over at Pennington, only to find his friend grinning at him. "What is it now that's got you so amused?"

"Did you at least enjoy that kiss? Because, from where I stood, you certainly seemed to enjoy it. I think *I* even enjoyed it."

Now it was Ioan's turn to smile. "Actually, yes, Penn. I enjoyed it very much, thank you for asking."

"Good."

"What is good?"

Ioan smiled as he turned to see his mother crossing into the music room. "We were simply talking about Miss Montgomery and how she is quite acceptable to me."

"Oh, well, *that's* a relief," the dowager drawled, rolling her eyes. "And here I was afraid I'd have to cancel everything."

"Mother, you know what I mean."

"No, actually, I don't." She held up a hand. "And I'd prefer to keep it that way." Her gaze slid to Pennington. "Good afternoon, Pennington. Don't you ever simply stay at Pennington House?"

"Not if I can help it." He shrugged. "Mother and Father keep trying to marry me off as well, and it's only gotten worse since word of Miss Montgomery's arrival has spread through Berkshire."

Ioan covered his grin with one hand as his mother rapped her cane against the parquet floor. "As well they should. It's high time both of you boys took on the responsibility of marriage and fatherhood. Neither of you is getting any younger."

"Ah, but there isn't a lady in all of England I've any desire to spend the rest of my life with," Pennington declared, rising from the bench. "Boring, the lot of them. I'd much rather travel to America and find my own heiress, like Blackthorne."

Ioan looked from Pennington to his mother, fighting back a laugh at the stern frown on her face. "He's joking, Mother."

"I'm not." Pennington shook his head. "I'm afraid English girls pale in comparison to your lovely little American."

The dowager shook her head. "That would kill your mother on the spot, you know."

"Most likely, so I suppose I'll have to let her think I'm about ready to court someone and then drag it out as long as I can."

"You are incorrigible," the dowager told him. "Utterly incorrigible."

Ioan lowered his hand. "What brings you in here, Mother?"

"Right," she said, turning back to him, "I thought we should probably host a ball or party to welcome the Montgomery family, to celebrate your engagement, and see how she fares in society."

"All three?"

"Well, perhaps to welcome and see how she does. Then, if all goes well, we can bring up your engagement."

He sighed softly. "I'm not officially engaged to anyone yet."

"But you will be, so it's close enough."

Pennington let out a low whistle. "And if she doesn't fare well?"

The dowager shrugged. "We will cross that bridge when we come to it."

Ioan shook his head. "She will be fine, Mother. She's really quite an interesting woman."

"Well, I don't honestly care how interesting she is. As long as she doesn't embarrass us, she will suffice." His mother rapped her cane once more, then added, "But perhaps we should warn them all. Just in case."

"It might be wise." The piano bench creaked as Ioan stood. "When were you planning on hosting this party?"

"I thought for the eighteenth. It gives us time to polish any chinks in Miss Montgomery's armor, if need be."

Ioan exchanged looks with Pennington, and then said, "Very well. That will give us enough time to make certain our visitors from America don't slurp their soup or wipe their mouths on their sleeves, won't it?"

The dowager had the good grace to blush. "Very well, perhaps I was being a bit too judgmental. After all, they're Americans, not heathens."

"But I thought that, to you, they were one and the same?"

"Quiet, Pennington, or I'll have Marmaduke toss you out on your ear," the dowager told him without smiling.

"I was leaving anyway." As he passed by the dowager, he bent to press a kiss into the top of her head. "I do hope you'll be nicer to your daughter-in-law than you are to Blackthorne's best chum, Duchess Mary."

"Of course I will," she retorted. "I rather *like* her, after all."

"Well, now I'm hurt."

Ioan rolled his eyes as Pennington strode from the room. "One of these days, Mother, he's going to think you're serious."

"I *am* serious," she told him, all innocence as she turned toward him. "I do like Sophie. She's a bit too timid, but I like her. Her mother, on the other hand—"

"Good." Ioan interrupted. "Then let's not foist all of London society on her at once, shall we?"

"She will be fine," the dowager assured him. "You will make sure of it."

CHAPTER NINE

When they first arrived at Blackthorne Hall, Sophie was amazed at how... *immense* everything seemed to be. The grounds. The house. Everything was just on such a grand scale, unlike any she had ever seen. Back home, buildings were tall. Townhouses were tall. Everything was tall. But nothing could prepare her for such grandeur.

And this would one day soon become her home. She didn't think she would ever be used to that. Of course, she told herself differently. She needed only to give it time and she would adjust, just the way she did when they first moved into Willow Point. Well, she'd been a Blackthorne Hall for several weeks, and she *still* had yet to adjust.

How could she, when all she could think about was how delightful Ioan's kiss had been. At various points over the past three days since that moment in the music room, it came rushing back, although she'd yet to find herself alone with him again. Which was a disappointment, really. She'd enjoyed that kiss and wouldn't mind kissing him again, should the right moment present itself.

If only it would.

She sighed as she strolled along the mezzanine. Unlike her home in New York, this was open, she could lean against the marble rail and peer down into the main hall, about which the mezzanine ran in a perfect square. Enormous potted ferns were set here and there, and the hint of flowers hung in the air. Roses, perhaps? There was a greenhouse not far from the ballroom, and he'd made mention of an orangery, but she didn't know what one found there, aside from perhaps oranges. They'd never quite made it to the orangery that first day, or any since.

Two of the maids appeared below, dressed in staid house dresses of green cotton, with snowy white aprons and matching caps. One carried a bucket in one hand, a mop in the other, while the other carried a box cluttered with other cleaning supplies. They chatted softly as they crossed the main hall and disappeared down the hallway. A low laugh rolled toward her, which made her sigh again. She didn't know where her parents had got to, didn't know where the dowager lurked.

She didn't know where Ioan had gotten to, either.

Ioan.

Her thoughts returned to that afternoon in the music room. What had possessed him to kiss her? And not just to kiss her, but to do so thoroughly and deeply, until she almost forgot her own name?

And drat it all, why did Pennington have to interrupt?

She leaned against the cool marble railing, hands clasped as she stared down at the marble floor, which looked so very far away. What would have happened, had Pennington not come into the music room? Would Ioan have pulled her into his arms, or swept her up from the bench? Would he have tugged her down onto the velvet settee? Would he have continued kissing her, or would his hands have begun to roam?

Would she have stopped him?

A shiver ran along her spine. It had been a lifetime since she felt that delicious thrill of being in the same room with a man she found attractive, of knowing he found her equally desirable. She'd forgotten how heady it was, to be kissed by someone who knew exactly how to kiss. It didn't happen often, but it had happened, and Ioan's kiss was far headier than any she'd ever received before. Somehow, she didn't think she'd mind being married to him, to be subjected to those skilled lips. She could only imagine what their marriage bed would be like.

Heat filled her. She shouldn't think such things. Only harlots and other loose women thought such things. At least, that was what she'd been taught. The only wisdom imparted by her mother was to grit her teeth and wait for it to be over, which sounded terribly bleak to her, though she kept *that* to herself.

But she couldn't help herself. He crept into her mind more and more and now that she knew was it was like to kiss him, she couldn't *stop* thinking about him. Grit her teeth over what? Was kissing the only good part about… about… *that*?

Damn it. She wished Joy were here. That was the worst part about being so far away from home. She needed Joy's guidance and her level-headedness right now. She couldn't talk to her mother about these newfound feelings. She'd rather die. Besides, her mother was far more interested in the fact that her daughter was about to become a duchess and would forever secure both of their places in society. When she and Sophie's father returned to New York, they would be welcomed into the upper echelons of society. That they were *nouveau riche* would no longer matter. They were part of English nobility. That would open so many doors to them that Sophie wouldn't have been surprised if her mother chose a pruny old man for her to marry. In fact, had the St. John family not accepted their offer, she could very well have found herself with just such a man. A horrifying thought, to say the least.

With another sigh, she turned to head to her room. She didn't know what else to do. She certainly couldn't go back to the music room. She didn't know if she'd be allowed to ride alone. And really, what else was there? Aside from Ioan and Pennington, the only people near her age were the servants. They were friendly, they were polite and cordial, but they were also staff and as such, she couldn't count them as friends. Blackthorne offered up a lonely existence for someone who didn't know a single person outside of the walls. It was worse than New York, where even if she didn't know them, people along Fifth Avenue still smiled and bid her a good morning. They didn't shun her, they simply didn't include her if they didn't have to.

New voices echoed around her, and she peered down once more, this time smiling as Pennington and Ioan strolled toward the front doors. Even from her height, it was easy to see how Ioan towered over his friend. He was a good three or four inches taller than Pennington, although he was just as solidly built.

From a distance, they could almost pass as brothers. Pennington's hair was almost as dark as Ioan's, and although his eyes were blue and not green, that would hardly matter. Both men were broad shouldered and too handsome for their own good, and yet neither one seemed at all aware of their looks. Neither one struck her as particularly vain or arrogant. Both made her feel welcomed at Blackthorne Hall. That first day aside, she didn't feel as if Pennington mocked her at all.

"You should warn your duchess to be," Pennington said as they passed by beneath her. "She might not appreciate meeting all of your friends at once."

"Friends?" Ioan snorted. "Mother's friends and bridal hopefuls, you mean."

Sophie's heart skipped a painful beat. As far as she knew, their engagement was all but final. But was that so? Or were other women also in the running, each hoping she would be chosen to be the next Duchess of Blackthorne? Was she to be one of many, to learn her fate in a public setting?

As if he heard her unasked question, Pennington asked, "Bridal hopefuls? As in more than one?"

"Well, no. Not as far as *I'm* concerned," Ioan replied. His voice grew fainter as they strode off away from her, so all else she heard was, "But one never knows with that group…" before it faded out entirely.

So, she was to have all of London society foisted upon her and within that group, a subset who still harbored hopes of catching the eye of an oh-so-eligible duke. How was she to compete with those ladies? True, she wouldn't be considered *nouveau* anything here, but somehow, her being American would surely work against her. Would she come up lacking compared to them? Would she seem, as Pennington had first assessed her, a quaint colonial?

"Wonderful." She reached up to rub her forehead, as the beginnings of a headache took root. "So, I'll be outcast on two continents instead of just one. How comforting."

"Sophie?" She winced at the sharp tone in her mother's voice, and looked up to see her approaching. "Where have you been?"

"Sorry, Mother. I was in the music room. I didn't think anyone would mind."

"Well, you need to come and dress for luncheon. The dowager has invited us to join her."

Sophie bit back a sigh. Not only was she not hungry, but she really wanted only to go and lie down for a while. Maybe then, her headache would resolve itself. "Mother, must I? I'm not feeling well."

"Not feeling well?" Her mother's forehead creased as she closed the space between them to press her palm against Sophie's forehead. "You aren't with fever."

"I never said I was. I have a headache and would like to take a nap if at all possible."

"Perhaps later," her mother replied, tugging on her arm. "For now, we are having luncheon with the dowager. She and I were discussing a party to introduce you to all of the right people here in England, and it would benefit you to make certain you learn all you need to in order to make a wonderful impression. These people are going to admire you, Josephine, but only if you act as if you are one of them. No, as if you are *better* than they are."

"But, I'm *not* one of them, Mother, and I have no desire to be one, either. And I'm *not* better than anyone. Not one bit."

She didn't expect her mother to understand and wasn't at all surprised when her mother scowled. "And that is precisely the *wrong* way to look at this, Josephine. Not only should you want to fit in, you want them to envy you. To wish they were you. That is the only way this marriage will ever be a success. You certainly don't want the duke being embarrassed by you, do you? To have him think you are nothing more than a backward American?"

Sophie swallowed hard, her cheeks growing warm as she shook her head. "Of course not."

"Good. Now, let's get you changed and then sit down with the dowager. She will make certain you are a success. Worry not."

There was little point in arguing with her mother and besides, she was probably right. Ioan had been raised in this life, with certain expectations. Especially where his wife was concerned. The last thing he wanted was for her to embarrass him, and the last thing she wanted was to do just that. If anything happened to make Ioan change his mind... Sophie would never forgive herself for disappointing everyone around her, and her mother would never allow her to forget she'd done so.

****

After Pennington took his leave, Ioan made his way back to the music room. His mother had gone. No servants were to be found.

Sophie wasn't there.

Sophie.

He sank onto the piano bench and let his fingers come to rest on the keys. He owed her an apology for pouncing on her the way he had the other afternoon. Although, the more he thought about what Pennington had to say, the more he found himself wondering if perhaps, marriage wasn't an altogether awful tiding? His mother could have done far worse than finding Miss Montgomery. Of that, he was certain.

Notes tinkled into the air, but they were flat and by

rote, with none of the passion he'd put into them when he played the same piece for Sophie. He simply didn't care.

"Oh, Your Grace, I beg your pardon."

He spun on the bench to see one of the housemaids in the doorway, arms laden with cleaning supplies. "Please," he held up a hand, "there is no need to beg my pardon at all. Amy, isn't it?"

"Yes, Your Grace." She dipped into a curtsey.

"Please, don't." He rose from the bench. "I hadn't realized anyone would be in here today. I'll be out of your way."

"There's no need for that," she told him, setting her supplies on the floor. "I can always come back."

"No. That won't be necessary." He smiled at the tiny redhead in prim green and white. "I can also always come back. Tell me, though, do you happen to know where Miss Montgomery has gotten to?"

"I believe she is in her chambers, Your Grace. She was supposed to have luncheon with the dowager and the Montgomerys, but she said she had a headache and went to lie down."

"Thank you, Amy."

Another curtsey. "Of course, Your Grace."

He bit back his rebuke and then left the maid to the music room. He certainly couldn't go up to Sophie's chambers now. The last thing he wished was for his servants—and hers, one day—to gossip about her. That would undermine her authority from the beginning, and that simply wouldn't do.

A luncheon, though. His mother made no mention of a luncheon with Mrs. Montgomery and Sophie, so obviously he was not needed. What was she up to now?

With that, he made his way to the dining room, where the low, flat pull of American voices reached his ears before his mother's voice. Mr. Montgomery seemed agitated, saying, "Are you suggesting we wouldn't know how to behave before your puffed up peers?"

"I've said no such thing, Mr. Montgomery," the dowager replied stiffly. "And if you would calm down, you would realize I am only concerned with Miss Montgomery's well-being."

"Randolph, please," Emily Montgomery broke in impatiently, "you are *not* helping."

"Well, forgive me," he snapped back, "but I will *not* sit here and be told I am not good enough for the likes of—"

"No one said anything of the sort, and you are still not helping!" Emily retorted, sounding very near tears. "And it isn't at all insulting besides. Sophie has no idea what is expected of her, and I think it would do her well to have a few lessons. After all, we don't want her falling on her face."

"Falling on her—this entire charade was *your* idea, Em. You will kindly remember that."

Ioan paused just beyond the doorway as Emily replied, "She has no other options in New York, Randolph. At least, until she becomes the duchess. Then, every door in New York will open to her."

"And *my* hard earned money will keep this museum up and running."

"It will also keep this estate up and running," Ioan broke in as he rounded the doorway and smiled blandly at the American upstart glowering in his direction. He'd recognized his mother's patience-stretched-thin voice and was not disappointed to find her scowling at the

Montgomerys. If one didn't know better, they would never guess how close the Americans were to being told to go to hell—nicely, of course. But, the dowager was almost to that point, judging by her stiff carriage, steely gaze, and the fact that her knuckles were almost white from clenching her goblet so tightly.

Both Mr. and Mrs. Montgomery looked equally unhappy, but in a different way. Mr. Montgomery scowled, as if spoiling for a physical battle, while Sophie's mother looked ready to cry. From the looks of things, he'd timed his arrival perfectly.

"Not to mention, your grandchildren will have the finest of educations and a firm hold in society, as will your daughter."

Randolph Montgomery didn't so much as flinch as he retorted, "Which they would have had regardless. We are hardly paupers, you know."

"Be that as it may, their lives will be far easier on this side of the ocean," the dowager said, lifting her wineglass to take a sip. "Where they will be welcomed into society. Both here *and* in New York."

"What goes on here, Mother?" Ioan asked, keeping his voice as pleasant as possible even as he glared at his mother. "It isn't often you set up a luncheon and fail to tell me about it."

She didn't look at all troubled or guilty as she sipped her wine, then lowered her glass to say, "I thought you wouldn't want to be troubled with this, Ioan. It's quite silly, really. I thought it would be nice to hold a party to introduce Miss Montgomery to our friends, and I also thought it nice to give our guests a fair bit of warning of what such an event entails for them and their daughter. They chose to take it completely wrong."

"We chose no such—"

Emily interrupted her husband. "And it is a fine idea, as I thought perhaps some of your customs differed from ours. There is no reason why we cannot simply combine the two worlds. After all, it isn't as if Sophie will become English overnight. She will always remain American."

Ioan pressed his lips together to hold back his smile as his mother openly winced. "She does have a point, Mother," he said softly. "And our children will be as much American as they will be English."

"Please"—the dowager offered up a wan smile—"do not remind me."

Ioan glanced at Randolph, who offered a scowl that didn't disappoint. "I beg your pardon?"

"Well, I realize no one is perfect," the dowager said, lifting her wineglass once more, "but you can hardly fault me if I consider them more English, can you?"

"Absolutely not," Emily said, her voice light and pleasant, "just as they will be more American when they come stay with us in New York."

The dowager offered her an incredulous look. "Whyever would they want to do *that*?"

Now both Emily and Randolph looked thoroughly insulted, so to keep the situation from escalating, Ioan cleared his throat and said, "And they will be perfectly happy to be in either place, because their grandparents will want nothing more than to spoil them rotten before handing them back to their parents. Now"—he came completely into the room and moved to the empty chair at the head of the table—"considering these children haven't even been conceived as yet, perhaps we might save this argument for another day?"

All three older people looked properly embarrassed

as they nodded and Emily Montgomery said, "Of course. It is rather silly to fight about it now." She glanced at her husband. "And I think Sophie would benefit from a bit of a refresher in English customs. I want her debut into English society to be as successful as her debut into New York society was."

Randolph rolled his eyes as he lifted his wineglass. "If it had been successful, we wouldn't be sitting here in England about now, Em."

"Hush, Randolph," she snapped. "You know what I mean."

Ioan exchanged grins with his mother but held his tongue before the situation flared once more. "Good. I'm glad to see compromise is possible all around. Now, has anyone spoken to Miss Montgomery about this, or were you all simply planning on foisting it upon her?"

No one replied, but all looked guilty, which gave him his answer. "Very well. *I* will go and tell her. If it wouldn't be too much trouble, I will also tell her when. It's the least any of you could do, you know."

He didn't wait for any answers, but turned to stride from the dining room. As he made his away above, he realized he didn't know which room was hers. So, muttering a curse to himself, he went back into the music room, where Amy was busy wiping down the hearth. "Excuse me?"

She whipped about. "Oh, Your Grace, you startled me!"

"I beg your pardon, of course, but could you tell me which rooms are Miss Montgomery's?"

She offered up a surprised look. "Your Grace, you shouldn't be up there!"

"Please, which room?"

A hint of a blush crept into her cheeks. "Of course, Your Grace. She is in the green room."

"Thank you."

"If you like, I can fetch her for you."

He shook his head. "That won't be necessary."

"If you're sure."

"I am." He smiled. "Thank you."

"You're welcome."

The green room was in the east wing, where Blackthorne Hall's more important visitors stayed. Sophie's room was at the far end of the hallway, where sunlight poured through the Venetian window. Her door was closed, and when he rapped gently on it, the sound exploded into the empty corridor.

He waited several minutes. Nothing, Not even her maid came to the door. So, he knocked again. This time, footsteps sounded, followed by a sleepy-sounding "Yes?"

"Miss Montgomery? It's Ioan."

"Oh." The sleepiness left her voice. "Of course."

He smiled as she all but yanked open the door. "Easy, Miss Montgomery, and I apologize if I woke you."

"I but meant to rest my eyes," she replied somewhat sheepishly, rubbing one said eye. "What can I do for you?"

"I'll let you wake up a bit first." He gestured into the room. "May I? I promise you, my intentions are completely honorable."

She let out a soft laugh and opened the door wider. "Of course, Your Grace. Do come in."

He stepped around her, casting a glance at the rumpled bed. The coverlet and quilt were tossed to one side, but they were the only things out of place in the entire room. If it weren't for that bed and the woman standing before him, he'd swear the room was unoccupied. "First off, I wished to apologize for my behavior in the music room the other afternoon."

"Oh, please don't." She offered up a sleepy smile, her hand going still. "It was actually a very lovely kiss."

Her words were so unexpected and so very honest, that he couldn't help but grin. "I beg your pardon?"

"I didn't mind it, Your Grace. There is no need to apologize."

"Are you certain? I mean, I rather pounced on you."

"You did no such thing." She moved to the bed, tugging the coverlet back into place. "I'm so sorry the room is in such disarray. As I said, I didn't mean to fall asleep."

"It's all right. I don't mind and this is hardly disarray. You ought but see *my* chambers. They often look as if a strong wind has blown through."

She paused, straightening up to look at him. "I find that hard to believe, actually."

"Why?"

"Because you always look so put together."

"I have a valet who can work miracles." He moved over to catch her by the wrist as she made to tug the quilt into place. "Please, I assure you, it's all right."

She peered up at him, a hint of a blush along her cheekbones. "I'm sorry. I know I say that a lot, but… I have no desire to offend you."

"And no chance of doing so, either. I assure you."

"Your Grace, I—"

"Ioan."

Her eyes widened. "I couldn't."

"I'm fairly certain I've given permission. More than once, actually."

"I know, but… my mother said I was to be sure to not use your name when others are around. That it wouldn't be proper."

"I don't give a damn what you call me, Miss Montgomery. And I don't give a damn what someone else thinks of it, either. Besides, there is no one else here to worry about it." He reluctantly released her hand. "It's quite tiresome, being Your Grace instead of being Ioan. I rather liked it when I was but the heir and people didn't necessarily treat me as if I were a fragile bit of glass."

"You mean to say you aren't?"

"Not one bit. Did I shatter when you elbowed me at the piano?"

"No. But I was afraid you might."

"Liar."

"Very well. No and truth be told, that was the first time I've felt comfortable here."

"Good. Because you should. We don't know one another just yet, but we will. And in time, I do hope you will always be that comfortable. Here. With me. With my mother from time to time."

She shook her head. "I don't know about that. Your mother frightens me."

"Oh, don't ever let Mother know that. She will never let you forget it."

Her eyes almost sparkled as she looked up at him. Damn, her eyes were so dark, if he didn't know any better, he'd swear they were as black as onyx. Black and mysterious and all at once, the urge to kiss her returned. Only this time, he didn't want to stop at kissing her. That kiss had awakened something in him, something as dark and mysterious as her eyes. For the first time since learning he was expected to marry her, he found himself looking forward to the wedding.

"I'll let you return to your nap, then," he said, gesturing to the bed. A mistake. Now, the thoughts creeping into his mind had everything to do with her in that bed, and nothing to do with sleeping. Heat swept through him, every sinew tightening, much to his surprise.

Then he wondered if her thoughts had taken the same turn because it might have only been his imagination, but her cheeks looked a bit on the pink side as well. However, she merely smiled and replied, "I'm afraid if I sleep any more this afternoon, I won't sleep a wink tonight."

I'd be more than happy to keep you company.

He didn't know where that came from, but fortunately, he managed to hold it in check as he said, "Then if you wish to return to the music room, I promise I'll not interrupt you again."

"Thank you, but I think I'll write a letter to a friend back in New York. She asked that I keep her up to date on what goes on here."

"A close friend?"

She nodded. "My dearest friend in the world." Her eyes darkened. "I miss her terribly."

"So, extend an invitation," he said without hesitation, wanting to see her eyes brighten. He wanted to see her smile, since the mention of her friend seemed to sink her spirits. "She is welcome to stay here for as long as it makes you both happy."

A smile tugged at her lips. "Thank you, Your Gra— I mean, Ioan."

"You're quite welcome. All I ask is that you let me know when she expects to arrive, so I can arrange transportation from Paddington." He moved to the doorway and tugged open the door. "You know, I *did* have a reason for interrupting your nap," he said, grinning at his own forgetfulness, "and that was to warn you. Mother has decided to host a party to announce our engagement and to introduce you to our society."

Her jaw went slack and her eyes widened. "What?"

"Don't look so terrified." He closed the door once more to lean against it. "I think you'll do just fine. It's mostly names you'll have trouble with, I think."

"But… when? And… do my parents know?"

"They do. They are in the midst of planning it, even as we speak. I felt it only fair to warn you and reassure you that you've nothing to worry about."

"Nothing to worry about? How can you possibly say that?"

"Because." He winked as he pushed away from the door to open it. "You will be the belle of the ball, as you Americans say, Miss Montgomery. I've complete faith in you and will be proud to have you on my arm.

"Now," he said, then inched around the open door, "I'll leave you to your letter writing."

"Thank you again."

"Of course." He smiled as he stepped out of her room and closed the door behind him before he did something completely out of character, such as sweep her into his arms to spirit her to the bed.

CHAPTER TEN

Activity in Blackthorne Hall increased as the staff began preparations for the upcoming party. Sophie tried not to think about the fact that she would be thrown into English society without any true preparations. The dowager duchess mentioned the party in passing, assuring her that it would be no different from any parties she might have attended in New York, but that was all she said. She must've known Ioan had told her about it already.

By the night of the party, she was a bundle of nerves, and not in a pleasant way. She couldn't decide if she looked forward to that the evening held, or if she dreaded it with every fiber of her being.

It was only too unfortunate Sophie's experience with such gatherings was pitifully lacking. Her family might be invited, and even greeted by the host and hostess, but that was about it. She and Joy spent each evening on the side of the room, watching as the cream of society danced and enjoyed themselves. On the rare occasion where a man asked her to dance, it seemed it was only because he'd been dared to by one of his friends. The last time it happened was the most embarrassing of them all. His name was Charles, and it happened the previous summer. Sophie never would have known the true reason, had she not heard the oaf laughing about it with his friends later that night.

Every time she thought about it, her cheeks burned with shame at the memory. Not only had he been dared to dance with her, his friends had also placed bets on whether he could sweet-talk her into lifting her skirts for him. The plan was to get her alone in the rose garden behind the house. Fortunately for her, her mother interrupted them before Charles could convince her to take a walk in said rose garden.

She was terrified the same thing would happen at Blackthorne. True, she didn't think Ioan could be so callow, nor did she think Pennington would be either, but she didn't know any of their friends. She could only hope Englishmen weren't as crass as so many American men could be.

One way or the other, she would soon find out.

She stood at the windows, gazing down at the coaches lining the drive. "How many people were invited?"

Her mother, seated at her dressing table, shrugged. "I've no way of knowing, Sophie. The dowager didn't ask for my approval on the guest list."

"And you let that stand?" Sophie's father emerged from his dressing room fussing with his tie. "I'm shocked, Em. Absolutely shocked."

Sophie saw her mother's scowl reflected in the glass and heard it in her voice. "Rand, you would take care to watch yourself this evening. You do realize, the duke can still back out of this. And if you ruin this—"

Sophie winced as her father replied, "Of course I realize it. How could I *possibly* forget? You remind me at every turn."

"This is important." Satin *schwiffed* softly, probably as her mother rose from the vanity bench. "Without this marriage, we will never belong back home."

"I am also well aware of that," he replied evenly. "As is Sophie. Aren't you, Soph?"

Sophie turned away from the windows with a nod. "I am and I will do my best not to embarrass either of you."

Her father's eyes fairly sparkled as they met hers. "I never worry about that, Sophie. Not ever, and neither should you. And you've a powerful ally in the dowager, who also thinks you will be quite the success."

Her mother, however, sniffed. "You should worry about it, Josephine. You have but one chance to make a first impression and that is all."

"Em, leave her be. She knows and she isn't stupid."

"No, but she also has never been in this position. A duchess, Rand. Our daughter will very soon be a duchess." Emily's voice brightened. "I cannot wait to see the look on Patricia Cavendish's face when we return home with this news."

Sophie bit back a sigh. Ever since the post from the dowager arrived, accepting her father's offer of a sizable dowry to wed the duke, all she heard from her mother was how Sophie's new station would make all of the others who did their best to keep her out, to keep her away from their eligible sons, eat crow. Frankly, Sophie didn't care if she ever returned to New York or if any society matrons ever ate crow. Her life would be in England now, and she'd seen enough of the Cavendish family to last her a lifetime. It was their son, Charles, who thought to try to ruin her in the rose garden for a lark. The entire family could burn in a hole for all she cared.

But since she certainly couldn't say that to her

mother, Sophie forced a smile to her lips. "She will be puce with envy, Mother."

"That she will. Her daughter married a Morgan. *Mine* will marry a duke."

Her father cleared his throat as he closed the space between him and Sophie. "And you will steal the duke's breath from his chest, love," he said, catching her by the shoulders. "For you are a sight to behold."

"Thank you, Papa," she replied, her stomach calming at his reassuring wink. She wasn't exactly comfortable in her ballgown of cream-colored silk, overlaid with moss green velvet. It was beautiful, decorated with small jade glass beads along the bodice, but since she had no idea what awaited her, even her own skin made her uncomfortable at the moment. Hopefully, it wouldn't last long once she went below. "I feel like a fraud, however."

"Well, don't," he told her, giving her shoulders a squeeze. "You are every bit as worthy as any young lady in that ballroom this evening, or in any ballroom between here and New York."

She managed to smile, despite her now-roiling stomach. "I hope so."

"You are. And His Grace will be lucky to be able to claim you as his wife." He leaned in and brushed her forehead with a light kiss, then offered up a reassuring wink as well as his arm. "Now, shall we go and make your England debut?"

"Wait!" Her mother stretched across the bed to grasp the moss green velvet wrap and pressed it toward her. "It's most likely drafty in that ballroom. Nothing about these English houses is warm. I should hate to see you catch a chill and fall ill."

Sophie took the wrap to drape about her shoulders. So she wasn't the only one who always felt chilly unless she stood near the hearth. It was one of the great differences between Willow Point and Blackthorne Hall. Blackthorne was cold and damp, and she didn't look forward to the middle of winter, when she had no doubt the house would feel even colder and damper.

Still, she kept those thoughts to herself as she slipped her hand into the crook of her father's arm and let him escort her down to the great hall. There, her mouth went dry as she caught sight of Ioan, dressed in a formal suit of the blackest black she'd ever seen. His shirt front almost blinded her by its brightness, his tie blended almost perfectly, and the cut of his coat emphasized his broad shoulders, while the cut of his trousers did the same for his lower regions. He stood, chatting with a woman dressed in plum, whose dark hair had been piled atop her head, with what looked like a strand of diamonds woven through that pile. She was almost as tall as Ioan, her neck long and elegant, her body long and shapely as well. From the back, she looked like an hourglass, and as Sophie approached, she couldn't help but wish she was taller than barely five feet. *Elegant* was not a word anyone would use to describe her, while the lady in plum was elegance personified.

Ioan looked up and his serious countenance melted into a smile as he said, "I was wondering if you'd gotten lost on your way down."

"I beg your pardon, Your Grace," Sophie's father said, his voice uncharacteristically low and calm. "My wife took a bit longer than anticipated."

Although her mother smiled, Sophie didn't miss the dark arrows her eyes shot at her husband. "I beg your pardon as well, Your Grace. I lost track of the time."

"It's quite all right." Ioan stepped around the woman in plum to catch Sophie's hand and lift it to his lips. "You look stunning, Miss Montgomery. Quite elegant, indeed. That color suits you."

"Thank you, Your Grace," she replied, her stomach twisting sharply. "You look quite handsome, yourself."

"She's right, you know," said the woman in plum said, her voice soft and lilting. "You will have every lady in the room plotting to sneak a moment with you."

"I highly doubt that." Ioan smiled as he tucked Sophie's hand through his arm. "Miss Montgomery, I'd like to introduce you to Lady Nora Etheridge. Lady Nora, this is Miss Montgomery. Her family has come to visit from America. New York, to be exact."

As the lady smiled, Sophie's heart sank into the soles of her moss green satin slippers. Lady Nora was, quite frankly, stunning. Ever since they were children, Sophie always thought Joy was the prettiest woman in New York City, with her dark hair and blue eyes, but Lady Nora put Joy to shame. She was strikingly beautiful, with high cheekbones, and eyes that looked to be almost violet. Thick black lashes framed those unusual eyes, delicate ebony brows slashed above them, and her hair shimmered like a raven's wings in the candlelight. Everything about her was… perfect.

Still, Sophie managed to smile. "It's a pleasure to meet you, Lady Nora."

"And you as well," Lady Nora replied, her eyes friendly as they met Sophie's. "Pennington has told me so much about you."

"Has he?"

"Oh, yes." She smiled up at Ioan. "And I understand

this party is to announce your engagement?"

Ioan nodded. "It is. Although, we aren't supposed to say anything as yet. You know how Mother likes to get one over on people."

"That's because she does it so well!" Pennington's voice boomed above the other chatter, and he burst through the crowd to join them. "Lady Nora, you are beautiful as always. Promise me at least one dance?"

"Don't I always?" She turned her perfect smile up to him.

"It never hurts to make certain." He grinned down at Sophie, who barely came to his chest. "And you look lovely, Miss Montgomery. I daresay, will your husband-to-be frown if I ask you to dance as well?"

Ioan chuckled. "If I say yes, will it stop you?"

"Not for one moment." Pennington winked at her. "She's perfectly safe with me. You"—he gestured to Nora—"are fair game, however."

"Pennington!" Lady Nora playfully punched him in the shoulder. "I daresay you wouldn't flirt so if your mother were within earshot. You'd have your marchioness before you knew it."

He recoiled in mock horror. "The hell you say! I will give up bachelorhood only if I'm brought kicking and screaming before a reverend. There are far too many ladies out there who catch my eye for me to settle with just one yet."

"Take care, you reprobate," Lady Nora warned, gesturing toward Sophie. "You'll offend Blackthorne's guest."

"Oh, that isn't a problem," Sophie said with a smile. "It will take more than some coarse language to offend me."

"That's right," Lady Nora said. "You're American. I suspect your standards are a bit different over there."

She said it lightly, but Sophie didn't miss the barb within those words. As pleasantly as she could, she replied, "Different how?"

"Oh, it's just not as... formal... as we might be. America is so wild and all."

"It's not as wild as you might think," Sophie replied, forcing her smile to remain in place. "We have customs and manners and everything in between. You would be surprised."

"Yes, I imagine I would." Lady Nora's eyes narrowed ever so slightly. "If I had a need to actually go there. Thankfully, I don't see that happening any time soon."

Ioan's hand came to rest at the small of Sophie's back, which she took as a warning, so she let her sour retort die on her lips as he said, "Perhaps we should go into the ballroom now? I imagine the orchestra has warmed up and is ready to play."

Lady Nora shot Sophie a look, but then smiled at Ioan. "I do hope you will save a dance for me as well, Duke."

"I'll do my best," came his noncommittal reply, "but I make no promises."

Lady Nora sniffed, but then went on ahead of them into the ballroom. Pennington fell into step with Sophie and Ioan, leaning close to whisper, "Take care, Miss Montgomery. Nora is an enemy you do *not* want to have."

"What is that supposed to—" Her question died on her lips as Pennington also went ahead of them. Since it appeared Ioan hadn't heard the exchange between her and the marquis, she drew in a deep breath and just let him escort her into the ballroom.

CHAPTER ELEVEN

The ballroom's vaulted ceiling seemed a mile away, and soft ivory light bathed the entire room. Tables and chairs had been set up around the dance floor, the tables draped in snowy white linens, with centerpieces of stunning purple roses in golden bowls in the middle.

"Where did you find roses at the end of October?" she asked Ioan as he led her toward the front of the room, where the biggest table had been set up.

"They were cultivated right here, in our greenhouses," he replied, tugging out one of the chairs for her. "Later on, remind me and I'll show them to you."

She smiled. "That sounds lovely."

He offered up a wink as he settled into the chair beside her. "How are you feeling? You looked petrified when you first came down."

"I *was* petrified," she admitted, smiling up at one of the footmen as he came up to fill her glass with white wine. "Thank you."

"You're quite welcome, Miss Montgomery." He moved to fill Ioan's glass, then moved away.

She lifted the glass, the crystal as delicate as anything she'd ever seen. The wine, light and refreshing, offered up a hint of comfort and helped steady her nerves. "Does Pennington flirt with every woman he meets, or only a select few?"

Ioan chuckled. "He likes to think of himself as a rake, I'm afraid. It kills his mother, who has grand designs of marrying him off as soon as possible, but in my opinion, it's never going to happen. Pennington likes the chase, but isn't exactly interested once the sun comes up."

"Your Grace!"

"What? Have I said something shocking?" He grinned at her. "Miss Montgomery, Pennington isn't going to settle down any time soon."

"Why do you say it like that?" She spotted Pennington on the far side of the ballroom, now deep in conversation with a petite blonde in sapphire blue. "Does he know everyone in England?"

"Our social circle has not changed since we were but children," he explained, lifting his own wineglass to his lips. He sipped, then lowered it to continue. "And Pennington? Well, he prefers the chase, and not much else when it comes to ladies."

"And you don't?"

His smile faded. "I did, at one point." He set the glass down, tracing his forefinger along the delicate stem. "But, I have responsibilities that he doesn't as yet. So, he is able to enjoy that chase. I, however, have to think about what comes tomorrow, and next week, or next year."

"Because of the trouble your family is in."

It was the wrong thing to say. His back stiffened, his finger went still, and his jaw tightened. "Yes, you could say that."

"I'm sorry. Perhaps I should—"

"You speak the truth, Miss Montgomery," he replied, his voice low and taut, "and I cannot be angry with you over it, for it *is* the truth. My father was a product of his time and not very good at much beyond visiting gaming houses, houses of ill repute, and running up debts. He was also a poor husband and an even worse investor. And now, here we are."

As he spoke, his gaze wandered across the room, and she followed it to see Lady Nora at the end of his line of sight. She was deep in conversation with a man in black formal clothes that were almost as elegant as Ioan's. She pressed her lips together as she brought her glass up once more. It was plain to see that *here* was not where Ioan wished to be. Instead, he most rather wanted to be *there,* with the beautiful Lady Nora.

"Now, here we are," she murmured before sipping her wine. Ever since he'd kissed her, Sophie saw Ioan in a different light. Whereas she'd once been apprehensive about marrying a man she barely knew, she'd begun to look forward to their wedding.

But now, as she watched him stare at the beautiful woman in plum silk, that anticipation vanished. He'd kissed her, yes, but it wasn't because he felt anything for her. She was there. It simply happened.

Her spirits sank. It was so much easier to pretend he would come to care for her than it was to be faced with the notion that her husband would be so in name only and that his interest lay elsewhere and that elsewhere was currently wrapped in plum silk.

She tried to ignore those dark feelings as the dowager welcomed everyone and the orchestra began playing. But then, the dowager smiled at her and Ioan as she said, "And of course, we are all here this evening to celebrate the engagement of my son, Ioan St. John, the Duke of Blackthorne, to Miss Josephine Montgomery of

New York!"

Sophie's cheeks felt poker-hot as it seemed everyone in the room turned to gape at her. Her mother and father beamed from their seats at the table just before the one she and Ioan shared, and she forced herself to smile. Thankfully, the orchestra began playing once more and Ioan smiled down at her. "Would you care to dance, Miss Montgomery?"

It was the last thing she wished to do, but since she certainly couldn't say such a thing, she smiled demurely up at him. "I would love to."

"Good." He rose from his chair and held out a hand, drawing her to her feet as she rested hers against his palm. Aware of all of the eyes upon them, Sophie nonetheless managed to keep her smile in place as the orchestra struck up a waltz.

The candlelight danced along Ioan's dark hair, which was as windblown-looking as usual. She craned her neck to peer up at him. "May I ask you something?"

His eyes glinted in the low light. "Of course."

"Does she mean something to you?"

"Does who mean something to me?"

"Lady Nora." She nodded in the lady's general direction. "You've been watching her since we came into the room."

Her heart skipped a beat as he glanced over his right shoulder, to see Lady Nora dancing with the man with whom she'd been speaking. Her throat tightened, her mouth grew painfully dry as he turned back to her. "No. She is but an old friend, Miss Montgomery."

She swallowed hard. "So, why do you stare at her that way?"

"I hadn't realized I *was* staring." He gave her hand

a squeeze. "And I apologize if you thought I was."

She wasn't so certain she believed him, but this was neither the time, nor the place to argue about it, so she managed to smile up at him. "Perhaps it's only my nerves. There are so many people here this evening."

To her surprise, his eyes softened and the hand on her hip tightened. "If you think this is a crowd, wait until our wedding. It will put this party to shame."

"Will there be many people?"

"Many people is an understatement. But don't worry, I promise not to lose you in a crowd or leave you to fend for yourself for too long."

"Oh, well *that* is a relief." The words popped out on their own, but when she looked up, it was to find him smiling down at her. "What?"

"Do all Americans simply say what they think, or are you the only one? Because I must confess, no one warned me how blunt you might be."

He said it in the same light, somewhat playful tone, but for some reason, it felt a bit like a rebuke. "Blunt? I've never thought of myself as particularly blunt before."

"Make no mistake, I like it." He smiled now, which did much to ease that feeling of being scolded. "I just wasn't expecting it. You will shake things up a bit around here, won't you?"

"Shake things up?"

"Once you're the duchess. I expect there will be quite a few changes you'll wish to see." He gestured with both their hands toward the ceiling. "Around Blackthorne Hall, I mean."

She glanced around. "I hadn't really given much thought to it," she replied slowly, coming back to meet his gaze. "I mean, this is your home."

"And it will soon be yours, so I do hope it doesn't take long for you to come to think of it as such." He gave her hand another squeeze as the music faded away. "And I fully expect you will wish to make it your home in some way as well."

With that, he pulled away, but kept her hand in his as he said, "Let's introduce you about, shall we? I promise you, they won't all bite."

"Wonderful."

He winked at her over one shoulder. "Trust me, Miss Montgomery, by this time next month, these people will be eating out of the palm of your hand in hopes of an invitation to one of your gatherings, whether it's here or in London itself."

Sophie didn't know if that comforted her or horrified her, and before she had time to dwell on it, he brought her across the ballroom toward a clump of people who all seemed to know one another and showed little more than a passing curiosity in their visitor from America.

****

As the night wore on, Sophie began to look forward to escaping to the peace and quiet of her chambers. She'd never met so many people in one evening, and although the guests peppered her with questions, she had the feeling not a single one really listened to her answers. Not only that, but within a few minutes of meeting them, she promptly forgot their names. There were simply too many of them, not to mention many names made little to no sense to her. She was far too tired to try to make sense of any of it at all.

Of course, everyone she met was pleasant to her,

polite to the point where Sophie second guessed their genuineness, but she really couldn't find fault with too many of the men and women she met. They seemed nice enough, but as Ioan had pointed out, one day, they would clamor for an invitation to Blackthorne Hall. So, how much was true interest and how much was social climbing?

By eleven-thirty, she was beyond tired. Ioan was every bit the attentive fiancé, whisking her out onto the dance floor at every opportunity, and she didn't miss how her mother beamed at her father each time Ioan spun her past them. Even the dowager seemed pleased by the match. Everyone was happy. Or so it seemed.

Everybody but Lady Nora, that is.

More than once, Sophie thought the lady looked bereft whenever she caught sight of her with Ioan. Not angry, but incredibly sad. But, she couldn't seem to find the words to ask Ioan again, since he'd already explained to her once about Lady Nora.

"May I have this dance?"

Sophie looked up to find Pennington standing before her. Like Ioan, his hair was mussed, although his was not nearly as tousled as Ioan's, and his forehead was shiny from exertion, as he seemed determined to dance with as many of the ladies as possible. She'd even seen him whisk the dowager out onto the floor, much to the dowager's displeasure, if her scowl was to be believed.

"Of course." She laid her hand in his, allowing him to draw her up beside him and lead her onto the floor. His hand came to rest on her hip, his other warm about hers as the music melted into a waltz.

"So, if I point people out, can you name them yet?"

She couldn't help her laugh. "Oh, I highly doubt it.

After the first dozen, I'm afraid I'm lost."

"Worry not, I've known some of them my entire life and *I* can't name them still."

"Now I think you're pulling my leg."

His dark blue eyes danced with merriment. "Try me."

"How? I don't even know a single one of them. You could call them anything you like, and I would never know if you were right or not."

"You will know them all in time." Pennington nodded toward a clump of ladies dressed in various jewel tones. "They are the Machet sisters. Eleanor, the one in green, is the oldest and is married to a man three times her age and four times her size. They have four children, believe it or not, and the rumors are her husband is not the father of any of them. Now, I'm not much one for gossip, but I will say, I tend to believe them, simply because the youngest one looks like her, but the other three don't look like anyone in that family. Instead, the firstborn looks very much like Lord Pomperton over there in the corner, and the second one looks vaguely like he might be a Canfield instead."

She had no idea who the Canfields were, but she surmised Lord Pomperton was the very important looking fellow in the corner, who kept looking at Eleanor as if he'd like to devour her. Meanwhile, Eleanor smiled up at man who did in fact look old enough to be her grandfather and wide enough that he could seriously hurt her if he fell on her. Fascinating.

"The other two are unmarried and on the hunt for a title. At one point, only dukes and marquesses need apply, but now, even a knight would suffice. Their mother is *that* desperate to marry them off at this point, since they passed spinster about ten years ago."

"Oh, that's a horrible thing to say."

"You don't know them," came his dry reply.

"True." She turned back to him. "And what of Lady Nora?"

"Ah… Nora…" His voice took on a faraway tone. "A man's fantasy brought to life and she knows it."

"So I gathered."

He gazed down at her. "She and I and Blackthorne have known each other since we were children. Has he told you about her?"

A small knot tightened in the pit of her stomach. "Told me what about her? I asked him if she was important to him, and he told me not at all, that she was but an old friend."

To her horror, his eyes grew serious. "She is an old friend. To both of us. But…" He paused, then glanced over his shoulder toward the glass doors leading out to a terrace.

She followed his line of sight, and her heart sank. Just beyond those doors, on the terrace, she could make out the silhouette of a lithe woman with a pile of dark hair atop her head. She couldn't see who was with Lady Nora, but then she turned back to Pennington and caught sight of Ioan on the opposite side of the room, speaking with his mother and Sophie's father.

"But what, Lord Pennington? You told me I do not want her as an enemy. Why would you say such a thing?"

He turned his attention back to her. "Take care, Miss Montgomery."

"Why?"

"Just… just take care."

"Please." She tightened her hand on his shoulder,

her voice barely a whisper. "I need to know the truth, my lord. Why should I take care? What didn't he tell me?"

A hint of a flush crept into his pale skin, swept along his sharp cheekbones, and he looked distinctly uncomfortable. "At one point, he had thought to ask Nora to marry him. We all thought he was going to do it. They were quite the cozy couple, you know."

Those knots in her belly twisted until bile rose in her throat. She winced as she swallowed hard against the brackish taste filling her mouth. "No, my lord. I didn't know. But thank you for not taking me for being completely stupid."

"I wouldn't, Miss Montgomery." He gave her hand a gentle squeeze. "I rather like you. And Blackthorne does as well."

"Of course he does," she replied, her voice breaking and her throat growing tight. "Because of me, he won't have to leave this grand house, or give up any of his precious horses, or his house in London. What is there to dislike? And it isn't as if marriages of convenience are so rare here, are they?"

To his credit, Pennington flinched. "That isn't exactly what I meant. I mean, he does *like* you."

"But he loves *her*."

"Oh, I don't know about that," Pennington said, shaking his head. "He's never spoken of loving anyone. At least, not to me. I'm not so certain he loves anyone at all or that he knows *how* to do so. You don't understand our life yet. It isn't the same as yours. He wasn't cherished and adored by his parents. He was groomed and taught what was expected of him. It's only in adulthood that he and Duchess Mary are friendly to one another." He pulled her slightly closer, as if in attempt to hug her without anyone else noticing. "I don't want to see you hurt, but you do deserve the truth."

"And I thank you for that honesty, my lord."

"Please, call me Stephen. Or Penn, as Blackthorne does." He offered up a smile. "I like to think you and I are friends."

"Thank you, my lord. I mean" she managed to smile back, "thank you, Penn."

"There, see? That wasn't so difficult, was it? Now, if you don't mind, I would love to steal you for a second go around this floor."

She glanced over at Ioan, who stared their way, a distinct scowl on his face, and then over toward the doors. Lady Nora came through them and strode purposefully toward Ioan.

That was the only push she needed as Sophie turned back to Pennington. "I would love to."

CHAPTER TWELVE

It was well after one in the morning by the time the last guest took their leave. Sophie's parents had gone up around midnight, the dowager had taken her leave not much later, and although she tried to sleep, Sophie simply couldn't make her mind go quiet enough for that to happen.

A clock struck three and she gave up, rising to slip into her wrapper. Perhaps a book from the library would help, so she padded her way below, and rounded the corner, only to stop dead in her tracks.

Ioan was already there. Apparently he'd had trouble sleeping as well, for he was stretched out on one of the damask sofas nearest a hearth, a book open and propped against his chest. He'd shed his shoes and coat, his shirtsleeves rolled to his elbows, his shirt open at the throat, and his silk socks wrinkled. He started, sitting up. "Who goes there?"

She also jumped, then chuckled at her foolishness. "I beg your pardon." She came around his sofa. "I didn't mean to startle you. I couldn't sleep."

He smiled, closing the book. "You're welcome to choose a title, if you wish. It seems sleep is in short supply this morning."

Without thinking, she gathered her wrapper at the throat as she sank onto the sofa across from him. "I didn't mean to disturb you."

"You aren't. Please, don't trouble yourself." He leaned over to set his book on the table. In the soft glow of the firelight, his skin was burnished ivory, the hollows beneath his cheekbones giving him an almost ethereal look. His shirt bagged away from his chest to offer up a glimpse of that expanse sprinkled with dark hair. His eyes glittered like dark emeralds as his gaze alit on her. "Did you enjoy yourself this evening?"

"I did, actually. It's been a while since I last danced the night away." She couldn't hold back her smile, even as hint of sadness crept through her. "That's a lie. I've never danced the night away. I've only ever spent them on the side, wishing I was dancing."

"Is that so?" There came a soft crushing sound as he rose and held out a hand. "Come dance with me, Miss Montgomery."

"There's no music."

"We don't need music." He wiggled his fingers at her. "Come now, it isn't polite to keep a duke waiting, you know."

"But, there's—"

He bent toward her to catch her by the wrist and tugged her up. "Are you always so stubborn?"

Her cheeks grew warm as he pulled her flush against him. "I beg your—"

"You'll do no such thing," he growled, his voice low and smooth. He did nothing more than sway with her in his arms, but that was fine with her. There was something to be said about being held by him. His arms were tight about her, but not uncomfortably so, and when she looked up, he said, "You looked stunning tonight, you know. I daresay, you were the most beautiful woman that ballroom has seen in ages."

A pleasant heat warmed her cheeks. "I thank you, Your Grace."

He leaned toward her and whispered, "Ioan."

"Ioan…"

Her heart skipped a beat as she realized he was going to kiss her again, but she managed to purse her lips and lift them just as his came to rest upon them. His kiss was soft and gentle, his mouth moving ever so slowly against hers, a caress unlike any other she'd ever felt.

The tip of his tongue came hot and pointed against her closed mouth. She parted her lips, her toes actually curling in her slippers at the silken heat of his tongue skimming along hers. He kissed the way he danced, slow and sensual, bending her back enough to press her breasts into his chest as his tongue tangled with hers, then drew it back into the wet heat of his mouth.

Without thinking, she flattened her hands against his back, against those two sheets of solid muscle. She pulled him closer still as he continued his sensuous assault on her tongue, on her lips. His hands slid down, cupped her backside, lifted her against him, and her eyes widened at the first touch of his arousal against her.

He broke the kiss then, smiling down at her as he let his fingers trail along her arm, toward the inner hem of her wrapper. His fingertips brushed her bared skin, swept the silk wrapper aside to display her silk nightrail. He traced along the neckline, which was scandalously low, but she never cared before because who would see it?

Now she knew. His gaze grew hotter as it slid over the inner curves of her breasts, on full display by that scandalously low neckline. "I like this," he murmured, his voice oddly husky as he looked up to meet her eyes once more.

"You don't find it… find too—too revealing?"

"Heavens, no." He shook his head and then, without warning, dipped to press a kiss against the curve of her left breast.

Fire shot through her at the caress of his lips against flesh she hadn't known was so sensitive. He didn't stop there, however. He moved down, into the shadowy valley between both breasts.

Then he moved outward.

"Oh!" She couldn't hold back her gasp as his mouth closed about her nipple, the tip of his tongue flaying it through the silk. It was unlike anything she'd ever felt before, and it made her insides tighten all at once. Those knots started in her belly, but quickly dropper lower to form an almost unbearable tightness deep within her, one that had her arcing her hips toward him, one that had her twisting her fingers in his thick dark curls. One that had her clutching him to her as he swirled his tongue about a nipple that now felt tight and achy.

He flicked his tongue against her through the wet silk and she shivered as he then slid a hand up along her inner thigh, dragging her nightrail up as he moved. She bit down hard enough on her bottom lip that she actually flinched when his fingertips brushed curls no man had ever seen, let alone touched.

"Ioan!" She couldn't hold back her cry as he breached her, sliding a finger inside her to stroke her in the most erotic way possible. He came back up to seize her mouth with his, that finger inside her swirling to make her shiver, to make her gasp and rock against him, her body pleading for more of the same. The knots tightened. They multiplied. They sent sparking hot pleasure ribboning through her.

She couldn't think. Couldn't speak. She could only meet his kiss and tightened her grip on him. That finger inside her moved faster, made her breath come harder and ragged about the edged. Her head spun. Her body ached. Relief was so near... she didn't know how she knew, but she did.

Then it happened.

She shattered, her entire body trembling as fire filled her, spread through her to leave her hot and hungry and desperate to make the bliss last. She shivered against him, her fingers twisting in his hair, his name a hoarse whisper on her lips, her body limp against his as the wave crashed over her then swept her out to sea.

He caught her, his finger slowing, his lips tender as they caressed hers now. A laugh came soft against her lips as she breathlessly protested when he slid that finger free, and he held her tenderly, whispering, "Sophie..."

Her head spun with pleasure, with the need to tease him the same way, to make him moan and rock against her. She might have been a wallflower, but she knew what to do and so slowly kissed her way along his neck, smiling at the breathless sigh rising to his lips.

He didn't stop her, didn't even try as she reached for the button of his trousers. It gave easily, and she looked up to find him smiling at her, his eyes almost all pupil as he traced a fingertip along her cheek. He knew what she was about to do, and from the looks of it, was not about to stop her.

Her heart hammered against her ribs at her boldness, at what she was about to do, and she carefully opened his trousers, sank to her knees, reached for him—

"Your Grace, is something the matter?"

Sophie froze as Ioan tensed against her. Thank the

Maker the sofa blocked her from Marmaduke's sight. He probably had no idea the duke's trousers were open and that he had a woman kneeling before him, about to taste him in the most intimate way possible.

She almost smiled at the strain in Ioan's voice as he managed to reply, "Not at all, Marmaduke. Simply doing a bit of reading before bed."

"May I fetch you anything?"

"That won't be necessary."

"As you wish. A good evening, Your Grace."

"And to you, as well."

She peered up at Ioan at the sound of fading footsteps. "Has he left?"

Ioan offered up a pained grin. "He has and that isn't all that's gone, I'm afraid."

She bit back her chuckle, even as disappointment crashed over her. Now, she felt incredibly foolish there, on her knees, before him, and so slowly stood. "Are you all right?"

"I will be, in a few minutes," he told her, reaching down to refasten his trousers. "It would have made the servants giggle like schoolchildren, had he seen you."

Heat touched her cheeks and this time, there was nothing pleasant about it. "I'm so sorry, Ioan, I thought—that is, I wanted—Oh, what I mean is…"

"It's quite all right, Miss Montgomery," he told her softly. "There will be other nights."

He bent toward her once more, brushing her lips with his, then said, "I should go up, before someone else decides to come and see if I'm all right."

With that, he stepped around her and, his book forgotten, made his way to the library doors.

"I did have a lovely time tonight," she called softly.

As his gaze met hers, she cleared her throat. "At the party, I mean."

"As did I," he told her. "And I had a lovely time here as well. Perhaps next time, there will be no interruptions."

He didn't give her a chance to respond, but disappeared through the doorway, leaving her to smile after him. Perhaps everything was going to work out just fine between them and their marriage might not be such a cold arrangement after all.

****

Sophie was the last one down the next morning, as it was nearly eleven before she awoke. All traces of last night's festivities were gone, tidied up by Blackthorne's very efficient staff. In fact, the only remainder was the hollow feeling in the pit of her stomach whenever Pennington's words echoed through her head.

What was Lady Nora to Ioan? Did she really want to know the truth? Theirs wasn't a love match, and there was no reason on earth for her to expect him to be faithful. She rather *hoped* he would be, but had no right to demand it. She wasn't daft enough to think otherwise.

Of course, she could simply ask Ioan.

Ioan.

Just the thought of him made her entire body go warm. And she certainly would never see the library quite the same way again. With any luck, Lady Nora would simply fade into the past and Sophie wouldn't have her to worry about again. All she had to do was ask Ioan.

Didn't she?

She argued with herself the entire way down into the breakfast room, where everyone but the dowager gathered around the table. Ioan looked up from the newspaper in his hands. "A good morning, Miss Montgomery."

As he spoke, mischief danced in his eyes and a slow smile played about his lips.

Then he winked.

"Good morning, Your Grace." Thankfully, her face only grew warm and not hot. It didn't feel warm enough to be a full-on blush, so hopefully, it wouldn't give her away. She quickly turned to her parents. "Mother. Papa."

"I was just about to send Edith up to fetch you," Emily said without looking up from her plate. "You don't normally sleep so late."

"I'm afraid I kept her up far too late," Ioan said, winking at Sophie as he added, "We were talking in the library long after I should have let her go up to sleep."

"Talking?" Emily looked from her to Ioan and back. "Talking about what?"

"Authors," he replied without missing a beat. "She asked me for a few recommendations, that's all."

"Oh... well, then." Emily turned back to her. "That was quite generous of the duke, wasn't it?"

Sophie couldn't hold back her smile, and meeting Ioan's gaze wasn't at all difficult now as she replied, "Oh, he was more than generous, Mother."

Ioan winked again and ducked back to his newspaper. "I do apologize for how late I kept you up. I could go on for hours about... authors."

"I have no complaints." Now the warmth grew hotter, so Sophie moved to the sideboard to take a plate. A full breakfast had been laid out, from bacon to eggs and all points in between. However, she wasn't exactly hungry, and so only took a small pastry to bring back to the table.

Now Emily looked up. Looked up and wrinkled her nose. "That's what you're eating?"

"I'm not very hungry this morning, I'm afraid."

"It's just as well," her father chimed in, tugging his cup and saucer closer. He leaned over to peer into the cup and seemed almost disappointed to see tea still in it. He preferred coffee, but Blackthorne Hall had none in its stores and wouldn't have any until someone ventured to London for it. "Isn't that seamstress coming today?"

Emily nodded. "She is. She'll be here for one." She looked over at Sophie. "It's probably wise if you put *that* back as well. You won't fit into your clothes, with the way you've been eating lately."

This time, the warmth in her cheeks had nothing to do with Ioan or their encounter in the library and everything to do with the squirming discomfort of embarrassment. The pastry fell back to her plate with a dull *thud*, her appetite gone to dust.

Ioan looked from her to her mother and back, his brows knit as he said, "I beg your pardon, Mrs. Montgomery, but Miss Montgomery has a bit of a way to go before she needs worry about such a thing."

"You would be amazed at how quickly she plumps up," Emily replied with a tinkling laugh. "And there's nothing worse than a plump bride."

To Sophie's surprise, Ioan replied, "Either way, it isn't very kind."

"Perhaps not, but it *is* true."

Sophie stared down at her plate, her vision blurring as tears filled her eyes. What little appetite she had vanished completely, and even her tea no longer had any flavor. "Excuse me," she whispered, pushing her chair away from the table to rise. When no one objected, she skirted the table to leave the room.

Footsteps sounded behind her and out in the hallway, Ioan caught her by the elbow. "Miss Montgomery, wait."

"Wait?" She swiped at her eyes. "Whatever for?"

"You haven't eaten a bite." He held out the same pastry she'd left on her plate. "You must be hungry."

"I was, but then Mother reminded me it would be a sin to grow plump."

He rolled his eyes, then pressed the pastry into her hand. "You're fine the way you are, and it will take more than a silly croissant to make *you* plump, no matter what your mother might think."

She looked up at him, her cheeks still hot, but at least her eyes dried. She broke off a piece into her mouth. It was every bit as delicious as it looked. Light. Flaky. It practically melted on her tongue. "I think she would beg to differ."

"Let her. It changes nothing." He smiled. "Delicious, isn't it? Our cook knows her way around baked goods. Her father was one of Paris's finest pastry chefs."

She broke the croissant in half and held out one portion to him. "Share with me."

He took the other half. "We'll grow plump together."

She tried to scowl, but couldn't quite make her face obey. "You are terrible."

"I have my moments." He waited for her to finish her half, then offered up his arm. "Come," he nodded in the direction of the hallway before them, "walk with me to my study."

She nodded and let him tuck her hand into the crook of his elbow. "Why, though?"

"Because I have things needing my—"

"No, I mean why do you wish me to walk with you?"

"Because I happen to enjoy your company, Miss Montgomery." He grinned down at her. "And our wedding is but twelve days away, and perhaps we should come to know one another a little more before then."

"And you think a walk from here to the other side of this house will accomplish that?"

"Have you seen how big this house is?"

She chuckled. "Fair enough, Your Grace."

"So, tell me, is your mother always so—"

"Opinionated?"

"Well, I was going to say blunt, but that works as well."

She bit back a sigh. "I'm afraid so. She isn't well-liked back home."

"You don't say," came his dry reply. "I'm shocked to hear it."

Boldness surged through her as she gave his arm a playful squeeze. "That's terrible, you know."

His free hand came to rest atop hers, his fingers warm as they curled over hers. "You've met my mother. I think they might be long-lost sisters of a sort."

She smiled. The dowager was every bit as... blunt... as her mother, and yet she wasn't nearly as off-putting. "Perhaps, but your mother is also different. People respect her and she treats them with equal respect. Back home, people see Mother as pushy and demanding, as if she thinks she is entitled to whatever she wishes because my father is wealthy."

"I take it New York society is as accepting as ours."

"We're *nouveau riche* as far as New York is concerned and too uppity for our own good. And Mother only reinforces it, I'm afraid. People simply don't take to her."

"So, *that's* why you've agreed to do this."

She peered up at him. A smile played at his lips, but his expression was still quite serious. Drat it all, she had such a difficult time telling whether he joked or not. She walked a fine line and could only hope she didn't come down on the wrong side of that line. "It wasn't exactly my decision, Your Grace. Mother means well—I think—but her dream is to be acceptable back home, for the Rockefellers and the Astors to see her as one of them. And having a daughter who also happens to be the Duchess of Blackthorne…"

"Will make that happen much more quickly."

She nodded. "That and she's hoping the mothers of eligible bachelors are all gnashing their teeth over their loss of me as a daughter-in-law. As if they'd actually do that at all anyway."

"Well, I would certainly gnash my teeth if you were to marry someone else."

"Your Grace!"

A low laugh bubbled to his lips as he turned toward her. "What? I would. And, if you like, when we visit New York, I will make a point of extolling your virtues for the world to hear. A true lady who loves and knows the arts, literature, music. Who plays Mozart. Who champions the downtrodden. And," his eyes darkened, "who is an utter vixen besides. Why, you are quite the perfectly acceptable sort."

Her cheeks burned once more and although he only teased, his words made her entire body as warm as her face. "I don't think that last bit is something anyone will believe."

"Why not?" He smiled down at her. "I know what you were going to do last eve, what would have happened, had Marmaduke not spoiled it. You should only know how arousing the mere memory is to me. And of course, watching you enjoy yourself was enough to make my entire body tingle, Miss Montgomery. And it does still tingle today. To a certain extent, anyway."

"Your Grace!"

"What? It does." To her surprise, his hand came up to curve against her cheek. "And I must also confess, I look forward to many more of those sort of nights. You've a gift, you know."

"A kissing gift?" She couldn't keep the snort from her words. "I think that might be an exaggeration."

"It is anything but. One day, you'll see." He winked and bent to brush her lips with a quick kiss. "Now, if you will excuse me. I've work to do and you've a trousseau to assemble. I daresay you will be anything but plump on our wedding day."

With that, he left her in the hallway, whistling softly as he took himself off into his study and closed the door softly behind him.

She stood there for a long moment, smiling. He wasn't the only one who looked forward to those nights.

CHAPTER THIRTEEN

The preparations for the wedding of the Duke of Blackthorne and Miss Josephine Montgomery set the entire household into a frenzy. There were flowers to arrange, meals to prepare, and rooms to ready for the influx of guests who would stay at Blackthorne Hall, as well as reservations to be made for those guests who would stay in the village instead. Seamstresses worked tirelessly to ready Sophie's gown for the momentous occasion. A photographer from London was due as well. With each passing day, Sophie lost more of her appetite, and by the morning of the wedding, she'd lost enough weight that Miss Danvers fretted about having to take in the bodice of the ivory satin gown.

The morning of the wedding dawned clear for the first time in what seemed like weeks. Sunlight streamed through the trees, dappled the lawns around Blackthorne Hall, and as Sophie peered through her window, down at the elegant coach adorned with white roses and stephanotis, her belly did the oddest flip. That coach awaited her arrival. To bring her to the church in Blackthorne Village, where it seemed everyone in the world would gather to watch her and Ioan marry.

She tried not to miss Joy, as when her mother sent the invitations, the Townshend family had mysteriously been left off the list. And of those sent to the families Emily tried her damndest to impress? It seemed several responses went missing and Sophia thought her mother might actually pop when the dowager calmly informed her the Astors had already accepted *her* invitation instead, as had the Morgans and the Vanderbilts. Sophie had to bite back her smile as her mother grew more and more sullen. Guilt accompanied Sophie's amusement, but at the same time, she'd had quite enough of her mother using her to break into society. She actually looked forward to her parents' return to New York. Somehow, she knew she'd sigh with relief when it happened. She'd be able then to concentrate on being a duchess and Ioan's wife. Perhaps then she'd figure out just who she was supposed to be.

She turned toward the bed, where her gown awaited her. Ivory satin. Tulle veil attached to a tiara glittering with diamonds from the dowager duchess's personal collection. Ivory satin slippers. Silk hose. She felt very much like a princess as Edith came in with two other maids to help her dress.

Her mother had gone ahead to the church, but as she descended to the first floor, she saw her father waiting for her, and when he looked up, his jaw went slack while his eyes grew shiny. "My word," he whispered. "My little girl no more."

"Do I look all right, Papa?"

"Darling daughter, you are breathtaking. Blackthorne won't know what hit him." He offered his arm. "Shall we?"

She shifted her small bouquet of roses, stephanotis, and gardenias—all in varying shades of white and all grown in the Blackthorne greenhouses—to her left hand so she could slip her right through her father's arm. As they made their way to the coach, she couldn't decide which of them trembled worse, and so decided it was him. After all, she had no cause to be nervous. This was a good match, for both her and Ioan. Everything would be just fine.

The ride to the church was a blur. People lined the main road, cheering as they rocked by, but that was all she remembered as they alit outside the church. She clutched her father's arm tighter, taking great pains to tread with care so she didn't trip over the flowing gown, and as the church doors opened, she swallowed hard and allowed him to escort her inside.

The scent of roses filled the air, and she forgot about being stared at as she crested the aisle and her gaze fell on Ioan, dressed in dove gray trousers and morning coat, his waistcoat almost blinding in its whiteness. His dark hair looked windblown as usual, but it was his expression that made her heart skip a not-so-painful beat.

He gazed at her as if in awe and didn't so much as blink as she made her way to him to slip her arm through his. As she turned toward him, she lost herself in that gaze, only hearing the vicar in time to recite her vows. She only barely heard him pronounce them man and wife, and then Ioan leaned in, lifted her veil from her face, and kissed her ever so softly on the lips.

He smiled, tucking her hand through his arm to escort her back, and she couldn't help but smile herself. Everyone in the church cheered and clapped, and the sound followed them out into the sunshine. This time, when she climbed into the coach, it was her husband who sat beside her and not her father, and Ioan seemed out of breath as he swept a dark curl away from his forehead.

"So, we did it," he said, threading his fingers with hers to give her hand a squeeze. "Josephine Montgomery

St. John, the Duchess of Blackthorne."

A shiver tickled along her spine. "So, I am now formally Josephine Blackthorne, am I right?"

"You are, love." He leaned over to nuzzle her. "But we won't worry about the rest of it now. There's plenty of time for you to learn it, and I trust you will."

A laugh broke free as he swept her into his arms and onto his lap. That curl toppled over his left eye once more, but when she went to brush it back, he caught her by the wrist, then pressed a kiss into her palm. "Leave it, darling," he murmured, his voice oddly husky, "and kiss me."

He didn't wait for her to respond but leaned in to capture her lips with his. They moved against hers, soft and warm, the tip of his tongue flicking against hers until she parted them. Then, her toes actually curled in her delicate slippers as his tongue snaked along hers and his arms tightened about her.

The gentle pressure against the outer part of her thigh had her opening her eyes. She knew was it was, of course, but it surprised her just the same. When Ioan slid one hand along her satiny bodice to skim along the outer curve of her right breast, that pressure increased.

It moves on its own?

Although she knew the basic workings of the relations between men and women, she wasn't entirely familiar with a man's arousal. He cupped her breast.

It twitched against her.

He squeezed it gently.

Was it getting bigger?

His thumb traced a slow circle around her nipple.

It's actually poking *me!*

He broke the kiss, his eyes smoky green as he

murmured, "I look forward to this evening, love."

Without thinking, she blurted, "So I gathered."

He simply stared, then to her surprise, burst out laughing. "Yes, he's a pesky fellow at times, demanding attention and all that. Ignore him and he'll go down."

"He'll?"

"Shall I name him?"

That struck her as wildly amusing. "Do men do such a thing?"

"Some do." The hand that had cradled her breast so lovingly slid back down along the curve of her waist and around to the small of her back. "I'm not one of them. Although, we could, if you like."

She pressed her lips together as her cheeks grew warmer. He gave her a gentle squeeze. "I was but teasing. I didn't mean to embarrass you."

"No, you didn't. Embarrass me, I mean."

"You're blushing."

"I know, but… that's because I was thinking, I really need to see what it looks like before I can settle on a name, so—" She paused as he threw his head back and his laughter echoed all around them. "What? What is so amusing?"

He gathered her closer still. "You are, Duchess. And don't ever lose it, please."

She smiled up at him. "I'll do my best, Duke."

"Good. Now, kiss me again. We're almost to Blackthorne Hall and won't have a chance to sneak away until everyone has worn themselves out and left."

****

If Sophie thought the party to celebrate their engagement had been grand, that was nothing compared to the reception the dowager hosted back at Blackthorne

Hall. Sophie had never seen so many people in one room, and Ioan confessed even he didn't know half of those in attendance. But it was a grand party, and she danced so much, she wore holes in her delicate slippers.

Everyone seemed to enjoy themselves, indulging in food and drink and wonderful music. Pennington seemed particularly delighted when he cut in between Sophie and Ioan with a toothy grin. "I'm but borrowing her for a round or two, Blackthorne. You will have her back in no time."

Smiling, Ioan shook his hair out of his eyes. "I'll hold you to that, Pennington. I'm going to get a bit more champagne. Darling, would you care for some?"

"I would love so—oh!" She burst out laughing as Pennington swept her away from Ioan and out onto the dance floor. "You didn't allow me to finish!"

He didn't look at all remorseful. "He will fetch you the champagne, you needn't worry." He paused, his expression growing somber. "He seems happy. Happier than I've seen him in a long time. Years, even."

She let her left hand come to rest on his shoulder, the muscle beneath his morning coat firm. "Does he? Good. I understand this year has been a difficult one for him."

"Quite a shock when the old duke died." Pennington nodded, glancing in the direction where Ioan had gone. "He'd been sick, but the doctor thought he'd bounce back. Pneumonia, you know."

"I didn't. I've never felt comfortable enough to bring it up." She also looked in Ioan's direction, only to find him in conversation with Nora Etheridge. Her stomach twisted, but she tried to ignore it and focus instead on Pennington. "I don't wish to upset him. Were they close?"

"Not particularly." He turned back to her. "The old duke made some poor choices, and he was not the strongest of men. He was rather weak, to be honest. He and Ioan butted heads more often than not. Unlike his father, Ioan is a very strong man. Hard-headed and with a firm delineation of right and wrong."

"I see. And one of those poor choices was losing the family fortune, wasn't it? And that's why he needs my father's money. To save Blackthorne." She looked back over at Ioan and Nora, who now looked upset. She had ahold of Ioan's arm, her eyes wide and her lips moving frantically.

Pennington looked over his shoulder again. "What are you—oh…"

"She seems upset."

"Probably another broken engagement. It happens at least once a month with Lady Nora. She is quite skilled at becoming engaged, less so at staying that way. Quite fickle, she is."

But for some reason, Sophie didn't think the lady was upset over a lost fiancé. Judging from the way her eyes slid in Sophie's direction every few minutes, she had the feeling Nora was more upset over the fact that Ioan had married. When Nora looked over at her once more and her eyes became slits, Sophie knew that was exactly it. Pennington's warning about having Nora as an enemy roared to the forefront of her mind, even as she tried to quash it. No, she didn't want to think about it. Didn't want anything to mar this otherwise perfect day. Besides, it wasn't as if Ioan's marrying came as a surprise. At least, it shouldn't have.

Even so, as she watched Ioan yank his arm from

Nora, Sophie couldn't help but wonder just what Nora might have bubbling inside her brain, and whether Sophie would find herself the target of some oddly conceived form of revenge.

CHAPTER FOURTEEN

As the celebration went on, Sophie caught sight of Nora, and each time, the lady looked less upset and more angry. She cornered Ioan once more, and although Sophie couldn't hear them, his reaction was more than enough. He jerked away from her and stalked back across the room, where one of the footmen stood with a tray of fresh champagne.

He snatched two glasses and strode in Sophie's direction. By the time he crossed to her, a smile replaced his scowl. "I see Pennington has finally let you be. I was beginning to think I might have to fight him for your attentions."

"Oh, don't be jealous," she teased him as he pressed a crystal flute into her hand. "He is a sweet man."

"I am not at all jealous, darling. I trust Pennington. I always have, you know."

"Good." She sipped the crisp wine, then lowered her glass. "Is everything all right with Lady Nora?"

Darkness flashed through his eyes. "Everything is fine."

"She seems upset."

"She is. Her engagement to Lord Pomperton has gone by the wayside."

Sophie only vaguely recalled the man Pennington had gossiped about at the engagement ball. The one rumored to have fathered Lady Eleanor Matchet's child.

"Oh? I hadn't known she was engaged to him."

"Well, she was and is now no longer so."

She glanced up at him. "Why are you annoyed with me?"

"What?" He shook his head. "I'm not, love. It's— this is *our* wedding reception, and I should like to dance with my wife once more. That is," he said, as he plucked the flute from her hand, "if she has no objections."

"Of course she doesn't," Sophie replied with a smile, laying her hand in his. "She isn't mad, after all."

****

It was nearly three o'clock in the morning before the last guests took their leave. Sophie's stomach felt as if it were filled with frenetic butterflies as she and Ioan bid the last of their guests farewell. It wouldn't be much longer before he would escort her above, to what would now be *their* room, and they—

"There is one last thing I need do," Ioan said as they stood at the foot of the grand staircase. "So, you go on up, and I'll be there in but a few minutes."

"Of course."

He bent to brush her lips with his. "I'll be up soon."

She nodded and they parted ways. Upstairs, she bit her lip as Edith came in to help her ready for bed.

"You needn't be nervous, Your Grace," Edith said as she drew the ivory silk wrapper about Sophie's shoulders. "I'm certain His Grace will be gentle."

"I'm not worried," Sophie assured her, and even managed to smile in the mirror to better convince Edith.

"Well, you look lovely, and he is a lucky man."

Sophie's smile went from forced to real as Edith lit the candles, then took her leave. Those candles flickered in the silver candelabras set up about the room, and they caused shadows to dance along the walls. Sophie sat at her dressing table—moved from her room earlier that day—her silver comb in one hand, just staring at her reflection in the glass. The candlelight bathed everything ivory, made her hair shimmer like molten copper as it tumbled down her back, and her eyes looked almost black. And the woman staring back at her looked far calmer than she actually felt. Any minute, and Ioan would be coming through the door. He would sweep her into his arms, spirit her to the bed and then—

And then what? She knew what to expect, more or less, as her mother certainly tried to impart a bit more knowledge before they'd left for the church, but she'd stammered and stuttered so badly, her face the reddest Sophie had ever seen. And she said nothing about emotions, focusing only on reiterating the mechanics of what happened between men and women. Sophie couldn't very well tell her mother she already knew about those mechanics. She could only imagine her mother's response to *that*.

Of course, knowing and anticipating didn't make the waiting any easier, however.

She glanced down at the ring on her left hand. The sapphire sparkled with each movement of her hand. The Duchess of Blackthorne. Joy would be beside herself with giddiness over Sophie's title.

Joy.

She missed her friend and wondered if Ioan would be averse to her inviting Joy to come and visit for the summer. It might make Berkshire seem a little less lonely, since she still knew so few people. He'd told her Joy would be welcomed, but it would be best to ask him once more, just to be certain.

The door opened with a slow creak, and her heart skipped at least one beat. Ioan came into view in the mirror. In the semi-darkness, he looked almost austere in his formal clothes, his mane of dark curls as untamed as ever. He fairly radiated sin and seduction, and for the first time in weeks, she wasn't apprehensive over what was expected of her this night.

"May I come in?"

"Of course," she turned on the brocade bench to face him, "seeing as how it's your room."

She turned back to the mirror as he pushed the door closed. "It's *our* room now, Duchess, and it's quite all right for you to think of it as such."

The floorboards groaned with each step he took. She actually felt them dip as he came up behind her. Her spine stiffened on its own when his hands came down upon her shoulders. Heat sank into her through her chemise. "Did I mention how beautiful a bride you were, Duchess? Every man in that ballroom wished he was me this evening."

"I think that is a bit of an exaggeration," she told him, tilting her head back to peer up at him. "But, thank you."

His teeth flashed in a smile, then he bent toward her, his lips soft and warm as they claimed hers. His fingertips brushed her throat, grazed along her shoulders, down her arms all the while his mouth moved against hers. The tip of his tongue nudged against her lips, parted them, then his tongue slid like hot silk along hers. Slow. Teasing. Drew hers back into the welcoming heat of his mouth.

Her heartbeat quickened. Her pulse did the same. She could actually feel the blood warm in her veins.

Knots tightened in the depths of her belly. Her skin seemed to come alive, tingling with each teasing caress.

His hands slid over hers. He linked fingers with her to tug her gently to her feet. His kiss deepened even as he turned her toward him, and without thinking, she wound her arms around his neck, pressed herself flat against him. His breath hitched at the contact while his hands curved about her hips. They tightened to pull her firmly into him.

He broke the kiss, sweeping his lips along her cheekbone as he whispered, "Sophie…"

She smiled as her eyelids grew heavier and her eyes refused to open. Then, she felt it. The firm ridge of what was the beginnings of a very powerful erection. Dear heavens, this was really going to happen. She would finally get to see what this magnificent man looked like naked. What it felt like to make love with him.

Please let it be everything wonderful.

He pulled back, his eyes glittering in the candlelight as he reached for the ribbon holding her chemise closed. A gentle tug, and the ribbon slid free. Heat filled her at the way his eyes darkened when he caught the edge of the chemise to move it out of his way.

The cool air danced along her skin as he bared it, and as the silk swept against her nipple, she sucked in a sharp breath. Even that felt wonderful.

"Dear Christ," he murmured, his voice husky, "even your breasts are perfect."

As he spoke, he brought his left hand up to cup her right breast. She bit down on her bottom lip as his thumb did a slow circle about her nipple, which tightened into a hard, surprisingly sensitive nub. Heat filled her like smoke, white and wispy, spiraled through her from the pit of her belly outward.

Sophie had to force her eyes to open, and when they did, it was to see Ioan smiling down at her as he continued to tease her nipple. The pleasure spun through her, her breath quickened.

He loomed over her, all broad shoulders and chest, and bent toward her once more. As their lips met, the fingers on her breast tightened. The gentle squeeze sent a ribbon of fire through her, and without thinking, she arched her back to press her breast deeper into his hand.

The fire grew hotter still with each caress, each gentle knead, until she thought she'd go mad from the pleasure eddying through her. Her fingers grazed the nape of his neck, stretched up into the soft fall of those dark curls. Ioan eased her chemise over her shoulders, and she lowered her arms to allow it to slip free and spill to the floor, where it pooled about her feet. A second later, he swept her into his arms.

The mattress yielded to her as she settled against it. Ioan covered her, his weight welcome and not nearly as heavy as she'd thought a man of his size would be. He kissed down, over the curve of her chin, along the slope of her neck. The tip of his tongue flicked into the hollow at the base of her throat.

He moved down, his lips warm, teasing, as they caressed the inner curve of her right breast. Her eyelids grew so heavy, but she fought to keep them from sliding shut. She didn't want to miss a single moment of this, of him, of all of it.

Candlelight danced along his mussed dark curls. Several of those curls spilled over his forehead, and without thinking, she gently swept them back, away from his face. All for naught, it seemed, for they tumbled right back to where they'd been. She moved to brush them back once more, when he caught her by the wrist. "Don't trouble yourself, love," he rumbled, his voice husky and low.

When he looked up, his eyes were almost as dark as his voice, but she had the feeling if there were more light in the room, she would see his eyes were bright green. His gaze held such heat, it was almost a physical touch, and she shivered when he pressed a soft kiss just above her navel without averting his eyes.

Her fingertips grazed along the fine fabric of his morning coat. Morning coat? Drat it all, how was it she was naked, while he remained fully clothed? That didn't seem at all fair. She wanted to see him, practically *ached* for it.

He kissed along the slope of her right thigh, pausing when he reached the fluff of chestnut curls between her legs. "Beautiful," he whispered without looking up.

Then, he dipped his head to her.

"Oh!" She couldn't hold back her gasp, her fingers tightening on the pillow beneath her head as white-hot fire shot through her. That fire was the sweetest thing she'd ever tasted, billowing through her with each slow, maddening caress and made her forget the imbalance in their state of undress. Pleasure unlike any she'd ever known filled her, scorched her, had her calling out his name as she thrust one hand into the thick mass of dark curls—the only part of him she could reach—while the other one twisted and tugged at the pillow.

"Oh… oh… dear he-heavens…" The words were so slow and thick to come to her lips. Her hips rocked toward him of their own accord, desperate for… something. She didn't know what, but her body certainly seemed to know. She writhed beneath him, the knots in her belly tighter with each slow, teasing flick of his tongue.

She pulled the pillow clean out from under her head as those knots all exploded at once and that sweet fire erupted into an inferno. She went over the edge, soared out over the chasm, her blood singing, her skin tingling, her lips pursed with his name balanced on them.

"Ioan!" The rush tore through her, threatened to blow her apart entirely as she felt every heartbeat, every last bit of pleasure as it burned through her. Then, she couldn't bear the sensations any longer. They were too much… she was far too sensitive… she needed air.

She needed him.

Without thinking, she tugged on his hair. Hard. Not once, but twice. If it hurt him, he didn't say anything. Instead, he obliged and let her tug him up to meet her greedy kiss. She had to touch him, had to let her hands roam over him, to make him gasp and quiver just as she had done.

The falls on his trousers gave her a fight, but it was a fight she won, and when she found him, his hitched breath was music to her ears. Instinct mingled with curiosity. She wanted to caress him, to explore him, to push him onto his back so she could tug down those cumbersome trousers and see him for herself.

He didn't disappoint, hard and proud, his desire evident as she wrestled his trousers down to let them fall into the abyss alongside the bed. She could only stare at that part of him she'd imagined, but never saw before, and with a soft laugh, he murmured, "I pass muster?"

"Oh, yes…" she breathed, tearing her gaze from his manhood to meet his amused gaze. "You are beautiful,

Your Grace."

He sat up to tug his shirt from his back. "Ah-ah, love. When we are here, like this, there will be no formality."

"No formality…" Her words were a whisper as she stared hard at him. She hadn't imagined the muscle sculpting his shoulders, his upper arms. Dark hair swirled across his chest, down over his belly, narrowed into a trail that then joined another thatch of dark curls. Dear lord, he was beyond beautiful.

She reached for him, trailing her fingertips down over the sculpted muscle of his chest, down along the ridges of his belly.

He sucked in a sharp breath, his eyes closing as she traced gently along his manhood. Shy at first, she could only bring herself to brush him with just the tip of her forefinger. Sleek. Smooth. Unlike anything she imagined it would feel like.

A soft sigh bubbled to his lips as she traced back along the same path. Then, with a deep breath of her own, she curled her fingers about him. Her first stroke came slow and teasing, and it made him shiver above her.

Her shyness fled as she tightened her hand about that part of him to caress with increasing speed. He arched to meet her, slick and hot, and with each thrust into her grasp, her own body responded. A tightness took root deep within her, a sensual heat built to spread through her veins as if her blood was actually on fire. That heat grew, steamy and damp, and when he bent toward her to kiss her, she couldn't hold back. She wanted him and wanted him to know just how powerful her desire for him was, and so when his tongue dipped between her lips once more, she caught it, drew it deep, and teased him with both her tongue and her hand until he was breathless above her.

He broke the kiss, his voice rough as he whispered, "Duchess…"

"Ah-ah," she broke in with a grin, "there is to be no formality. Remember?"

A soft laugh rent the air. "None whatsoever."

As he spoke, he lowered against her, smiling as he dipped between her thighs. "You will call me anything but Duke or Your Grace, Sophie."

She shivered as he eased his hips between her thighs. The tips of his fingers brushed her. Then, one slid inside her. She bit down hard on her bottom lip while her fingernails bit into his bare shoulders. He teased her with that finger, stroked fast, then slow, and whispered, "My beautiful wife," as he slid free.

Then he moved slightly, easing his hand between them to position himself He pushed. Breached her. *Oh, my…*

The pain wasn't entirely unexpected, nor was it ungodly. A brief *pop*, a sharp sting, and then he filled her. To her surprise, he shuddered against her, a low moan in his voice as he breathed, "Dear Christ…. You feel *amazing*…"

Then, he moved.

Oh, my…

He thrust again.

She bit down on her bottom lip. Again.

Another thrust.

Another.

Each thrust felt more wonderful than the last. He moved easily inside her, stirred those same delicious feelings that his tongue had. Oh, yes, this was nice. So very nice, indeed.

Then, he let out a low moan, heaved against her, and groaned, "Oh, damn it…" as he collapsed against her, fighting for air.

She couldn't help but feel a pang of disappointment. Surely there was more to this for her, wasn't there? True, her mother, upon explaining it, never mentioned Sophie should actually enjoy herself. No, she always spoke of it as a duty, almost likening it to a chore to be endured rather than enjoyed.

Looking up at Ioan, she wanted to voice these thoughts, wanted some sort of reassurance that it would get better when they came to know each other more intimately. But she simply could not make the words form. Shyness rendered her incapable of voicing her questions. All she could do was hope it either improved for her or she managed to *not* be such a mealy-mouthed ninny. Hopefully that too would come in time.

"Duchess," he whispered, kissing the side of her neck, "I beg your pardon, of course. This was a surprise for me."

"A—a surprise?"

He eased away from her, but gathered her in his arms as he replied, "It wasn't supposed to end quite as quickly as it did."

"It—it wasn't?"

He shook his head, tracing his fingertips along the side of her head. The motion was so light, so gentle, that drowsiness crept over her. "Not at all."

"I didn't know."

She curved against him, her eyelids heavy and her entire body on the languid side. Despite her disappointment, she was quite comfortable, there in his arms, tucked against him so perfectly.

"What else is there?" she asked after several minutes of comfortable silence.

"Pleasure," he replied, his fingers going still for a moment. "And wonder. And awe. And you wondering if I am, perhaps, some sort of god when it's all over."

"Wondering if you're a god?"

"It would be nice."

Sophie lifted her head to find him grinning. "You shouldn't tease me that way." She scowled. "I thought you were serious."

He chuckled, gathering her closer still. "You should expect pleasure and perhaps laughter at times. And intimacy. That should be there as well. But, most of all, you should always look forward to the next interlude." He pressed a kiss into the top of her head. "I can only hope I leave you as satisfied as you leave me."

She chewed on that for a moment. Her pleasure was important to him. That surprised her, since her mother's speech mentioned nothing about her finding pleasure in her marriage bed. She'd always thought it was unimportant for the wife.

Then without thinking, she let her fingers trail along Ioan's belly, up over his chest. As her fingertips swept over his left nipple, he sucked in a sharp breath. She did it again, smiling as he reacted the same way, only this time, a sleepy smile came to his lips as well.

She bit the inside of one cheek as she traced a circle about that nipple. Ioan growled low and soft in his throat.

She swept over it.

The sheets rustled as he came up to cover her, his body warm against hers. His eyes were soft, tender, holding hers as he curved his hands about either side of her face. His lips found hers, his kiss long and lingering, and enough to set her head spinning and her heart racing.

She slid her arms about his waist, trailing her fingernails along his bare back, and to her surprise, he shivered against her. She did it again. And again. Once more until he exhaled hard against the slope of her neck and whispered, "Vixen," as he swept a kiss up along her neck toward her ear.

He caught her lobe between gentle teeth, flicked it with the tip of his tongue, released it to swirl his tongue along the shell of her ear. It was her turn to shiver again as he swept a kiss down, along the slope of her neck, over the rise of her breast.

Her nipple tightened and she bit down hard on her bottom lip as he met her gaze just as he swept the tip of his tongue over the hard nub. *Flick. Swirl. Flick. Swirl.* Her head spun with each teasing stroke, her back bowed sharply when he caught the nub between his teeth. The knots returned, the dampness between her thighs hotter and slicker now. Her eyes closed of their own accord as he brushed his fingertips down along her belly, into the fluff of curls, into her heat.

His stroke was slow. Teasing. Her hips arched on their own as he teased another nub, this one far more sensitive than the one at the tip of her breast. This one made the fire brighter, the dampness slicker, and little by little, tingles swept through her, hot and sweet, and brought his name to her lips in a breathless moan.

Heat filled her. Desire washed over her. She had to touch him, had to explore him, had to make him feel even one iota of the pleasure he sent smoking through her. She wanted to explore him the way he explored her. Wanted to touch and tease and taste every last inch of him.

He didn't halt her as she pulled away to press a kiss into his chest. His hand fell away from her, still as she swept her lips along the flat plane of his belly.

She flattened her hands against his chest and pushed to urge him onto his back. He complied, a smile playing at his lips as he murmured, "What are you about, darling?"

"You'll know soon enough," she whispered back, leaning over to brush her lips over his left nipple. He sucked in a sharp breath as she did it again, and this time, flicked her tongue over it. Then, she pulled back to kiss her way down, over his stomach…

"Oh, Christ…" He actually shuddered when she inched down to his hips and her lips closed about him. He was hot and smooth, hard and sleek at the same time. Above her head, he let out a low moan. His hips rocked slowly toward her, drew back, thrust again as she swirled her tongue along his length. Her curiosity got the better of her, her fingers moving gently over the base of his manhood, along the curves and planes of his maleness, using his moans, his shudders, as her guide.

He pulled away with a strangled, "Wait…" then caught her by the hand to tug, urging her over him.

She held back. "What? Why do you wish me to stop?"

His eyes sparkled. "I don't, love. But I think you'll thank me in a moment or two."

"Thank you?" Darn it. She hated being so damn naive sometimes. What did he want her to do and why would she thank him?

"Trust me." He gently tugged her hand. "Come here."

"Ioan…"

He caught her by the hips to angle her over him. Then, with one hand, positioned himself and whispered, "Ride me."

As he spoke, he tightened the hand still on her hip to coax her down. As her body met his, she sucked in a sharp breath, sheathing him in a single, silken caress.

"Oh…" she couldn't keep the wonder from her voice as the sensations swept through her. He felt so full inside her, and yet, she didn't quite know how to respond to it. Her body urged her to move, so she rocked forward, ever so slightly.

"Oh, yes…" he growled, his hands tightening on her thighs. "Nice and slow, love… nice and slow…"

She rocked again, drew him deep, savored the delight it sent shooting through her. Was *this* the pleasure he meant? She certainly hoped so, because it was delicious. Besides, she didn't think it could possibly feel any better than this. It simply was not possible. This was nothing anyone could have prepared her for, and she didn't want it to end. Not ever.

His thumbs pressed into her thighs, his voice soft as he whispered, "Don't be shy, Sophie. You feel so wonderful, darling girl…"

"But I… I don't know what to do…" She arched forward now.

A muscle bulged in his jaw. "That is just fine…"

Back and forth, up and down, she settled into a rhythm that had him moaning and arching into her, and had her own body singing with pleasure. The need to climax bore down on her, delicious and sweet, and she braced her hands on his chest for more leverage.

He thrust hard, and that was all it took. Her body took over, the need for release overpowering her as she moved faster, her fingernails bit into his chest, his hands gripped her thighs. He filled her, throbbed into her, and then he went rigid beneath her as his body spilled into hers, as his climax became hers, as his body became hers.

"Sophie!"

She threw her head back as she met him, wrapped around him, her release mingling with his. Her entire body tightened about him, drew him as deep as she could into her, and when the waves receded, she collapsed into him, fighting to breathe.

Ioan wrapped his arms about her, his breathing rough and hard as he gritted, "Oh… beautiful woman… what you do to me…"

Her eyes closed of their own, her head spinning so widely, she thought she might actually faint. Ioan didn't seem to mind her there. No, he kissed the top of her head and held her as if afraid someone would try to steal her from him.

CHAPTER FIFTEEN

She was in the wrong room.

Sophie stared up at the ceiling, with its inlay of gilded *fleur de lis*, and for a horrifying moment, wondered where she was. But then, a low sigh reached her ears and she smiled. No, she wasn't in the wrong room. She simply was unaccustomed to *this* one. The one she now shared with her husband.

Another sigh floated into the air, and a solid leg brushed the back of hers, followed by the arm that draped about her waist. Ioan's hand was relaxed, his long fingers only just brushing her belly. Without thinking, she reached up to slip her hand into his and those fingers tightened about hers, his thumb grazing along hers. His arm tightened, pulled her back into his chest as he whispered, "I wondered when you were going to wake."

Her smile came of its own volition as she carefully turned toward him. "Have you been awake long?"

"Long enough." His eyes were still heavy-lidded, giving him the same seductive look he'd had the night before, when he'd introduced her to all of the wonders to be found in the marriage bed. She couldn't recall a night where she'd slept more soundly, although perhaps that was because he'd simply worn her out, and truth be told, she certainly wouldn't mind ending each and every night that same way.

She gazed up at him. A dark hint of beard shadowed

his jaw, his hair was as mussed as ever, and her stomach fluttered. This magnificent-looking man was her husband. Even her mother could relax now. Her daughter was officially the Duchess of Blackthorne and Emily's place in society, both in England and in New York, was safe and secured.

The skin at the outer corners of his eyes crinkled as he smiled at her. "You look as if you've something quite heavy on your mind," he murmured, drawing her hair away from her face with his forefinger. "What is it?"

"I'm having difficulty believing this is really happening," she confessed, her cheeks growing warm.

His laughter came warm across her bare shoulder. "Why?"

"Well, because… yesterday I was but an ordinary American and today I am a duchess. It simply does not reason."

To her surprise, he tightened his arms about her and gently tugged to bring her atop him. "Of course it does. You only need to adjust a little. Perhaps we could take a walk about the house and the grounds and you can tell me what you'd like to see changed or updated."

"What?"

"Well, it's your house as well, and I've the feeling you've been rather underwhelmed by it."

The heat in her cheeks worsened. Had she been so obvious? She thought she'd hidden her dismay at the lack of heated running water and the terrible draftiness quite well.

Apparently she'd thought wrong.

"It's not so much underwhelmed," she hedged, letting her head fall forward so her hair spilled forth to hide her scarlet cheeks, "as it is… surprised. The house my family calls home is only a few years old, so we have all of the modern amenities, while Blackthorne has almost—"

She cut herself off by clamping her lips together. Dear heavens, what was wrong with her? She was on the cusp of insulting her new husband's ancestral home.

"None of them," he finished for her softly. He didn't sound upset or angry, or even insulted, but simply very matter of fact. "I understand that it doesn't. You might not have noticed, but the English are not exactly racing to greet the future with open arms. We prefer tradition, I suppose. We tend to fight progress as if our lives depend on it."

"I beg your pardon if I've offended. I meant no harm."

"Nor did you offend me." He trailed his fingertips along her back, and when they brushed over her buttocks, she shivered at the unexpected tickle. He did it again, grinning as she squirmed against him. "Oh, does that bother you, love?"

"It tickles," she managed around her chuckles.

"Does it?" He did it again, and again, then sighed softly. "I like how this feels, darling girl. Would you care you indulge a little this morning?"

"In the daylight?" She couldn't keep the horror from her voice.

"Sophie, you have nothing to fear from the daylight." He curved his hands against her bottom to pull her into him, which sent a funny flutter through her. "Trust me, you are stunning no matter the light."

To her surprise, his words sent a heat that wasn't at all uncomfortable streaking through her. Until meeting him, she never thought of herself as particularly pretty, never mind stunning, and she was content with that. Joy was the beauty. That was how it had been since they were girls, and she'd long since accepted that. Men would never fall all over themselves trying to impress her, or go out of their way to win her attention the way they did for Joy. Although, she often wondered what it must be like to be a woman like Joy, Sophie tried hard not to dwell on it. It was far too disheartening.

But now, seeing how he, this undeniably handsome, sought-after duke, looked at her now, she almost believed she was as stunning as he claimed. Now she knew. The feeling amazed her.

"You blush," he murmured, his fingers now trailing up, over the small of her back. "Why?"

"You say things no man has ever said to me before."

"I say things that are true, Sophie. Here suits you. England suits you." He rolled to pin her beneath him with the soft *schwiff* of twisting linens. "And I wish to love you from stunning top to adorable bottom and all points between, Duchess."

As he spoke, he moved down, into the valley between her breasts. His dark hair caressed her skin as he moved over the inner curve of her left breast, working his way toward the beaded crest that already anticipated his touch.

She drew her fingers through those soft curls, the urge to arch her back and press her breasts into him overpowering her. The things this man made her feel were unlike anything she'd ever felt before, unlike anything she even knew could exist. If someone had told her back when these arrangements had first been made, that she would be as happy as she was the morning after their wedding, she would have told them they were mad.

Yet, she was happy. So very happy indeed. When pleasure swelled through her and her husband made love to her in the soft light of dawn, his eyes never leaving hers as his body claimed hers until their shared climax erupted, she surrendered to the moment, to the new life, and welcomed both with open arms.

****

"So, where shall we begin our tour?" Ioan came up behind Sophie as she sat before her mirror, combing the most recent knots from her hair.

"Our tour?" She smiled. "It's about time you remembered."

"Remembered? I never forgot."

"Is that so? Then why is it we're only doing this now?"

He grinned. "We've been rather busy, haven't we?"

"Oh, just admit, you forgot."

He leaned over to press a kiss into the top of her head. "Very well. I admit. I forgot. So, will you allow me to make up for it now, seeing as how all of that wedding hullabaloo is behind us."

"Yes. Yes, I will." She peered at him in the mirror. He was dressed for the cool weather in buff-colored trousers and an elegant shirt of snowy white lawn. Highly polished Wellington boots encased his feet, and his great coat lay draped across the foot of the bed. "Is it so cold out yet?"

"There's a hint of snow in the air, believe it or not." He stepped back to lift the coat and shrug into it. "I do believe our Christmas will be white."

She smiled. "I would like that so much." She turned on the bench toward him. "Do you really wish to hear what I'd change about Blackthorne Hall?"

"Of course I would." He paused in buttoning his coat to meet her gaze. "I've made my peace with the fact that there are facets of this old house that don't suit you, and I'm curious to see what you have in mind. Unlike some of my peers, I'm not entirely beholden to the past."

She turned back to the mirror. Although he certainly seemed to have made peace, it still felt odd to her, to walk around the house that had been in his family for so many generations and point out what she thought was wrong with it, and what she wanted to change about it.

Still, the old house was terribly drafty, and she would love to have a hot bath without waiting for maids to lug buckets of water up from the kitchen. Aside from that, she really did love Blackthorne, found it filled with charm and atmosphere. There wasn't much she would change. Of that she was certain.

"Will we walk about or ride?"

He smiled. "It's a lot of walking, touring both the grounds and the house. I thought we could ride. Unless," he gestured to her, "you'd prefer to walk."

"Riding would be lovely. I haven't been on a horse since we arrived." She rose from the bench and moved to the wardrobe, to take out her one pair of riding boots. If they were going to ride regularly, she'd have to see about having at least one more habit sewn for her, and obtaining at least one other pair of boots. Her current outfit was tidy and nice, but faded to a certain degree.

Her boots were also in need of polishing, and when she looked up at Ioan, she said, "I beg your pardon for their shabby appearance."

"Nonsense. They only need be polished and they'll be right as rain. When we return, I'll give them to William to buff until he can see his reflection in them."

He strode to the door and tugged it open. "Take your time and I'll meet you in the stables. Do you remember how to get to them?"

"I think so."

"Good." He winked. "This morning was lovely, Sophie. I look forward to a repeat performance this evening."

The butterflies teased the inside of her stomach at the purred seduction in his deep voice. "As do I, Your Grace."

One dark brow crept up ever so slightly. "I beg your pardon?"

She couldn't hold back her smile. "I mean, Ioan."

He winked. "That's right and you would do well to remember it. You certainly did when you scratched your fingernails along my back earlier."

Heat filled her at his reminder, although it was no doubt a sweet heat. "You promised you'd never speak of that!"

"I lied. You should only know how arousing it is, to know I have that effect on you." He winked. "Do hurry, though, before the snow begins."

"Yes, Ioan."

His laughter remained even as he drew the door shut behind him, leaving her to smile at it as she murmured, "How did I become so lucky? It's almost too good to be true."****Ioan whistled softly as he made his way toward the stables back behind the main house. The air was heavy and cold, the skies leaden with the promise of snowflakes before much longer. For the first time in a long time, he found himself looking forward to the snow, looking forward to the Christmas holiday only a few days out. It was the first Christmas since his father's death, and until recently, he'd dreaded the holiday, despite his complicated relationship with his father. Having Sophie there softened the blow, made the unbearable perfectly bearable now.

How funny was it that now that the wedding was over, and all was said and done, he wasn't nearly as unhappy as he thought he'd be? Somehow, he didn't think conceiving his heir was going to be quite the chore after all. Sophie was a lusty woman once she let go of her inhibitions. Sensual and brazen, she treated him to sights and sensations he'd never dreamed could exist. She was wanton and beautiful, eager to explore, with a body created for sin. He would almost be sorry once she conceived, and would most likely move back into her chambers until the child's birth. Unless, of course, he could convince her that perhaps she should continue to sleep beside him every night. He hadn't realized how much more soundly he'd sleep with Sophie at his side.

His boot heels echoed against the stable's floor as he stepped into the pungent semi-darkness. "Regan? Are you about?"

The groom, well over six feet tall and with flaming red hair, emerged from the tack room. "Of course I am, Your Grace. Which horse shall I saddle for you?"

"I'll need both Jupiter and Lady Anne saddled. The duchess will be accompanying me today."

"Very well, Your Grace."

While he waited, Ioan stepped back out into the brisk cold. He could almost *smell* the snow in the air. How perfectly everything fell into place, as if it had been meant to happen this way. He had the feeling Sophie would delight in the picturesque landscape Blackthorne Hall would offer up once blanketed in pure white. He couldn't wait to share it with her.

Horse hooves on gravel caught his ear, and he turned to see Nora Etheridge seated upon her coal-black mare, Susie. She was a regal sight, in her brilliant red habit and glossy black boots, not a hair out of place. "Good morning, Duke," she greeted, her teeth flashing in a warm smile. "I'd wondered if you'd be up and about today."

"What brings you here so early?" He strode over to take Susie by the halter. "I'd have thought you would sleep in this morning. You seemed to enjoy yourself quite a bit yesterday."

"Did I?" Leather squeaked as she carefully dismounted and let the reins lay loose in her hand. "Well, I awoke this morning feeling quite like a new person. Although, I must confess, I'm rather surprised to see you alone." She peered first over her left shoulder, then her right. "I would have thought your duchess would be out here as well."

He didn't miss the darkness that flashed through her eyes as she said *duchess*. Despite her apparent nonchalance, his marriage still troubled her.

"She'll be along soon." He smiled, glancing toward the house without thinking. "She was dressing when I left."

"Dressing." A shadow seemed to fall behind her unusual eyes, but it faded so quickly, Ioan thought he might have only imagined it, especially when her smile returned. "So, does it feel differently? Being married, I mean."

"There are no words." He had no desire to expound on how or why it was different, even if he could find the best words to describe those newfound feelings. They were too new, too raw, for him to share with anyone. Still, he couldn't hold back his smile as the first snowflakes whispered against his face. "Perhaps we're to have a white Christmas this year."

"It would be nice." She stepped closer to him, reaching to catch his hand between both of hers. "Are you happy, Ioan? I mean, are you truly happy?"

He didn't pull free of her grasp, as he met her gaze evenly. "What do you mean, am I happy? Why wouldn't I be?"

"You didn't want this," she replied, her fingers tightening about his. "You didn't want any of this, if memory serves. Remember? You said it yourself you had no desire to settle down as yet."

"That was before."

"Before?"

"I don't expect you to understand, Nora." Now he eased his hand free of hers and stepped back.

"So, you mean to tell me that you spend one night with this woman and all of the sudden, you are madly in love with her?"

He shook his head. "As I said, I don't expect you to understand."

A hint of triumph shone in her eyes. "You didn't say yes."

"Nora…"

"She's American. She knows nothing about us or our ways." She closed the gap between them, one hand coming to lay against his chest. "My grandmother was your grandfather's mistress. Let me be yours."

Her voice was a low, throaty purr, her hand warm despite the layers of fabric between it and him. A knot formed in the pit of his belly as her fingertips swept against him. Once, he would have leaped at the offer, at the promise in her voice. Lady Nora Etheridge was one of the most desirable women in all of England and until now, had kept him at arm's length, hadn't wanted to risk their friendship when she knew he would offer no more than that.

So why had she changed her mind? She hadn't married yet, and there were still several acceptable titles left dangling before her, even if she had no interest in the older men bearing them. She was the daughter of an earl, a marriage to an equal or greater station was all she would accept, and unfortunately, he had been the last unmarried title of her age, unless one counted Pennington.

"If I agreed to that, you would never marry," he told her, covering her hand with his to draw it away from him. "And I couldn't do that to you."

"I would make the sacrifice."

Of course she would. Becoming mistress to the Duke of Blackthorne meant a lifetime of ease and comfort. A townhouse in London, a dressing room overflowing with gowns from the finest couturiers in France, and it meant being the hostess of some of the most sought-after salons in all of England. Sometimes it was preferable to be the mistress instead of the wife, especially when it was that or be faced with marrying a man twice her age and being forced to share a bed with him.

"I'm not asking you to make any sacrifice."

"We belong together. We always have." She met his gaze and a smile played at her lips. "The last barrier was that my family couldn't save yours. Well, you don't need it now, and you told me that once you married, you'd be free again."

"Nora, I—"

"And you've yet to let go of my hand."

"I could never ask you to do that, to give up your chances of marrying as well."

"I don't care, Blackthorne. I don't. Pomperton broke off our engagement, and that leaves only Lord Mayfair, and I'd rather live as your mistress than as a broken-down old viscount's wife. He's a decrepit warhorse who wants only to talk about orchids and mulch. And Lord Pennington is like a brother to me. And—"

He sighed, letting go of her hand now. Where once, he would have dragged her into the barn to pin her in a pile of soft hay, now he wanted only to find Sophie. "No. Nora, things have changed. I'm sorry, but they have."

"You don't love her. You know you don't." Those violet eyes grew shiny beneath a veil of tears. "And I won't believe you if you suddenly declare otherwise, either. You love me, Ioan, you have since we were children and you know it."

"Nora, I—"

She silenced him by flinging herself at him, her arms around his neck, his lips smothered by hers. Her body, willowy and lithe, flattened against his. Her lips were demanding, her tongue determined as she tried to slide it between his lips. He twisted to break away, to free himself, and tell her just what he thought of her.

"Am I interrupting?"

He jumped back, spinning about in the same motion to see Sophie at the edge of the drive, dressed demurely in a pale blue habit. Her expression was neutral, but her eyes betrayed her—wide and luminous and gleaming with hurt. His gut kinked sharply. He felt sick. "Sophie,

I didn't hear you coming."

Nora stepped back, demurely drawing her fingertips along her lips as she said, "Nor did I, Duchess."

"So I gathered." Twin spots of color appeared on her cheekbones as she turned her eyes to Nora. "What brings you here, Nora?"

Ioan didn't miss how Nora's back stiffened and her brows pulled low. She seemed on the verge of correcting Sophie, but then caught herself. Sophie was no longer her inferior, but rather, the roles had reversed. "I was out for a ride and thought I'd pay a call."

"To the stables?" Sophie's voice remained mild. "Interesting."

Ioan cleared his throat. "Shall we go, love?" he asked, catching her by the elbow. "I can explain this all as we ride."

"Why, I don't think there is anything to explain," she told him, and his stomach sank as he met her gaze once more. Gone was the hurt, replaced already by hard, icy fury. Then, she shook her head. "And I find I don't feel much like riding any longer. So, if you will both excuse me."

As she turned, Ioan stepped toward her. "Sophie, please, let me—"

"No. There is nothing to explain." A cold hardness flattened her eyes as she glared up at him. "Go and enjoy your ride. I am perfectly capable of walking back inside alone, Duke. I found my way here alone, and I will be more than able to find my way back. Alone."

"Sophie, if you would just—"

She threw up a hand as she marched away, while Ioan stood there, fists clenched, and watched her go. He forgot Nora still stood there, until her arm slipped through his and she murmured, "See? She understands."

"She under—" He spun about to glare at her. The knots in his belly loosened and with that, came fury. He couldn't recall the last time he'd felt such anger toward anyone, much less a woman. "Have you gone completely mad, Nora? Do you even have any idea what you've done?"

"What *I've* done?" She pressed a hand against her chest. "I just gave you your freedom back, Ioan. Don't you see? Now, everything is exactly as we'd hoped it would be."

"You're a madwoman," he snapped, throwing her off him as Regan emerged with both horses saddled and bridled. "Stay away from me, Nora. Stay away from me and stay away from Sophie."

"Your Grace? Has Her Grace come out yet?"

Ioan swallowed the blue streak threatening to erupt from his lips as he faced the groom. "No. And I beg your pardon, but there's been a change of plans and I'm afraid we won't be riding today."

Regan looked puzzled. "I don't understand, Your Grace."

"Put them back in their stalls." Ioan bit off the last words as he turned heel and left both the groom and Nora staring after him.

CHAPTER SIXTEEN

By the time she returned to Blackthorne Hall, Sophie could barely see through the haze of tears flooding her eyes. Still, she managed to hold them back until she was safely ensconced in her room, where she flung herself facedown across the bed to let them fall.

To her surprise, though, that didn't happen. Instead, what began as icy cold heartbreak became fiery hot fury. She knew Ioan didn't love her, but the last thing she expected was to find him in another woman's arms the day after their wedding!

The nerve of that woman to show up at Blackthorne Hall and—

And what?

She didn't do anything that Ioan didn't allow her to get away with.

Damn it.

A sharp knock sounded. "Miss Sophie—ah, I mean, Your Grace? Is everything all right?"

Sophie scowled up at the canopy. "Go away."

The door handle rattled. "Your mother said you came running up here and you looked upset. What is it?"

Sophie's scowl deepened. Of course her mother had sent the maid up to check on her. Now that the wedding was over and she had successfully landed the duke, she became someone else's concern. "Please... just go away."

"Miss—that is, Your Grace"—the handle rattled again—"please let me in."

Sophie swallowed the oath tickling her lips as she sat up and stomped to the door. She yanked it open with such force, her hair actually fluttered. "See? I'm fine. Now, report back to Mother that I haven't thrown myself out the window and leave me in peace, if it isn't too much to ask."

Unperturbed, Edith brushed by her. "What happened? And don't tell me nothing, because I know you and I know when you're upset."

Sophie just stared at her. On one hand, at least *someone* cared to know why she was upset, but on the other, she just wanted to be left alone. "You've some nerve, Edith. Do I need to remind you of your place?"

"Not at all. And I know you won't, either."

As she spoke, Edith strolled to the wardrobe, as if that had been her intended destination all along. She tugged open one door and peered in. "Now, are you going to tell me or not?"

"Not." Sophie closed the door to lean against it. "And what the devil are you doing?"

"If I'm here, I might as well begin laying out what you'll wear later, when you have dinner."

"I'm not going down to dinner. I'll have a tray up here."

"The day after your wedding?" Edith spun about, the wardrobe forgotten. "But, won't that raise eyebrows? They'll expect you to come down."

"I don't care. I'm not having dinner with that man and his family."

"That man—" Edith's forehead wrinkled. "Your Grace, what happened?"

"I don't wish to discuss it."

Edith crossed back to her. "What is it?"

"I just *said* I didn't wish to discuss it."

"But, you're so upset. It isn't like you."

Sophie struggled to contain her emotions, to force them into submission. Her hands trembled from the force of her fury. Her belly churned. She wanted to lash out, to hit someone, to make them feel as awful as she did right then.

Although she knew he didn't love her and that theirs was a financial arrangement alone, it still hurt more than she thought possible to see him with another woman in his arms. It hurt. It humiliated her. It drove home the fact she was in a loveless marriage and what was worse? Her husband waited less than a day to stray on her. Perhaps she had been wrong, to assume he'd at least be discreet in his infidelity. Never, in her worst nightmare, did she think she would happen upon him in the act of being unfaithful. In a *stable*, no less. The gossips would absolutely salivate over this *bon mot*. A duchess less than a day, and she'd be the laughingstock of society.

Wonderful.

Worse still, she had no one in whom she could confide. Joy was three thousand miles and an ocean away. Her mother had gotten what she wished: a daughter who was now nobility. She certainly wouldn't want to hear any of this. Her father? How could she possibly confess that her husband had tired of her less than a day after wedding her? The humiliation alone stung like a thousand tiny cuts.

That left Edith, and it seemed far beyond pathetic to confide in her maid, no matter how understanding Edith might be. She might even offer up amazing advice, but still, Sophie simply couldn't bring herself to do it.

"Your Grace?"

"I said, I have no wish to discuss it, and I don't. So, please, leave me be."

Edith's face fell. "Of course. I beg your pardon."

Sophie mashed her lips together as her maid nodded and turned back to the wardrobe. Now, on top of everything, she'd hurt her as well, and Edith had always been nothing but a friend to her.

No. That wasn't true. She wasn't a friend. She was a maid, paid by first her father and now her husband, to be at Sophie's beck and call. If the duke decided tomorrow to fire Edith, she'd be gone without a look over her shoulder.

Her mind whirling, her emotions warring, she moved to the windows, overlooking the lush lawns and what would be the enormous gardens come spring. Now, it was barren. The grass was more yellow than green, the trees were mere skeletons and the gardens patches of brown. In the distance, deer meandered, grazing peacefully.

The first flakes swirled past the window. She and Ioan were supposed to be out there, enjoying a bit of quiet time before the hustle and bustle of readying for the holidays and then their wedding trip, which was to begin in the new year.

She'd been so excited about the trip, being able to see places she'd only ever read about before. France. Prussia. Austria. Italy. It would be nothing short of a grand adventure. And what made it even more enticing? She'd be seeing them with Ioan. She'd looked so forward to that, to coming to know her husband in a way few others would.

"I caught the duke with that awful Lady Nora," she whispered, sinking onto the window ledge.

Edith spun about once more. "What?"

Sophie nodded. "Just now. At the stables. They were kissing."

A dark blue silk day dress draped over her forearm, Edith came over, pausing long enough to lay the dress out on the bed before joining Sophie at the window. "Are you certain?"

She shot her maid a look. "I *do* know a kiss when I see one."

"No, I mean, are you certain he was kissing her back? It takes two, you know."

"I'm certain. She had her arms about him and everything and I—I don't know what I'm supposed to do. I know this is no love match, but still… I always thought my husband would be faithful beyond the first twelve hours of our marriage. And if he strayed"—her cheeks burned as she tried to come up with the best words that wouldn't horrify Edith *too* badly—"if he strayed, he would do so in a far more discreet manner. Or so I'd hoped."

"But, why would you think he would…" Now color came to Edith's pale cheeks. "Why do you expect he would ever do such a thing?"

"We both know why he agreed to this marriage, so let's not pretend it is anything other than a business arrangement."

Edith shook her head. "I'm not so certain of that. I've seen how he looks at you, Your Grace."

"It was but your imagination playing tricks, Edith. And nothing more."

Her maid didn't look at all convinced. "You should

talk to him."

"Whatever for? I told you, I *saw* them."

"You did, but perhaps you didn't see quite what you think you did."

"Edith, how many other things look like a kiss?"

"I know," Edith replied softly, patting her knee through her skirt. "But allow him to explain and then be angry, if necessary. It might not be what you think it is."

"I don't see how it isn't. It looked apparent to me."

"Your Grace…"

"I know," Sophie replied softly. "But, what if I'm right?"

"What if you aren't?"

"But what if I am?"

"There is only one way to know, and that's to talk to him."

Sophie turned back to the window. Edith was right, of course, but somehow, hearing it from Ioan's lips would hurt far worse than simply seeing him and Lady Nora together would. As long as he never confirmed it, she could still pretend otherwise.

Lady Nora. No, Sophie was well within her rights to address the lady as simply *Nora* now. By virtue of marriage, Sophie, an American-born heiress, now outranked the daughter of an earl. She'd be damned if she would show that harlot an ounce of respect now. It was only unfortunate that the same daughter of the earl could now boast about snagging the Duke of Blackthorne away from his bride within a day of that bride becoming the duchess. That smashed flat any hint of smugness Sophie felt at knowing she outranked Nora Etheridge.

Damn it all. New York might have been lonely and without much in the way of marriageable prospects, but being lonely didn't hurt nearly as much as being betrayed did. She knew where she stood where the bachelors of New York were concerned. Besides, she'd had Joy to commiserate with, to share that loneliness with to make it seem a little less lonely. For a short while, she even managed to forget it.

But here, in England, and in Berkshire especially, Sophie wouldn't be able to escape the knowing, smug looks Nora would most likely shoot her way. Sophie might bear the title of duchess, but Nora had the knowledge that she had managed to steal a kiss from the duke. She would always have that. All Sophie could do was hope Nora had nothing else to add to it.

All she could do was hope Nora never had anything else to be smug about.

CHAPTER SEVENTEEN

For Ioan, the walk back to Blackthorne Hall did nothing to cool his fury. In fact, by the time he was indoors once more, he wanted only to turn tail and go back out, to get on Jupiter and ride to Stanridge House, and throttle the precious Lady Nora blue. Did she have any idea what she'd done? Did she care?

Yes and no. He already knew the answers. Confronting her would do no good. It certainly wouldn't make Sophie unsee what happened in the stables, and it wouldn't undo the fact that he'd allowed Nora to kiss him. He'd never been so angry at himself before. He'd let it happen and now... damn it all to hell and back. He mucked everything up so terribly, and hadn't a clue as to where to even begin to try and fix it. In fact, he wasn't even certain it *could* be fixed.

What the deuce had he been thinking? Why had he simply stood there, like he'd gone suddenly idiot, and let Nora do that? How could he be so stupid? So bloody stupid? The moment she appeared, he should have called for Regan or just walked away. But no. He didn't, and now look at the mess in which he was now mired.

He found himself at the foot of the staircase, staring up in the general direction of the room he now shared with Sophie. He wanted to go above, to right everything with her, to assure her she didn't quite see what she thought she had. She was a reasonable woman and once she calmed down, that reason would return.

Wouldn't it?

There was only one way to find out, so he mounted the staircase.

At the top, he paused once more. What if she wouldn't see him?

Wait one minute… he had every bit as much a right as her to be in his own damn room. They needed to talk this out and damn it, that's exactly what they would do.

With that, he strode toward their chambers and threw open the door without preamble, "Sophie, you didn't—oh." He paused, catching sight of his wife's maid with her at the window. Edith's pale face remained impassive, but he had the feeling she knew the entire story. At least, the story as Sophie saw it. "Ah, Edith, I didn't realize you were up here. Would you give us a moment, please?"

"No," Sophie shook her head, "you are to stay right where you are, Edith. You are not the one who's leaving." She narrowed her eyes at Ioan. "*He* is."

"*He* is doing nothing of the sort," Ioan shot back, folding his arms as he held her stare easily. Without looking at the maid, he said, "Edith."

"Yes, Your Grace." She bobbed her head and ducked out of the room without a sound.

"How dare you dismiss *my* maid, you high-handed… man," she finished lamely. "Get out of here."

"I'll do no such thing. After all, it's *my* room," he reminded her, some of the heat draining from his voice. He didn't want to fight with her. He wanted to clear the air. "I want to explain—"

"Explain? Oh, yes, please do explain how it is you come to be kissing another woman the day after our wedding? I should *love* to hear the reason for it."

"She kissed me." He fought off a wince at how lame that sounded, but what else could he say? "I don't know what else to tell you but that. I did nothing to encourage her. Nothing to convince her I wanted her to kiss me. She simply did it."

Although he expected her eyeroll, he didn't expect her snort as well. Yet, snort is exactly what she did. "Have you gone completely mad? Is that supposed to make everything all right?" Her hands came to rest on her hips. "What is she to you? And do not even *think* to lie to me."

"Sophie, you have to realize—"

"What is she, Ioan? And don't tell me she is nothing because we both know *that* to be a lie."

"She is a friend."

"A friend? Oh, really?" She shook her head. "Then the English have an odd custom, for in America, we don't kiss our friends as if our lives depended on it."

"Sophie, I did nothing wrong."

"Please. You certainly didn't seem to be fighting to break free of her, now, were you?" She crossed to her dressing table and sank onto the brocade bench. "Although, it isn't as if ours is a love match. You've been more than upfront about that, so I don't suppose I really have grounds to be angry. I suppose it was rather foolish of me to think something like this wouldn't happen the very next day after our wedding, but there you have it."

He flinched as he moved to crouch down before her. "Sophie, what you saw, you weren't supposed to see."

Her eyebrows practically leapt into her hairline. "Oh, well, *that's* something, I suppose."

His gut curdled as the emotions warred across her

face. She most likely had no idea how easily she betrayed herself. Her eyes were wide and shiny, her lips pressed together. She was hurt, and he was responsible, and he hated how it felt. Not because it made him uncomfortable, but because he'd done it to her.

"I don't blame you for being angry," he began, choosing his words as carefully as he could.

He might as well not have bothered, for she leapt up from the bench. "You don't blame *me*? Oh, well, isn't that terribly generous of you?" she snapped, hands on her hips, eyes flashing with fire. "I am eternally grateful for that, Your Grace, although I fail to see how *your* kissing that—that *whore* is somehow *my* fault to begin with!"

"If you would but—"

She cut him off once more. "If I would but what? How do you stand there and tell me you don't blame me when you are the one who is in the wrong? I know I am but a quaint colonial, but I fail to see how *your* actions are *my* responsibility."

Irritation sliced thorough him. It shouldn't be this difficult, should it? "I didn't say they were, but I'm trying to fix this, Sophie. But, how do I do that when I've done nothing wrong?"

"Done nothing wrong?" Her voice rose with each word. "You were bloody *kissing* another *woman!*"

He almost smiled at her use of an English oath, but then she added, "But you don't blame me for being upset over it, which is terribly generous of you, you jackass."

The urge to smile faded and his gut twisted into a sharp knot. "I didn't mean it quite that way," he told her, reaching for her hand. "And you should know—"

She jerked back before he could touch her. "Yes, I should. After all, this is no love match. I've already fulfilled half of my duty by rendering your family solvent. And once I conceive, I will have fulfilled that duty as well. And when that happens, I will move back into my old rooms."

This was *not* at all how this conversation was supposed to go. Somehow, he had to calm her down, calm himself down, before tempers spilled over and they flung regretful words at one another. Before things went from bad to worse. "Sophie, wait—"

"No. This is fine, really. It is." She stood, her head high as she cleared her throat and added, "It's for the best, actually. So, that's how it will be. The air is clear, and I am perfectly clear as to how our life will be."

He straightened and shook his head. "You are being stubborn, Sophie. And foolish. There is no need to act as if I've somehow wounded you. She pursued me. She kissed me."

"Yet, you didn't push her away. And of course you didn't. She is everything that would suit you and I… well… we both know I'm not exactly your sort, am I?"

"You're not exactly—do you have any idea how stupid that sounds?"

She turned away. "All I ask is that you be discreet while you're here. I'd rather *not* be gossiped about, if it's all the same to you. And ask your whore to be discreet as well, if that's even possible."

He stared at her back, the irritation in his gut doing a slow burn. She already had her mind made up about what had happened with Nora and obviously wasn't interested in the truth at all. She was so determined to believe the worst about him, had so little faith in him, that it fired his temper now. "So, let me see if I have this straight." Heat crept into his voice. "Although, I've done nothing wrong, you are pushing me away. Pushing me *to* Nora?"

"She's the one you want, isn't she?"

"Damn it, Sophie, I—"

"I only ask that I be allowed to remain in this room until I become pregnant. Then, your life is yours to live as you see fit."

"As long as I am discreet."

She turned toward him to nod. "Yes."

"Well, I'd have to be a total fool to pass that up, wouldn't I? What man ever is presented with his cake so thickly frosted and all for him to indulge in?" She closed her eyes as he raised his voice with each word, squeezing them tighter as he added in a low growl, "Have it your way, Duchess. But I can assure you, you *will* regret it when you realize how you've punished me for something I didn't actually do. I hope you'll be able to live with your decision when you are sleeping alone and I am in Nora's bed."

Her flinch was almost imperceptible. Almost. Once more, that feeling of wanting to rip out his tongue and stomp on it surged through him. She held his stare. "I will live just fine, thank you."

"Is that so?" He shook his head. "Well, before you go thinking you've bested me, know this. We will spend every night attempting conception, and I don't give a damn if we kill one another in the process. Prepare yourself, Duchess," he growled, his hands clenching into fists. "Because you *will* come to regret this."

He didn't wait for her response, but slammed out of the room, not even wincing when he heard the shatter of glass against the closed door.

Damn it.

CHAPTER EIGHTEEN

Crystal clinked against crystal as Ioan yanked the stopper from the decanter and poured amber liquor into the glass. He didn't bother restopping the decanter, since he threw back the glass's contents and immediately poured another.

"Isn't it a bit early for this?"

He hadn't heard his mother come into his study, but he didn't so much as flinch. "I'm not a bloody child. If I want a drink, so be it. I'm having one."

"What's the matter?" She came into the room, closing the door behind her. "And do be quick about it. That dreadful Emily isn't far behind me, I don't think."

He filled his glass a third time. "I've no wish to discuss it."

He lifted the glass, but before he could take a drink, his mother caught him by the wrist. "What is going on?"

"It's none of your concern, Mother, and I'll kindly ask you to leave off."

"Ioan."

"I am not joking." He jerked his arm free and threw back the contents. A soft buzzing sound filled his head and softened his anger and with a sigh, he moved to sink onto the settee. "Perhaps this was a mistake."

"Three drinks in less than five minutes at one in the afternoon?" Her cane tapped quietly against the carpet as she moved around him to sit on the settee across from him. "Yes, I should think that is most definitely a mistake. One you might regret even more, if you keep this up."

"No." He gestured all around. "Everything. From that dreadful Emily to this farce of a marriage."

"Farce of a marr—Ioan, you've been married only a single day. What on earth happened? Why are you talking madness? What is going on?"

"Nothing I wish to discuss."

"Oh, dear… this sounds serious."

"Well, it isn't. Sophie and I know where we stand with one another. And once she's pregnant, it won't matter." He rolled his eyes as the dowager flinched. "Oh, stop. I'm hardly a child. You know how all-important a bloody heir is, remember?"

"No, you aren't a child, but there are still some things a mother need never know about her son, no matter how grown he is, and this most definitely belongs in that category."

"Oh, ho, is that so?" He rose onto unsteady feet to fill his glass once more. "But, that's all that matters, isn't it? The coffers are overflowing once more, and now I only need an heir. And last I checked, one does *not* find babies out in the cabbage patch, do they?"

"Ioan, you're being vulgar."

"*I'm* being vulgar?" He pressed his free hand into his chest as a dry, humorless laugh blew across his lips. "I married my wife for her money. I think it safe to say it hardly can be much more vulgar than that."

"What the deuce happened between last evening and now? You and Sophie were the picture of happiness yesterday."

"Happy? Mother, she and I barely know one

another! How the deuce are either of us supposed to be *happy* right now? She's a veritable stranger to me and I am one to her. Bah!" He slammed down the glass, which fortunately did not break, and gestured wildly about the room once more. "And you know I had planned on making Nora Etheridge my wife. You've known that since I was a boy."

"And within a year, you would have been destitute, selling our possessions at an estate sale. When that happened, I daresay, the fine Lady Nora would have already had her cap set for another suitor. One who is *not* a pauper!"

"Would have—you're right, Mother. Why wouldn't she? Unlike my wife, she doesn't love me, right? Spare me."

"And now you've lost me. What are you talking about?"

"I'm talking about this! The house! My title! My damn bloody heir! Because of my father's bloody mistakes, I'm stuck—for lack of a better word—with a woman who doesn't want me!"

"Are you completely blind? You've seen how she looks at you. Of course she wants you."

He rolled his eyes. "No. She wants my title. It makes her look better to her peers in her precious New York. That is what matters to my duchess and her family. The social standing that comes with the name Blackthorne."

His mother's eyes widened as his voice rose. Her back stiffened. She slammed her cane against the parquet flooring. The heavy thud rang out like a thundercrack. "And you wanted her money."

"No, *you* wanted her money." He leaned against the piecrust table holding the decanters. "I didn't care about any of it. The title. The money. The house. They are but things, Mother."

"Things that have been in the St. John family since Queen Elizabeth!"

"Things all the same!" His voice reverberated off the paneling, off the paintings of his forebears lining the walls. Christ, he'd made such a mess of everything, and he didn't even know how it happened. One minute, he was happy, thinking there was a chance for him and Sophie, that perhaps a marriage of convenience could become one of love and friendship.

And then Nora…

Damn it. Why the hell had she done that? And why hadn't he bloody well stopped her?

And why didn't he just go to Sophie and beg her forgiveness? To promise her he would do whatever it took to win her trust. Her heart. Her love.

Because she didn't want him.

No, that wasn't true. She wanted part of him.

An image of her, astride him the previous night, burst into his mind, and his entire body hummed to life as it had done when he was a boy and first discovered what arousal meant. Nora was beautiful, but her kiss didn't affect him half as strongly as the mere memory of Sophie did.

"There you are!" Emily Montgomery strode into the study as cheerful as the sun. "Where is Sophie? I thought you and she were going riding this afternoon?"

"We had a change of plans," he replied brusquely. "If you will excuse me, I've some papers that require my attention."

"But, I thought perhaps we—" Emily moved to grab his arm, but froze as he glared at her. "I beg your pardon,

Your Grace."

"Excuse me, Emily." He looked over at the dowager. "Mother."

This time, he didn't care if either woman had anything further to say, but stormed out of the study. He did have a few things which needed his attention, but those papers were stacked nicely on his desk in the study, and that was the last place on earth he wished to be at the moment.

The gallery was quiet, no sign of a maid or footman anywhere. His boots echoed against the marble, then the sounds died as he halted in the middle of the great hall. High above, the dark wood beams rose to meet the frescoed ceiling, and all around, on the pillars supporting the mezzanine, were the crests of the families of each previous Duchess of Blackthorne. Only one would remain blank.

That of Josephine Walker Montgomery St. John, the ninth Duchess of Blackthorne. The only American-born duchess in the lineage. Their children would be half-American as well. A sigh rose to his lips. Children. Only if their firstborn was a girl, for he had no doubt Sophie would bar him from her bed otherwise.

He sank onto one of the fainting couches in the gallery. Huge potted ferns dotted the perimeter, and above them hung portraits painted by some of the greatest painters who ever lived. Two had been done by Gainsborough, although only one was on display there. The other oversaw the smaller library. Everywhere he looked, he saw history, and wealth, and power. His predecessors rubbed elbows with the kings and queens of England. His children would be educated in the finest schools in England. His son would one day inherit one of the most powerful titles in Europe.

Unless, of course, his wife gave him no sons.

A dull headache took root behind his eyes. All wouldn't necessarily be lost, should he and Sophie produce only girls. The third duke had two girls, each married into a royal family, one here and one in France. But he couldn't trouble himself with that now. For now, he had to concentrate on fulfilling his duty and begetting the all-important heir. Somehow, he didn't think one night—no matter how passionate—had done it.

He just had to hope Sophie was at least receptive to that. After all, the sooner she conceived, the better. But, that thought left him feeling empty inside. He didn't know why, but somehow, the thought of taking a mistress no longer offered him the same amount of comfort it once had.

CHAPTER NINETEEN

For the rest of the afternoon, Sophie jumped at the slightest sound, convinced Ioan was coming to make good on his promise of attempting to conceive his heir. Part of her was apprehensive, but part of her—the wicked part, no doubt, was curious about his threat. Could he perform without emotion? As if it was no more than haircut or trimming his fingernails? Were men able to separate the physical act of love from those emotions? Would she be able to? More importantly, did she *wish* to be able to do such a thing?

She had no idea. Her wedding night had been romantic, and dreamy and wonderful. She didn't doubt the feeling of being cherished was not only in her imagination. The passion that raged between them had nothing to do with anger and everything to do with caring about one another, even if love didn't come into view.

But in the span of fifteen angry minutes, that was all gone. Lost in an argument over something that should have never happened to begin with, something she'd hoped would never come to pass.

When Edith came up to dress her for dinner, Sophie refused to unlock the door. "Tell everyone I have a headache," she called flatly through the door.

"Your Grace"—Edith rattled the handle—"please, let me in."

"Go away. I've no desire to see *him* or his mother,

and I have even less of a desire to explain this all to Mama."

"Your Grace—"

"I said, *no!*"

Edith went silent and the handle went still. After a slight pause, she then asked, "Are you certain?"

Rolling her eyes, Sophie nodded, even though her maid couldn't see it. "Quite, Edith. And I do not wish to be disturbed. Including by His Grace."

"I cannot possibly bar him from his own room!"

"You won't need to. I simply will not unlock the door. I've no qualms about telling him to go away, either."

"Your Grace, I think this is terribly unwise."

Hot tears stung Sophie's eyes, and she squeezed them shut as she pressed her forehead against the door. "This entire farce was terribly unwise, and yet, here we are. Now, leave me be."

"Of course, Your Grace."

Sophie waited until Edith's footsteps faded, then, with a low, shaky sigh, she turned away from the door to return to her perch in the windows. The snow had stopped earlier, turned to rain, and now a low fog hung over Blackthorne Hall like a shroud. The room remained damp and chilly, despite the fire crackling on the hearth, mocking her with its merrily dancing flames. The chill permeated her, sank into her skin and her bones, and no matter tightly she wrapped the quilt about her, no warmth followed. She felt hollow and numb, like a tree that had fallen victim to disease but hadn't toppled over yet. It was the worst feeling in the world, and she hated it, but there it was and she couldn't make it go away. She sat there, staring into the darkness long after the dinner gong rang, and no one came looking for her.

She lost track of time, jumping when the door handle rattled. "Sophie, open the door."

She winced at the low timbre of Ioan's voice even as she shook her head. "Go away."

"Open the door."

"No."

"Damn it, open this door."

"I said, no."

The dull thud of a fist hitting the wood echoed, but then silence fell. She breathed a sigh of relief as she stood and moved to spread the quilt back on the bed. The clock on the mantel read half past ten. Time to ready for bed.

Although she'd instructed Edith not to bother her, and although she knew self-pity was pathetic, Sophie couldn't help but feel sorry for herself as she sat before her vanity, removing the pins from her hair. She missed home, missed New York with a fury she never thought possible. She missed laughing with Joy, missed knowing her friends were close by and that she wasn't entirely alone. Joy would be the first one to devise a plot to either make Ioan suffer for his betrayal or to help her take revenge on Lady Nora for being such a whore to begin with, and right then, Sophie would have loved to come up with that scheme and carry it out. Joy had a bit of a cruel streak when it came to women who moved in on another woman's man. She was creative. They could be a dangerous combination.

But, Joy wasn't there, and Sophie had no one with whom she could plot. Damn it all. So much for having all the luck. If she'd ever had it, it had gone terribly sour in a short span of time.

She undressed, drew on her nightrail, and slipped

into a wrapper before returning to her vanity to remove the pins from her hair and brush it out for the night.

The door banged ope,n and she spun to see Ioan with a set of keys in one hand. "We have a master set, you know," he said by way of explanation, tossing the keyring onto the low chest just inside the door. "In case someone loses a key."

"That's good to know now," she retorted, turning back to the mirror. "But, be that as it may, you are still *not* sleeping in here."

"Is that so?"

"Yes."

"Well, I beg to differ, Duchess. This is as much my room as it is yours. In fact, more so, since it was mine from the time I graduated from the nursery, and you've been here but a few weeks."

"Good for you." She made a face at him in the mirror and went back to plucking out pins.

He closed the door and to her consternation, made an exaggerated show of locking it. "I should hate to be disturbed mid-coitus."

"I beg your pardon?"

She stiffened as he approached, leaned over her shoulder, and whispered, "In the midst of fucking."

Heat leaped into her cheeks, and she promptly poked her thumb on a pin. Damn it all. How many pins had Edith used anyway? "Oh."

"As cute and perky as your breasts are," he went on, tugging his shirt from his trousers as he moved to the wardrobe, "I'd rather no one else here see them."

That made two of them, but since she certainly couldn't say that, she merely made a noncommittal *hmph* sound.

"And of course, the rest of your body is equally lovely, but the same goes."

Certain she'd finally pulled out the last pin, she lowered her arms. "Are you trying to provoke me into an argument?"

"Me? On the contrary, I thought I was being refreshingly honest."

"What you are being, Your Grace," she said, then turned toward him, "is an ass."

He chuckled, tossing his discarded shirt into the wicker basket for the laundry. "Am I? Well, perhaps they are the same thing."

She rolled her eyes, unable to tear her gaze from the sight of his bare back. The muscles rippled beneath his skin as he stretched into the wardrobe, bunched along his shoulder when he reached up for something.

"It's quite all right if you have nothing complimentary to say about me," he remarked, peering at her over one shoulder, his left eyebrow rising ever so slightly at her stare.

She hadn't meant to be caught staring at him, nor was she about to take his bait. "Perhaps I find fault with you, Your Grace," she replied with a halfhearted shrug.

"Do you?" He turned entirely toward her as if challenging her. Well, she would accept that challenge, not averting her eyes as he added, "You would be the first woman to do so."

"That is low, you peacock."

"It's also true." As he spoke, he unfastened the button on his trousers and shoved them down. Her mouth went dry at the sight and she both sighed and swore inwardly as her entire body went hot.

There was no flaw to be found on his magnificent

body. Not a single one. Dark hair sprinkled across a muscled chest, down an equally muscled belly, over heavily muscled thighs and calves. Dear lord, he was a sight to behold, and she wanted only to run the tip of her tongue from just below his ear, along the slope of his neck into his shoulder, and down until she was on her knees before him. Her spine stiffened. Still, she hadn't forgotten she was furious with him.

"I find that difficult to believe," she replied. "They were simply too afraid to mention it, I'd imagine."

"Oh, of course." Clad in only his small clothes, he strode toward her. "Shall I help you undress?"

She glared at him in the mirror. "Are you foxed?"

"Not at all. Why?"

"You do not honestly think I'll—"

"I think exactly that. The bargain, love, remember? The entire reason you are here is—"

"Because you needed my father's fortune," she snapped, sliding off the bench away from him. Her belly churned as she looked from him to the bed with its rumpled quilt. He could easily lift her and toss her onto that bed, and it wouldn't take much effort for him to take her right then and there.

"And an heir. And you agreed to it, so"—he gestured to his small clothes—"shall I remove them now, or would you rather wait until we are both in bed?"

"The devil take you, Blackthorne," she snapped, one hand clutching the front of her wrapper as if that would be enough to prevent him from simply yanking it from her. Foolish, no doubt, but instinctual just the same. "I wouldn't sleep with you if you were the last man on earth."

"Of course you will. You will keep your word." He

skirted the bench, closed the gap between them. He didn't touch her, but simply loomed over her. "I can take you right here, if you wish, Sophie. You're tiny enough, I might even be able to hold you in one arm."

She held his stare even as warmth spread through her. He was probably right, but she wasn't about to let him know how she felt. He would never have that sort of power over her again. She backed away from him, pressing flat against the wardrobe. "You wouldn't dare."

Challenging him was a risk. He could so very easily overpower her. He towered over her now, all broad shoulders and chest, and although he seemed sober enough, this was a side of him she couldn't imagine brought out without liquor.

"Wouldn't I?" His voice lowered to a silky whisper, one that would have her sighing softly and almost swooning in his arms, were it used in any other circumstances. He brought his hands up to rest flat against the wardrobe doors, on either side of her shoulders. He surrounded her, threatened to engulf her, and her heart beat faster still as he added, "I thought you also wanted a child, Duchess? And there is only one way for that to happen."

"Leave me be."

"I cannot do that." He leaned toward her, and her heart tripled its pace as she waited for him to kiss her, to snatch her up into his arms and spirit her to the bed. There would be no anger the moment their lips met. And he would assure her that he would never throw her over for Nora again. "Haven't you figured out by now, I have a deuce of a time resisting you? Because I do, you know. In fact, it's almost impossible for me to do so."

Her heart gave a small leap at his words. He

certainly sounded as if he meant those words, his voice low and husky. She wanted only to melt into his arms and assure him he was equally irresistible. And she would, once he finally kissed her.

But, that kiss never came. Instead, his lips brushed her ear as he murmured, "If you like, I will turn you away from me before I'm inside you. You can close your eyes and I—"

Knots twisted deep in her belly, apprehension combined with anger to make her snap, "Can pretend I am Lady Nora?"

He jerked away as if she'd struck him. Fury darkened his eyes to almost emerald. "I beg your pardon?"

"If you don't see my face, I might be any woman." She refused to look away from those irate green eyes, but held his glare easily. "So you can pretend I am your precious Lady Nora?"

She didn't miss the tension winding its way across his shoulders. The sudden stiffness in his back. The way a muscles along his jaw suddenly bulged then went smooth. He simply stared at her and then gritted, "That would make it easier, wouldn't it?"

"Beast." Her face went hot. Then her body. Her eyes stung with tears, but she refused to let them fall. She wouldn't give him the satisfaction. "Get out. I do not give a damn where you sleep, but it will *not* be here."

"You needn't worry," he growled, snatching his dressing gown from where it lay draped over the foot of the bed. "I've no intention of staying here."

At the door, he paused, his eyes practically glowing as he said, "You are my wife, Josephine. And you will *not* turn me away again. Your duty is to give me a son.

You *will* fulfill that duty, lest you want to lose your money, your title, *and* your home when I divorce you."

"You wouldn't dare."

He drew the gown on and fastened it. "Are you so certain, Duchess? Because you don't know me nearly as well you have yourself thinking you do."

Her gut kinked sharply, and she swiped up the first object within reach, the book she'd been reading earlier, and fired it at him. She missed. The book hit the wall, chipping the plaster, which coated it with white dust as it hit the floor. "Bastard!"

"You would do well to remember that," he snarled, yanking open the door.

With that, he left, the darkness swallowing him whole, and she slammed the door behind him, twisting the key to set the lock. Then, she sank to her knees, buried her face in her hands, and broke down.

CHAPTER TWENTY

Sometimes, he truly was a jackass.

Ioan spent the remainder of the night tossing and turning on the narrow, hard bed in his dressing room. Sleep mocked him. He despised himself. Even with the fire on the hearth, his dressing room was too cold and too drafty. The bed was far too lonely. The entire house was too quiet. Too quiet and too damp. All he wanted was to go back to his room, crawl into bed alongside his wife, and apologize to her for being such a jackass. Once more to apologize for being a menacing, overbearing lout. For not shoving Nora under a coach. For everything that had happened in the last twenty-four hours. How the deuce did he manage to muck everything up so absolutely perfectly and then instead of righting them, only muck them up ten times worse?

What the bloody hell was he thinking? He'd gone above with the intention of seducing her, of driving her so mad with lust and passion that she forgave him his non-indiscretion. His intention had been to grovel as much as necessary to thaw her chill, to draw her into his arms and love her until she had no choice *but* to forgive him, to believe him. Then, he'd make it all up to her in any way he could think to do so. And it if took the rest of his life, so be it. He didn't care.

So what happened?

"You happened, you bloody jackass," he muttered

into the darkness. "That's what."

For the remainder of the night, he stared up into the darkness, or over into it. At one point, he pulled the pillow over his head and stared up at it instead. Finally, as the gray light of dawn split the darkness, he flung the pillow across the room and gave up.

It was a damp morning, clear and cool, with a hint of frost in the air. His breath emerged as a silvery close and grass crunched beneath his boots as he strode across the lawns, down the narrow gravel path that led from Blackthorne Hall across to the folly—an absolutely pointless marble recreation of a single wall of the Parthenon that stood alone in the field south of the gardens. The walk did much to clear his head, to help him try to make sense of his stupidity from the previous night. He had to find some way to make Sophie believe him. To make her understand Nora held no interest for him. At least, not any longer. That interest, whatever had remained of it, evaporated the moment her lips touched his. Her kiss was flat and dull, about as enticing as kissing one of his horses would be. Nothing like how a kiss was *supposed* to be. It didn't thrill him. Or set fire to him. Or do anything other than make him want to jerk back and wipe his mouth.

In other words, the exact opposite of how Sophie's kisses affected him. Hers were powerful enough to fire his lust with a simple peck on his cheek. Just the thought of her mouth on him, on *any* part of him, brought a stirring to his lower regions more powerful than any he'd ever felt before. When she kissed him, it was all he could do to remember his own bloody name. She made him tremble like a schoolboy come face to face with his first pair of naked breasts. She made his knees weak and his blood hot and his body ache for her.

So why the deuce couldn't he just *tell* her that?

Because she was far too angry with him, that's why. And despite his asinine idiocy last eve, he couldn't fault her. She knew he'd once wanted Nora. Knew that the Montgomery money was the motivating factor behind his proposal. So, what else could she possibly think, when the *day after they were married*, she saw him with Nora in his arms?

His groan emerged in a cloud of silvery frost. He paused on the path, turning to see Blackthorne Hall in the distance. Damn it all. This was his fault, and he just kept digging himself deeper into trouble.

Divorce. Sweet Jesus, he wanted to cut out his tongue for that idiocy. When had he become so damn stupid? He wouldn't divorce her. He didn't *want* to divorce her. He was an idiot, but he certainly wasn't mad.

And he'd *threatened Sophie with it*. What was *wrong* with him? He knew that single word would hurt her, would cut her to the quick, and yet he'd barreled on like an idiot and done just that.

He let out a heavy sigh, his breath still rising in a frosty cloud. "I need to set this right," he muttered, starting back toward the house.

The more he thought about it, the greater his sense of urgency. He would make it right, and tonight, when he came up to their room, it would be to sweep his wife into his arms, spirit her to their bed, and make love to her. Just as he should've done last night. Perhaps he could show her what he could not put into words—that there no other woman held his interest at all. Sophie was the only one he wanted. The only one he would ever want. Now, he had to prove it to her.

****

The pit of Ioan's stomach fell away when he returned to Blackthorne Hall, only to find Sophie nowhere to be found. Instead, he found the housekeeper in the gallery, deep in conversation with one of the maids.

"Mrs. Hopkins, I beg your pardon," he broke in, joining the two of them, "but would you happen to know where the duchess is?"

"I do, Your Grace. She and her mother went into London for the day." A tiny frown creased between Mrs. Hopkins's brows. "Something about seeing a man regarding the pipes here?"

He grinned despite his disappointment at missing her. "In America, the houses have hot and cold running water indoors. The duchess has remarked about how she dislikes waiting for water to be heated for a bath. And to be honest? I rather agree with her. It *is* tedious."

"But still, shouldn't you be doing this?"

"It's quite all right."

The maid—Amy, was her name?—smiled. "She also mentioned something about a furniture shop, Your Grace."

Mrs. Hopkins's frown deepened. "Your Grace, you should be with her if she is shopping for this house. After all, it is *your* home. You should be the one approving any and all changes to Blackthorne."

His smile faded as he looked from Amy to the housekeeper and back. "Need I remind you Blackthorne Hall is *her* home as well? She does not need my permission to make her new home as comfortable as the one she left behind. And even if you think she does, perhaps she and I have discussed the matter and I am perfectly fine with it?"

Mrs. Hopkins looked duly chastised. "I beg your pardon, of course."

"Good. Now, should either one of you see her first, please let her know I wish to speak with her when she has a free moment."

"Yes, Your Grace," Amy replied.

"Of course, Your Grace."

"Thank you both." He started down the hallway, then glanced at them over his shoulder and called, "And don't look so concerned. A new century will dawn in a few years, and far be it from us to dwell in the previous one longer than we must."

****

Emily Montgomery shook her head. "Sophie, are you certain this is wise? The duke might not appreciate your trying to remake his home, to change it from what it's always been. Perhaps you've not noticed, but the English aren't *exactly* keen on keeping with the times."

Ioan had said the same thing to her, but it was as he was encouraging her to change the house as she saw fit. Still, it was none of her mother's concern. She was leaving in a few days besides, so Sophie didn't care *how* her mother felt.

Still, she couldn't very well say *that*, so instead, she shrugged. "It's *my* home as well and considering it is also *my* money, I see no reason to ask him a single thing about it. And if he's upset, he will simply have to get over it, I suppose."

"Still, it seems to me—"

"Enough, Mother. As I said, if he's upset, he will simply have to get over it."

With that, Sophie shrugged and moved away from her mother to pore over the sample books. Mr. Abercrombie was the premier upholsterer in London, and she had a mind to redo every last one of the sofas in Blackthorne Hall. The old patterns were dull, the fabrics faded from years of being in sunlight. Some were actually threadbare, and she wanted to bring them up to date. From there, she would venture into Kensington Furnishings to replace the old, worn pieces in her private room with new and far more comfortable pieces. Pieces that *didn't* have springs poking her in the most uncomfortable places.

Shopping was one way to soothe her raw emotions. She'd already been to Madame Fontaine to update her wardrobe now that she was married. She needed new dresses and hats, new undergarments of the finest silk, new shoes, new accessories. Even two new riding habits, which promptly soured her mood as an image of Ioan and Nora flashed through her mind. It made her wince, but fortunately, her mother took no notice.

With each purchase, she told the proprietor to send the bills to her husband. Let him know that while he could threaten her person, she could threaten his accounts, and considering the money was hers, there was blessed little he could do about it. At least, she didn't think he could do much. If she was wrong, she had no doubt he'd tell her.

But, by the time she returned home, Sophie's sense of triumph faded. Ioan would most likely be furious at the amount of money she'd spent, as well as her decisions regarding his home and how she simply thought to change it without consulting him. Besides, it changed nothing in the end. Her husband still preferred another woman over her. Shopping helped in the moment, but left her feeling so very empty once she finished.

She set her parcels on the bed and sank into the armchair in the corner, where she simply stared at them. A low sigh bubbled to her lips. Things. With still more to come. She'd have more gowns than she could ever wear, would need an entire room for her shoes and hats and other accessories. When the bills came due, Ioan would go through the roof.

And yet, she still felt so empty inside. Nothing had changed at all.

The soft tap at the door made her jump, and she was certain her heart actually stopped beating when Ioan called, "May I?"

She nodded, then rolled her eyes. *Idiot. He can't* see *you.* "Yes. Of course."

The door opened and he poked his head in. "Am I interrupting?"

Sophie winced as she glanced over at the pile of parcels on the bed. "Not at all."

He came completely into the room, closing the door behind him. "I see you enjoyed yourself. Oxford Street?"

She nodded. "I'm afraid I went a little mad."

"And you had the bills sent to me?"

"I did."

"Good." He came over to her side of the room. "You should have them all sent to me. What all did you buy?"

She stared up at him. He didn't sound angry at all. Nor did he look it. Rather, there was a hint of a smile in both his eyes and on his lips. "I beg your pardon?"

"Mrs. Hopkins told me you'd gone shopping. And to see a man about installing heated water?"

Her cheeks grew warm. "I did."

"And did you find a man who can do this?"

For the first time all day, she smiled. "I had no idea where to look or what to say if I found one, so no. I didn't actually."

"Next time, we'll go together and find someone."

This was unexpected and she straightened. "I'm sorry?"

"Well, between the two of us, we can probably fumble through whatever we need to find someone qualified. Heated running water would be nice."

She just stared up at him as if she'd never seen him before. "You—you aren't angry?"

"Why would I be? I told you before we were married there would be changes you'd want and that I was fine with them. Why would that have changed?"

Her skirts rustled as she stood and moved to the window. Rain pattered softly against the panes. "I… I don't know."

He joined her, one hand coming to rest on her shoulder. "I'd like to apologize for what I said last eve. I meant not a word of it."

"Which part?"

To her surprise, his thumb moved lightly along the slope of her shoulder. "The threats. It shouldn't have to be said, but I will never force myself on you. Nor would I toss you into the streets. Those were both cruel and uncalled for."

"But the rest remains."

"The rest?"

"The bargain." Heat swirled through her with such force, she couldn't look at him, and so went back to staring out the window. "About a child."

202

"That stands, yes."

There was her window, her chance to win him back.

"Very well." She cringed inwardly. That was the best she could do? A weak *very well*?

"Very well."

She stared up at him, trying to find a way to say what was on her mind, but the words simply refused to come. Instead, she blurted, "Nora won't mind?"

"I beg your pardon?"

"Your mistress."

His eyes hardened. "So, you still choose to believe I was unfaithful." His voice was flat.

"I know what I saw. Believe me, choosing had *nothing* to do with it. I'd have never chosen to see what I did. No one would."

"I see. Very well." He stepped back. "I understand, and be certain to have any other bills sent to me as well. As your husband, it is my duty to see them honored, and I will, of course, do just that."

She closed her eyes as the tears threatened to overflow her lower lashes. "Of course, Duke."

With that, he left, closing the door softly behind him. For the rest of the night, she pleaded a headache, taking to bed, where she proceeded to silently berate herself until she finally fell asleep.

CHAPTER TWENTY-ONE

1 December, 1892
Dearest Sophie,

So by now you are a duchess*! And no, I am not at all jealous, although I must admit, I was a bit hurt that my family was left off the guest list, although Mama said I shouldn't be. We know why, and I will not blame you, especially if I am actually able to come visit you on your grand estate!*

Things here have not changed much since you left. Duncan, of course, does *resemble Tiny Tim and you should only know how hard I laugh over that whenever I think about it for more than a moment or two. But worry not, I haven't told him.*

I cannot wait to meet your duke, for he sounds like something out of a dream. But, I promise, when I do come visit, I will not *stare at him, no matter how handsome he is. You deserve a tall, dark, and handsome man to call your own. However, I would like an introduction to your marquis friend. He sounds adorable as well. Mama has been making noises about possibly doing as your mother did and trying to arrange a title for me to marry as well. Is your marquis friend in the market for a wife? Nudge.*

So, please write back and tell me all *about your wedding night. It is as magical as we both thought? Or is it a drudge, to be suffered thorough like a stoic miss?*

Actually, don't tell me if it is. I'd rather believe the romantic lie instead.

I cannot wait to see you, Soph! We have so much to discuss! You would not believe what happened with Charles Cavendish and Marie Jefferson. They were caught atop the piano at Waverly and by Charles's mother of all people. She and Mr. Castle were attempting to rendezvous in the same way, only to open the door to the music room and catch Charles and Marie in the act! Marie shot off that piano in a blink and Charles rammed himself into the side of said piano. I didn't know you could break it, but I'm fairly certain he did. Long story short, they were married last Tuesday, they expect a baby early next summer, and Mr. Cavendish is suing Mrs. Cavendish for divorce, while Mr. Castle has been doing his damnedest to get back into his wife's good graces, as she controls their purse strings. There is rarely a dull moment here, you know.

I hope you will write back with good news of your own, of perhaps the baby variety, but as long as you are simply happy, that will be fine, too.

Yours Always,

Joy

Sophie sighed softly as she reread Joy's missive. When she learned Joy's family had been left off the wedding guest list, she hurriedly wrote her to explain, but thankfully, Joy didn't need that explanation. She knew.

And she had a hard time mustering any sympathy for Charles Cavendish. Marie Jefferson had been trying to land him for years, but since his interests were more in sleeping with women than marrying them, it seemed only fair that he should find himself forced to right his wrong for once.

But, Joy also thought she, Sophie, was happy. She should only know that in the four days since her wedding to Ioan, Sophie had gone from the pinnacle of happiness into the deepest pit of despair.

Each night, she sat at her dressing table, combing out her hair, waiting for Ioan to appear and demand she fulfill her end of their bargain. But at each hour passed, he failed to appear. Still, she knew he would, and she knew she was bound to honor it as well. Trouble was, she didn't know how she felt about honoring it. It seemed to her, emotion and mechanics tangled inside her, and she wasn't at all certain she could separate them the way a man obviously could. And part of her wanted to make him suffer as well.

Suffer. She'd told him to go to his mistress, to actively seek out that awful Etheridge woman. How on earth was that making him suffer? She was so stupid sometimes.

"Your Grace?" Edith's voice floated through the door. "May I?"

"Of course." Sophie stowed Joy's letter in the top drawer of her dressing table as the door opened and Edith came into the room. "I hadn't realized how late it was. Has His Grace come up yet?"

"I believe he is in his dressing room." Edith appeared in the mirror behind her. "But, I don't know if he's readying for sleep or not."

As she spoke, Edith picked up the comb and went to work. She separated Sophie's hair into three smooth sections, then began braiding them. Her eyes met Sophie's in the mirror. "Do you wish me to fetch him for you?"

"Not at all."

"Very well, Your Grace."

Silence fell as Edith plaited, then secured it with a pale blue ribbon. "Is there anything else you need?"

"Thank you, but no. I'm just going to read a bit before going to sleep."

"Very well." Edith moved back to the door. "Good night—"

"Excuse me, Edith," Ioan appeared in the doorway, "but I'd like a word with my wife."

"Of course, Your Grace."

Sophie's stomach kinked as the maid stepped aside to allow him entry, and when he closed the door behind him, she folded her arms. "I've nothing to say to you, Duke."

"Well, I have something to say to you, so you'll do well to listen, Duchess."

"I'm not at all interested in anything you have to say."

Darkness flashed in his eyes. "Is that so?"

"It is." She turned back to her mirror. "Please, I should like to go to sleep now."

"And sleep you shall." The floor creaked as he strolled toward her. "Once we've finished."

Her mouth went dry, her belly kinked. "Finished?"

"Our bargain. Once you conceive, we each lead our own life. But, since you haven't yet... I will visit you three times a week until such time as you are pregnant. Once you are, I'll leave you be unless you give me a daughter. If our firstborn is a girl, once you are well enough to resume relations, I will once again visit you thrice weekly."

Her heart began hammering against her ribs. "And

if I have nothing but girls?"

"We keep trying until we have a son." He shrugged, his hands coming to rest on her shoulders. "So, it begins tonight."

"And what if, perhaps, I have a headache tonight?"

"I'll make it go away, Sophie."

"I'm tired as well."

"It will take but a few minutes."

"What if"—she scowled at him in the mirror—"I simply do not want *you*?"

"You will."

She fought down the urge to laugh in his face at that. "Think so, do you?"

"Think so?" His hand slipped down beneath the edge of her nightrail. He cupped her left breast, his fingertips brushing her nipple. "No, Duchess. I *know* so."

As he spoke, he teased that nipple, caught it between his thumb and forefinger to roll it slowly. She stared at the mirror, horrified to see her eyes darkening, to see how her cheeks flushed at that one simple caress. He watched her as well, his own eyes almost all pupil as he gently tugged her nipple.

Damn it all! Her body turned traitor on her, heat swelling as he worked her nipple into a tight, aching point. One simple touch and she melted for him. And he knew it.

"Rise." His voice rose as a low whisper, and she did as he said, fighting the urge to bite down on her bottom lip as he slid his hand free to skirt around her, taking her seat in the chair. "Now, come astride me."

She made to sit facing him, but he caught her by the hips, turning her away from him. "This way, Duchess," he growled, closing his legs to maneuver hers along his outer thighs. "Sit."

She did, now biting on that lip at the rush of air between her legs. He caught her nightrail, dragged it up over her thighs, and heat swept through her at the image in the mirror. Good heavens... she'd never felt so... exposed before.

Horror mixed with curiosity as he slid both hands along her outer thighs. His touch was light, a gentle caress that sent a rush of tingles sparkling through her. He brought her nightrail higher, and her cheeks burned at the sight of that triangle of dark hair between her thighs, of *her* reflected in the mirror. Then, he slid a hand between her legs, and she bit back a sigh as he slid those fingers through her curls, as he parted her, letting her see exactly what he stroked.

Perhaps it was only her imagination, but she thought his breath quickened. Her eyelids grew heavy as he slid through those curls, around that little nub that sent more tingles burning through her. He squeezed it ever so gently. Traced a slow, lazy circle around it.

She could feel her own dampness, could feel it in how easily he glided against her. Then, to her horror and delight, he slid a finger inside her and bent it to stroke.

"Oh..." Sophie hadn't meant to suck in a sharp breath, but the sensations he sent coursing through her rendered it unavoidable. Beneath her, his cock rose to press against her backside, and she was overcome with the need to touch him.

If only she could reach him.

She tried to move, only to have his free hand come up and cup that breast again, holding her in place as he tortured her in so erotic a manner. It was so heady, to see him teasing her body the way he did, to see herself as she moved her hips to generate more fire from his touch. He didn't hold her still, but let her rock against him as he rolled that aching nipple once more, as he kneaded a fullness into that breast she'd never felt before.

She tried to reach for him again. All for naught as he held her tighter and growled, "Sit still, Duchess."

"But—"

"Shhh…" His voice was almost a purr, low and sensual, and she wondered if, perhaps, this was *not* mere mechanics for him after all.

His touch was gentle and seductive. He teased her, he caressed her breast, he worked magic with his fingers inside her to make her ache with want. And she did want him, God help her. She wanted him in the worst way. Just seeing them in the mirror, seeing how flushed and aroused she was for him, *because* of him, was beyond powerful. Her body hungered for his, was starved for his, wanted to greedily devour his until they were both spent and sated and fighting to breathe. He touched her like a lover, like a man definitely concerned with her pleasure.

The woman in the mirror was wanton, her cheeks flushed, her body heaving as she savored the pleasure surging through her. He opened his legs slightly, the finger inside her going deeper as her legs spread wider as well. His thumb continued to brush that nub, gently at first, but then with more force.

He released her breast to shift her and then the hand between her legs came up as well. "Lift yourself."

She did, carefully lifting herself by bracing against the chair's arms, and then, in the mirror, she saw him position himself. She bit down hard on her bottom lip as he angled her over him and let go.

She came down onto him as slowly as she could

manage, smiling as he moaned softly. Her arms trembled, but she refused to go any faster. The sensations rippling through her made her head spin and her entire body tense. He was so full inside her, stretching her, feeding the fire that threatened to engulf her.

"Ioan…" His name rose as thick whisper. "I… oh… oh, my…"

He caught her by the hips to rock her ever so slightly. Fire tore through her with simplest of motions as her body tightened about him. He lifted her. He lowered her. She watched as he disappeared inside her, and it did something wicked and wonderful to her. Taking his cue, she found her rhythm, rolling her hips slowly to draw out the pleasure.

The sensations sparking along her pleasure points swelled. The knots inside her tightened. The need for release, the urge to climax, rode her as hard as she rode him. Behind her, he groaned low in his throat, the swelling inside her increasing. His hips rose to meet her thrusts. His hand slid between her thighs to torture that little knot that left her gasping and pleading with him to push her over the edge.

Seeing her own reflection, watching as she made love to him, as she rode him harder and faster, was almost as arousing as his hands on her skin. It was beyond heady, seeing how they fit together, watching as he slowly slid inside her, then back out, only to plunge deep again.

She found her rhythm, angled her hips to drive him deeper, to make the pleasure so much sweeter, to make the fire burn so much hotter. He moaned softly, his body trembling beneath hers. That fullness inside her demanded she move faster, that she drive them both over the edge into the sweet, maddening relief of mutual climax.

Every muscle in her body tightened. The flashpoint burst hot and sweet as she erupted around him, her entire body pulsing to the pleasure thrumming between her thighs. He growled. "Sweet Jesus," as he tensed. His arm clamped about her waist. He surged hard. Erupted to meet her. Shuddered as he peaked.

"Ioan!" She couldn't hold back her cry as she throbbed into him. Her eyes closed at the fiery bliss sweeping through her and as her climax ebbed, she sank against him, fighting to breathe, waiting for the soft kiss on her shoulder and an even softer "Duchess" in her ear.

But that never happened.

He shifted to slip free of her, and although he was gentle about it, he lifted her off him to ease down from the chair. He bent to tug his small clothes back up and then did the same with his trousers. "Sleep well, Duchess," he said as he refastened his trousers and moved to the door. "I will return on Monday, and we will do this again."

She could only stare at him, the remnants of her climax still tingling through her to mock her. How was it possible that he could make her desire him, despite her fury with him? How could he make her think he touched her out of any sort of caring instead of just to prepare her body for his entry?

That her body could betray her so easily, to make her wanton enough that, should he reach for her again, she would gladly ride him in the chair before the mirror and not think twice about it. And what was worse? He knew it as well. He felt his effect on her.

Hot tears stung her eyes as she watched him leave,

then she picked up the hairbrush and fired it at the door. "Bastard!"

****

The loud *thunk* of the hairbrush meeting the door made Ioan wince. God damn it, why hadn't he just given in to his impulse to wrap her in his arms when she sank against him? She should only know how arousing it was, how damn erotic it was to watch her find her pleasure in that bloody mirror. To watch her body accept his. To see the effect his touch had on her. To see her effect on him.

And bloody hell, why was he so damn determined to muck up everything at every turn? One moment, he was in his dressing room, a snifter of brandy in his hand to help him sleep. The next, he was fired up and ready to seduce his wife into letting him back into her bed.

How could he win her back, if he forced her hand at every turn? True, he'd shown them both how he could make her want him, could make her want him inside her, but he didn't want to have to *make* her do anything. He wanted her to simply want him.

A sharp pain stabbed him behind the eyes. He'd taken a bad situation and miraculously made it worse. Wonderful. He'd seduced her, all right, but not in the way he'd meant to do it and with his luck, tonight would be the night she conceived. One more thing he'd have to make up to her.

"Bloody hell," he muttered, stomping into his dressing room, where he slammed the door and then flung himself down onto the small sofa nearest the fireplace.

"Your Grace?" His valet, Baxter, rapped on the door. "Do you need any assistance?"

"No, thank you. I'm fine."

"Very well."

The footsteps moved away and died out, and Ioan rubbed his forehead as he stared into the fire. "Out of the pan and into the fire," he muttered, watching the flames dance on the hearth. "And now I've another mess to find my way out of."

CHAPTER TWENTY-TWO

The next morning, Sophie blushed as she sat at her dressing table and images of her and Ioan flashed through her mind. The steamy memory filled her with an uncomfortable heat and within a moment or two, had her squirming against the chair. Somehow, she thought that, under the right circumstances, making love in the chair with him might be worth revisiting.

Except the previous night was *not* lovemaking at all. It was breeding, for all intents and purposes, and come Monday, she would find herself in the same predicament. Or worse. After all, he'd told her there were many positions for a couple to explore and she had the feeling quite a few would involve little to no face-to-face contact at all.

But perhaps that was better. In some ways, not seeing his face—only seeing the forbidden parts of him—heightened her senses. And he wasn't exactly cruel toward her. Cold, perhaps, but not cruel. He hadn't forced himself on her, and he had made damn certain she was ready before he entered her. But still…

A sigh rose to her lips as Edith bustled in. "Is something the matter, Your Grace?"

"No, Edith. Nothing new, anyhow." She looked over at her maid. "Are my parents up and about?"

"They are. In the breakfast room."

Sophie rose from her chair, her eyes lingering on the

mirror where, for a moment, she saw her and Ioan in the grips of passion.

No. Not passion. It was mere rote for him.

She winced and turned away, which did not go unnoticed by Edith. "Are you certain you're all right?"

"Quite." Perhaps she should see about replacing that chair. After all, if she blushed every time she looked at it, Edith would eventually begin to wonder why.

She turned away from her dressing table, spying the lovely pale blue velvet gown spread across her bed. It was one of the dresses sewn specifically for coming to England and she hadn't had a chance to wear it yet. She dressed and prepared herself to go below.

The soft buzz of chatter coming from the breakfast room gave her pause, but she took a deep breath and forced herself to thrust open the door. The dowager was already there, as were her parents, but she breathed a sigh of relief when she didn't see Ioan anywhere. Good. She wasn't quite ready to come face to face with him just yet.

"Good morning," she greeted, forcing a smile to her lips as she strode to the sideboard to take a plate and fill with shirred eggs, crispy bacon, and toast with sweet butter and jam.

"Good morning, indeed," her mother greeted her, wiping her mouth on a pale green napkin. "I thought you and the duke would be taking breakfast in your room this morning?"

"Where is Ioan, by the by?" The dowager lifted her teacup.

Sophie paused, halfway to her chair, and said, "I'm... I'm not sure. He wasn't in our room when I woke this morning."

"Probably tending to his horses," Randolph said,

scooping up a forkful of eggs. "I've never seen a man so in love with all things equestrian."

"You say that as if it's something of which to be ashamed." China clinked as the dowager set her cup in her saucer.

"No, not at all." Randolph shook his head. "But, it does strike me as a bit wasteful. Money that could be better spent elsewhere."

Sophie's cheeks grew warm as the dowager simply stared at him. "I beg your pardon? Horses are quite gentlemanly."

But Randolph wasn't put off so easily. "And this is why you need my money. Am I to assume your son will waste *this* fortune as well?"

"Papa!" Sophie glared at him. "Mind yourself!"

"I won't," he told her. "I have a right to express my opinion when it's my dollars that keep the roof over your heads."

"I'm afraid you simply have no idea what goes into running an estate such as Blackthorne." The dowager straightened, her eyes cold and hard. "Not that I'm surprised, mind you. I find few Americans let not knowing something stop them from insisting they know what's best for all around them."

"Enough, both of you," Sophie snapped, slamming her hand against the tabletop hard enough to rattle everything on it. "I've had quite enough of the bickering, and Papa, you would do well to mind yourself in *my* home!"

All three pairs of eyes went round as they stared at her, and her father's cheeks flushed as he said, "Of course, Sophie," and went back to his newspaper.

"Is something the matter?"

Sophie froze as Ioan strode into the breakfast room. He looked at each one of them. "Again, is something the matter?"

"Not at all." The dowager pushed her chair back and leaned heavily on her cane to rise. "But I have a letter to get into the morning post, so if you will excuse me."

"A letter?" Ioan frowned at her. "Mother, what is going on?"

"Everything is fine, Ioan." She shuffled out of the room.

"Why did I hear raised voices?" Ioan looked first at his in-laws, then at Sophie. "I'll not ask again."

"Good. For the answer will not change." Sophie tried to ignore the heat sweeping thorough her at the sight of him. He was dressed as he usually did, in trousers and a fine shirt, but for some reason, he flashed through her mind with the falls of his trousers open, and that amazing part of him on display for her eyes only.

He narrowed his eyes at her. "Well, someone has found their spine, I see. Good." He moved to the sideboard and peered over one shoulder at her. "You look well-rested this morning, Sophie. I take it you slept well?"

"Fair, I suppose."

She held his gaze easily, but then he winked and the heat returned as he added, "You certainly looked sleepy enough last evening."

"I supposed I was." Her appetite faded, so she abruptly stood and pushed her chair in. "Last night was a rather tedious evening for me, so yes, I suppose I *was* sleepy."

He flinched ever so slightly, so she knew her barb found its mark, but then he merely shrugged and replied,

"Perhaps tonight will be livelier, then."

Her stomach did an odd flip, and although her mother and her father appeared to be oblivious to the conversation around them, engulfed by their reading, Sophie knew better than to reply what she truly thought. Instead, she shrugged. "Somehow, I doubt it. Now, if you will excuse me, I've asked Edith to accompany me to London."

Her mother looked up. "London? Whatever for?"

"I have a list of tradesmen I need to hire." Sophie shot a pointed look at Ioan. "This house is in terrible need of modernization, and I see no reason to put it off any longer."

Ioan cleared his throat. "Tell your maid she will remain here. This is my house and as such, I will go with you to hire any tradesmen."

She scowled. "Very well. If you insist."

"I do."

He said it mildly, but there was no mistaking the seriousness in his eyes. Now she was stuck with him for company in London, when she'd really only wanted a chance to do a bit of shopping for Christmas gifts to send to Samuel and Joy.

Wonderful.

****

It was one of the longest days Sophie could recall, and she was thankful when they were in the coach on the way back to Blackthorne. Ioan hadn't left her side, being overly solicitous as they hired the workmen needed to bring Blackthorne Hall up to more modern standards. Work would begin after the new year, which meant by summer, she would have access to indoor running hot water as well as a myriad of other conveniences.

"Are you hungry, Duchess?" he asked as they alit from the carriage. "We've missed supper, but I'll have Mrs. Frayne heat something if you like."

"Thank you, but no. I'm fine." She strode to the door, pausing when he didn't follow. "Aren't you coming, Duke?"

"Me? No." He glanced at the driver. "Take me into the village, please."

"Yes, Your Grace."

"Good evening, Duchess." Ioan climbed back into the coach and offered up a smug smile through the window as the coach rocked back down the driveway.

She stood there, watching as the coach rolled out of sight. What was he doing in the village this evening? No, it was probably best if she didn't wonder. Wondering led to her imagination creating scenarios and visions that made her stomach hurt and her head ache. She'd assumed Ioan spent the past nights in his dressing room, in that narrow bed alone.

But what if she was wrong?

What if he did exactly what she'd told him he could and he was going to seek out Nora. What if he whiled away each evening rolling about an inn bed with her? Or perhaps her family lived on the other side of the village?

She winced, her eyes stinging. Damn it all, she couldn't even be angry with him if he was; after all, she'd *insisted*.

Then again, if she'd protested, it certainly wouldn't stop him. Just as it didn't stop him from kissing that slut at the stables. All any of it did was make her look like a fool.

"Your Grace, is everything all right?" Mrs. Hopkins came out onto the drive, her forehead creased with worry. "Where is His Grace?"

"He went into the village."

"Went into the village? Whatever for?"

"How the deuce should I know?" Sophie snapped as she stalked past. "He didn't ask me for permission and give me a reason, you know."

"Well, of course not." Mrs. Hopkins fell into step beside her. "But that doesn't mean he didn't say."

"We missed supper. I expect he is going to eat at the pub."

"Shall I have Mrs. Frayne heat you a tray?"

"Thank you, but no." Sophie hurried on ahead, before anyone else happened upon them. "I have a terrific headache and want only to sleep."

"Very well, Your Grace." Mrs. Hopkins paused at the foot of the staircase. "If you change your mind, you need only ring."

Sophie didn't reply, but hurried down the hallway to her room, where she leaned back against the closed door and let out a heavy sigh. "Well done, Josephine St. John. You've gotten yourself into a fine mess this time. Now, let's see how you get out of it."

****

Pennington leaned back in his chair, exhaling a puff of grayish smoke. "Why are you here, when you could be home with your lovely little bride?"

"Because I'm hungry and I missed supper."

"Are you joking, Blackthorne? You need only say the word and you know Mrs. Frayne will rectify that."

"Yes, I suppose she would." Ioan traced his forefinger about the rim of his goblet. "But I think the faces here are friendlier."

"Here?" Pennington looked about at the Swan's

patrons. "I don't know about friendlier, but they certainly aren't prettier."

"Pretty isn't everything, you know."

Pennington leaned forward. "What did you do this time?"

"Where do I begin?"

"Perhaps at the beginning?"

"At the beginning." Ioan threw back the rest of his wine and signaled the barkeep to bring another glass. "My dear man, if I go back to the beginning, I'll bore you to tears."

"The last twenty-four hours, then."

"Ah… the last twenty-four hours." Ioan looked up at the pretty serving girl and winked. "Thank you."

"Of course, Your Grace."

Pennington kicked him in the shin. Hard. "God damn it, man!" Ioan yelped, clutching his lower leg as the serving girl chuckled and made her way to another table. "What the deuce was *that* for?"

"You're being an arse, that's what. You've a beautiful little minx home waiting for you and yet, you're here. Undressing a barmaid with your eyes, no less."

"Undressing—are you mad?" Ioan lifted the glass of cabernet and shook his head. "Last night… you should only know what happened last night."

"So tell me."

"Have you ever seen a woman so beautiful—so beautiful and seductive—you wanted to fall to your knees and thank the Lord for making you a man?"

"Not yet, I haven't."

"I have." He swallowed a mouthful of wine. "This beautiful, sensuous temptress was in my arms last night.

She treated my body to a pleasure I haven't felt in forever."

Pennington coughed. "This is a bit personal, Duke."

"Hush. You asked, now you listen. I made love to this woman in front of a mirror, *her* mirror. Watched every last sigh form on her lips, watched a flush spread through her entire body, watched her ride me into ecstasy. Do you know how arousing that is? Do you have any idea how hard I responded to her?"

Pennington shifted in his chair, propping an elbow on the table to lean closer. "I think you've had enough wine, chum."

Ioan drained the glass and signaled for yet another. "Not nearly enough, old man. That woman thinks I'm with Nora Etheridge now, and I have her blessing."

Pennington's eyes practically bulged from their sockets. "What?"

He nodded. "She thinks that I'm in bed with Nora right now, and she has given her permission. Her permission to plow another woman!"

"Why do I feel I'm missing something here?"

"She thinks she caught me with Nora."

"Why would she possibly think such a thing?"

"Because she did."

This time, when the barmaid came over, Pennington leaned over and swiped the goblet from him. "*What?*"

"Give over, Pennington, and get your own."

"No. Explain yourself, you dimwit."

"Yes. I *am* a dimwit. Nora kissed me and Sophie happened upon us." Ioan threw himself back in his chair, fighting to steady himself as two Penningtons vied for his attention. His brain felt thick and fuzzed over, as did his tongue, but he blundered on. "And now, once I get her pregnant... that's it."

He swept his arms outward in a grand gesture. "If it's a boy, I will never make love to that stunning, seductive woman again. But I'm free to topple Nora onto any flat surface that will hold us, at my pleasure."

Pennington cocked one brow. Actually, *both* Penningtons did. "And if it's a girl?"

"Then I have another chance, once she's able. But do you hear me? She thinks I was unfaithful."

"From the sounds of it, you jackass, you were." Now both Penningtons scowled at him. "And you sit here, oh-so-proud of yourself for this? What is wrong with you?"

"I am not at all interested in Nora. Don't you see?" Ioan lurched forward to snatch the goblet and downed it in one swallow, only to realize the mistake in doing so as the wine hit his belly and destroyed his brain. "But Sophie thinks I am. She thinks... she thinks..."

"You're an idiot?"

"No." Damn it, the words were refusing to come to his lips. His thoughts came slower, more sluggish as well. "I don't wanna... I just wanna... bloody hell..."

Pennington sighed softly as he eased from his chair and came around to grab Ioan's left arm to set around his neck. "Let's get you home, old man. Tomorrow, you tell me what mess you've gotten yourself into, only without the gibberish."

Ioan's legs felt rubbery, and the damn room tilted so sharply on him. He stumbled, but Pennington caught him easily. Ioan tried to force his eyes to focus. "You're my bes-besht friend, Stevie... I love you... I want you to know that I love you."

"I love you as well, Ioan." Pennington shook his head as he helped him out to the waiting coach. "Which is why I want to hear this entire story from sober you. Then, I'll kick your backside but good and tell you how bloody stupid you're being."

The coach tilted as sharply as the tavern had. He stumbled, then sprawled facedown against the velvet seat. Pennington climbed in, telling the driver, "I believe the duke wishes to return home."

"Of course, my lord."

That was the last thing Ioan remembered as the coach began moving and he passed out cold.

CHAPTER TWENTY-THREE

Opening his eyes was a horrid mistake. Ioan lay on the narrow bed in his dressing room, where Baxter had left him the night before, prior to hopefully showing Pennington to his room as well. At least, he thought Pennington was still there. He didn't honestly think he'd managed to make it home on his own.

Carefully, he eased onto his back. His stomach sloshed, but its contents stayed put. Thank the Lord. He lay there, staring up at the ceiling, trying to remember what he'd told Pennington the night before. Damn it all, he'd hoped Pennington would have advice, good advice, but honestly, he'd take anything at this point, in how he could woo his wife and win her over once more. He'd been married a week, and managed to muck it up not once, but twice since the wedding. And each time, he dug his hole that much deeper.

But all he could recall was the look of mild amusement on Pennington's face when Ioan described the night he'd made love to Sophie in the chair before her dressing table.

He frowned. Made love? Hardly.

Damn it all, he'd mucked it up three times, each time worse than the last.

"Your Grace?"

Ioan winced as Baxter rapped on the door. "What?"

He poked his head in. "Are you ready to go below

for breakfast?"

Ioan groaned, his stomach churning at the thought of food. "Good God, man, no. Leave me here to die."

"Very good, Your Grace."

Ioan almost grinned at the dryness of Baxter's voice. Carefully, he lifted his head. "Is Pennington still here?"

"He's in the Queen Anne room."

"Good. Go see if he requires assistance." He let his head fall back to the bed, wincing at the echo inside his bloody skull.

"Yes, Your Grace."

The door clicked softly shut, and Ioan lay there, contemplating life and death and whether or not he'd ever move again, when the door opened once more and Pennington said, "Are you dead?"

"I'm not at all certain."

"Well, you're talking, so there's some life left." The door clicked again and the floor creaked. "Do you remember anything from last night?"

"I remember hiring men to come install heated running water after the new year. I remember coming back here, and my wife allowing me to go in search of my mistress, and then I remember seeing your ugly face instead."

"What nonsense is that you're spewing about mistresses and the like?"

Steeling himself for the rush of nausea, Ioan slowly sat up. His head ached. His belly lurched. But he managed. And in a soft rush, he brought Pennington up to speed, ending with, "And that's how I found myself in this whole mess."

"So, your wife saw you kissing another woman, and you don't understand why she's upset by it?"

Ioan scowled, rubbing his face with both hands. "I was *not* kissing her. She was kissing me."

"Oh, because *that* makes a difference," Pennington scoffed. "You are a bloody idiot, do you know that?"

"Believe it or not, I actually agree with you." He let his hands fall away from his face. "The question is, how do I fix it?"

Pennington perched on the edge of the wide windowsill, arms folded, expression solemn. "Are you certain you can? Or that you want to? A wife *and* a mistress? All men should be so lucky."

"If your plan is only to mock," Ioan gestured toward the door, "take your leave and hie back to London. I'm in no mood for games."

Pennington sighed softly. "She's gotten under your skin, has she?"

"In the worst way, Penn. In the worst way." He shook his head slowly and got to his feet. "She is all I can think about. Day and night, awake or asleep."

"So, tell her."

"I don't think she'll believe me."

"Well, you've nothing to lose." Pennington rose from the sill and crossed to the door. "Don't be an idiot, Ioan. You will regret it for the rest of your life. Come find me later, and I'll help you if you still need it. But for the love of God, man, *don't* be a fool."

****

Each morning, when she went down for breakfast, Sophie's stomach churned like mad until she rounded the corner and saw only her parents at the table. Thank heavens, Ioan wasn't there. She didn't know where he'd spent those nights, but had the sickening feeling it wouldn't take much to figure out. There was no way she'd be able to sit across from the table and look at him, knowing he'd most likely whiled some of the time away with his mistress. She didn't know where or how, and thought she'd probably be sick if she were to find out. Either way, she'd ruined everything and could blame no one but herself for such idiocy. If he decided to take Nora as his mistress, she could hardly fault him. The blame would rest quite squarely on her own stubborn shoulders.

This morning, as Sophie stepped into the breakfast room, her mother looked up from the slice of toast she buttered. "Sophie? Are you all right? You look... peaked."

She scowled. Her head ached and her mood remained sour. "It's a bit early, Mother." She drew out her chair to settle into it. "Can we wait until luncheon to for you to start pointing out all of my flaws? And before you ask again, I am fine. I simply did not sleep well is all."

"Leave her be, Emily," her father said without looking up from his newspaper. "She is a newlywed, after all, and probably lost track of time." Now he peeked around the side to wink at her. "Right, Soph?"

To her horror, her cheeks grew hot. "Papa!"

"What?" He shrugged, his newspaper snapping as he straightened it once more. "We're all adults, and you're a married woman now. You are—how do they say it?—worldly."

"Randolph! There's no need to be crass!"

Sophie stared down at the china place setting, her face growing hotter by the moment. Perhaps the floor would open up and simply swallow her whole? Or was her luck not good enough for such a thing?

Why did she even question it?

"Good morning." Sophie swallowed a groan at the low pull of Ioan's voice, and she looked up to see him and the dowager step into the breakfast room. His eyes met hers, and for a brief moment, his darkened. But then, they were bright green once more and to her astonishment, he came around the table to brush her cheek with a kiss. "Good morning, darling," he said, his voice light and without care. "Sleep well?"

"I did. And you?"

"Like a rock." He moved to the sideboard to pick up a plate. "Emily, Randolph, all set to return to the States?"

"We are," Emily replied brightly. "But, we have thoroughly enjoyed our stay here, Your Grace. Thank you so much."

The dowager sat next to Sophie. "I thought you were planning to stay through the holidays?"

"While that was our original plan," Randolph replied, getting up refill his coffee, "I received a telegram this morning, and I'm afraid it's a matter that simply won't wait until the new year."

Sophie's spine stiffened. "Did something happen back home?"

"Nothing you need concern yourself with, love." Her father smiled at her as he settled across from her once more. "Simply a problem your brother is having. Nothing to worry about, but we will have to leave sooner than we'd originally planned."

"Oh." Sophie looked over at her mother, who seemed even less perturbed by the thought of trouble back home. "Mother? Will you come back and visit soon?"

"Of course, but I don't know when, exactly." Emily set down her spoon to lift her teacup. "Or, you and Ioan will are always welcome to visit us in New York. Have you ever been?"

Ioan turned away from the sideboard, his plate heavy with eggs and sausage and toast. "No. I haven't. I've only ever been to Boston, and that was when I was but a boy." He glanced over at Sophie. "Would you like to visit?"

"Perhaps. Maybe this summer?"

He sat next to her father. "We will have to see. By the summer, you may not be in any condition to travel."

Her cheeks grew warm as all eyes were upon her now. "I'm sorry, Ioan?"

"Well"—a sly smile came to his lips as he held her horrified stare easily—"most doctors would frown on a heavily pregnant woman traveling so far and since our first order of business is to—"

"That is quite enough, Ioan," the dowager broke in sharply as Sophie's face felt close to melting right off her skull, "and this is neither the time nor the place for such vulgarity."

"Vulgarity?" He turned innocent eyes to his mother. "Why, you were the one reminding me how important it is for me to get her—"

"I said, *enough!*" The dowager slammed her cane against the floor. "What on earth has gotten into you this morning, Blackthorne? You are downright crass, and it is incredibly uncalled for."

To his credit, Ioan's cheeks grew red. He dabbed at his lips with his napkin, then threw it down as he rose. "I beg your pardon, everyone. I'm afraid I didn't sleep well at all, actually. My judgment is not what it should be, and for that, I apologize. If you will excuse me."

He didn't wait for anyone to reply, but left the room,

and once he was gone, all eyes turned to Sophie now, whose entire body grew hot. "I—I don't know what to say," she admitted, unable to get her voice above a whisper. The need to leave, to become invisible, swept through her, and she practically knocked her chair over in her haste to rise. "Excuse me, please."

She darted out of the room, heading toward the rear of the house, where she stepped out into the gardens and welcomed the chilly air as it swept over her to take some of the shamed heat from her body. Despite the cold, it was a lovely day, with puffy white clouds rolling through the clear blue sky.

With that, she started off for a walk. She didn't know where she was going, until she found herself at the stables, and although she wasn't exactly dressed for riding, that didn't stop her from smiling at the confused-looking groom and saying, "Have you a gentle mare I could ride?"

"Of course, Your Grace. Daisy is the gentlest mare in the stable. If you'll excuse me."

She nodded. "Absolutely."

The groom went back into the stables and when he emerged, it was to lead a small gray and white horse out. "Daisy, this is Her Grace, the Duchess. Take care with her, as she's new around here." He smiled at her. "Your Grace, Daisy is as gentle as they come. Stay with the trails, keep the house on your right, and you should have no trouble at all. Shall I saddle His Grace's favorite?"

"That won't be necessary, Mr. Regan." She stepped up onto the mounting block, then carefully mounted the horse. "I'll be riding alone this morning."

"Just Regan will be fine, Your Grace." He rubbed Daisy's nose. "Does His Grace know you're here?"

"I'll be back for luncheon." She gathered up the reins and led Daisy from the stables. It was the first time since her arrival that she ventured out on horseback alone, and the solitude was exactly what she needed to clear her head.

She couldn't believe Ioan's nerve. What was he about that morning? Was he taunting her? Would he admit to her where he'd gone in the village? Would he be visiting her again tonight to continue his quest for an heir?

It would be much easer if she had some way to tell if she was pregnant without having to wait for weeks.

Then again, she'd be lying if she said she didn't want him coming to her bed again. Despite everything, she'd found such pleasure with him. He'd made certain that happened. So, did that mean there was more than mere mechanics behind his actions?

But did he do the same things with Nora?

She winced. *Damn it all already. Why should I worry about* that? *I don't care how many nights he spends with that… that whore. It doesn't matter.*

No, that was a lie. She *did* care. She cared so deeply, it caused a physical ache deep inside her. She didn't know where he'd passed those nights, nor did she know if he passed them alone. All she knew was that he wasn't with her.

Perhaps he *had* snuck off to tryst with Nora Etheridge each night instead.

She winced, and a sour taste flooded her mouth as images leapt unbidden into her mind. Had he spent the previous three nights holding her? Caressing her? Peeling her dress and undergarments from her body as he kissed his way down to—

"Stop it!" She shook her head as she guided Daisy around a rather deep rut in the path. "You'll make yourself sick."

But the images wouldn't leave her in peace, and her stomach tightened more with each one that slid into her mind. A sour taste rose in her mouth. That feeling of being ill swelled until she found herself tensing to hold it at bay. Damn it all anyway, why couldn't she have simply kept herself from feeling anything for Ioan, just as she'd originally planned? So many women of her class were in marriages of convenience. Did they pine for their husbands and grow ill at the thought of said husbands with other women? It seemed so terribly unfair that she should suffer, when she'd done nothing to deserve it.

They'd been married not quite a week. Had mere days passed since she felt she was the happiest woman in the world? Only days since Ioan pulled her onto his lap in their coach and kissed and touched her with such affection? Only days since he introduced her to the pleasures to be found in their marriage bed.

She winced every time she thought about how he so coldly promised her she'd regret her decision.

He was right. She did regret it. More so than any other she'd ever made.

But at the same time, she wasn't the one kissing another the *day after their wedding*.

"And that is all the difference."

"Talking to yourself, are you?"

She jumped, then chided herself for her foolishness as Lord Pennington came trotting toward her on a giant dappled horse. "Do you often sneak up on unsuspecting women?"

"You wound me," he told her, smiling as he drew up

and eased his mount around to fall into step alongside her. "I don't sneak up on anyone, unsuspecting or otherwise. How do you fare, Your Grace?"

"Please, I've never felt less like a duchess, and I'm still not used to having a title. If you can't bring yourself to call me Sophie, I implore you, Duchess is just fine."

His blue eyes danced with mischief. "Exactly how does one *feel* like a duchess?"

"Oh, don't ask me to explain it. I'm not at all certain I can."

"You look tired." He lowered his voice and inched his horse closer still. "In all seriousness, Duchess, is everything all right?"

It was on the tip of her tongue to lie. To paste on a false smile and assure him all was wonderful in her world. After all, what would he think, to learn his dearest friend had already broken his marital vow?

Of course, why she should care if she tarnished Ioan's reputation was beyond her. Her heart hurt too much for her to care, and it was always possible it wouldn't harm said reputation at all. For all she knew, mistresses were so common, no one batted an eye.

But such genuine concern wove through Pennington's words, it sliced through her just like a sharp blade. Her eyes stung with sudden and unexpected tears, so she bowed her head, her, "I'm fine," emerging as a broken whisper.

"Duchess?" Leather squeaked. Metal rattled. A gentle hand came to rest on her thigh. "Sophie? What is it?"

"Nothing is right, my lord. Nothing is right at all, and I wouldn't even know where to begin…"

"Come down here and we'll walk." He stepped back

and held out a hand. "The horses will be fine here."

Despite her blurred vision, she dismounted and let him take the reins for both animals. He looped them about a low branch, then moved to catch her by the shoulders. "What is it? What happened?"

"It's silly," Sophie managed to whisper, forcing herself to look up, to meet his concerned gaze. "It isn't as if this is a love match. He married me for my family's money, and I understand that, but…" She shook her head slowly, trying unsuccessfully to blink back the remaining tears. Impossible. They spilled over her lower lashes to course down her cheeks, one after the other, until they combined with the cold to sting her skin.

Without preamble, Pennington pulled her into his arms, wrapping her in a tender embrace. "What did that bloody fool do?" He growled, hints of anger creeping into his normally smooth voice.

"I—he—oh, I don't even know how to begin…" She let her head come to rest against his chest. For the first time in a week, she no longer felt alone, isolated, and the comfort he offered was wonderful.

She lifted her head. "I should go back to the house, I think. I should hate for anyone to see us and have the wrong impression."

Pennington released her, then dug about in the pocket of his greatcoat, coming up with a snowy white handkerchief. He pressed it into her hand. "Why don't you go to the beginning and tell me?"

She dabbed at her eyes with the soft linen. "Everything was wonderful, my lord. Absolutely wonderful. You saw us at the church. At the reception. He seemed happy, didn't he?"

"He did, actually. More so than I would have

thought, given he wasn't exactly in a hurry to marry." He flinched. "You know how I mean that, don't you? I meant no offense, of course."

She waved off his apology. "Of course. And you aren't wrong, either. I thought the same and, stupid me, I assumed it was because *I* made him happy. That he was happy to be there, with me."

"I've been to weddings of couples claiming to be in love that didn't appear as happy as you two did." Pennington gestured down the path. "Shall we walk some more?"

She nodded, dabbing at her eyes once more. The tears slowed, but hadn't stopped completely, and her throat still felt tight and raw. The cold air held a hint of frost, the iron-gray clouds threatened snow, and for one mad moment, she wondered if anyone at Blackthorne Hall even missed her. Somehow, she didn't think anyone had evem noticed she'd left.

"I caught him with Nora Etheridge," she said bluntly.

"*What?*"

She nodded. "The morning after our wedding. We were going to go riding, and he went down to ready the horses while I finished"—heat climbed into her cheeks—"while I finished dressing. And when I came down, there they were."

Something glinted in Pennington's eyes, something dark and fiery. "Dare I ask what they were doing?"

"He was kissing her."

"That son of a bitch."

His coarse language should have horrified her, but it didn't. She'd heard far worse from her father when he lost his temper. It did, however, surprise her. She would never have expected him to be angry on her behalf. "I beg your pardon?"

"He is such a fool. I told him to tread with care where she was concerned. And he swore she was the past."

"He did what?"

He nodded. "The night of your engagement ball. I took him aside and basically warned him." Every last bit of humor was gone in his eyes now, his voice low and even. "And he told me I had nothing to fear and no reason to worry. He had no intention of straying on you." His eyes were direct as they met hers. "Are you *certain* they were kissing?"

She offered up a long look. "I *do* know a kiss when I see one."

"Of course you do. You are hardly a fool." Pennington sighed, raking a hand through his dark hair. "I am so sorry, love. You say you caught them. What did he say?"

She shrugged, the last of her tears drying up. Her anger was gone now. Numbness crept over her. "He said she kissed him and that he tried to push her away. But, what else would he say?"

"Well, to be honest, Blackthorne's not one for lying, usually. Not even to save his own skin. He is disgustingly honorable that way, you know." Pennington leaned against the tree he'd tethered the horses to and gazed down at her. "Are you certain he isn't telling the truth? Is there any chance he was trying to free himself from Nora? She can be quite… clingy when the mood strikes."

"I *saw* them, my lord. I wish to God I hadn't, that I could at least fool myself, if nothing else, but I can't. If he tried, it was halfhearted at best." She sighed deeply, moving to lean against the tree alongside him. "May I tell you something?"

"I thought you already had."

"My lord, please."

"I beg your pardon, Duchess. Of course you can."

She glanced sideways up at him. "I was rather hoping she would take an interest in you instead."

He said nothing at first, and she had the horrible feeling she'd said something she oughtn't have. As the silence stretched, and his expression went from concerned to grim, her belly twisted with apprehension. "My lord?"

Then, he let out a heavy sigh. He pushed up from the tree and turned toward her. "I'm afraid I haven't been entirely honest with you, Duchess."

"What? I don't understand."

He caught her by the hands and for a moment, she thought he was going to maybe do something mad, such as kiss her. After all, they were alone and she really didn't know him all that well. Perhaps this was a mistake.

But then, he said, "I'm afraid Lady Nora is not exactly the sort I find attractive."

"I find *that* difficult to believe. She is every man's fantasy come to life. Isn't that what you said to me?"

"Yes, well, in my defense, I was just coming to know you and I wasn't entirely comfortable telling you about me. Far easier to allow you to think Blackthorne and I were the same sort of hot-blooded man."

Now she was *really* confused. "What are you getting at, Pennington?"

He grinned. "And now I know you are comfortable with me."

"I'm lost, that's what I am."

He gave her hands a gentle squeeze. "Ladies hold no interest for me. They never have. And aside from Blackthorne, you are the only other person in Berkshire who knows, and I do hope you will keep that in confidence."

In the weeks since her arrival at Blackthorne Hall, and all the time she'd spent with both Ioan and Pennington, this left her speechless and confused. She opened and closed her mouth several times, her thoughts falling all over one another as she tried to sort them. Finally, she just said, "Then what *does* hold your interest?"

"Lately? A rather handsome viscount from Bath." Pennington smiled. "I believe Blackthorne introduced you to him at your reception. Lord Mallen?"

"Oh…" She certainly did remember him. Tall. Blond. Rather handsome, indeed. But, wait… so that meant that Pennington preferred—

She glanced up at him. Back in New York, there were several men in her social circle who were whispered about when it came to their proclivities. But, she only knew one herself and he wasn't quite as… masculine as Pennington.

The women of Berkshire would be crushed if they ever learned the truth.

But on the other hand, he could do far worse than Lord Mallen. "So, you mean to tell me that you… and Lord Mallen… are…"

"We're lovers." Pennington nodded. "But, things being what they are, you cannot breathe a word of it. To anyone. Please. I told you this as a friend, and in the strictest of confidences."

"I—I had no idea. And of course, I shall take it to

my grave, if you wish."

He looked somewhat uncomfortable. "I only told you because I know what you thought, and honestly, if I was interested in her, if I was... *normal*, for lack of a better word, I would help you. I would help you in a heartbeat. You must know that."

"Does she know?"

"No one aside from Blackthorne knows. But, she would learn rather quickly, should she want something more than friendship. I'm afraid she would be—ah—disappointed by my reaction, or lack thereof, to her."

"Well, your secret is safe with me, Pennington. I promise."

"And you aren't disgusted by me?"

She looked up at him. He was charming and funny, and sweet and kind and a fabulous dancer. He made her laugh. Offered a shoulder to cry on. He was no different to her than he had been ten minutes earlier. She might not understand his leanings, but to her, they didn't change that kindness, that humor, that charm, *or* how wonderfully he danced.

"No. I couldn't be. Confused, perhaps, but not disgusted. I promise you that."

"Let me speak to Blackthorne," he told her. "He will be honest with me, if nothing else. And with any luck, you will find he was honest with you as well."

"Oh, I think it will take more than that." She sighed softly, and filled him in on what happened, from what Ioan had snarled to her in their bedroom all the way up through breakfast that morning. When she finished, she said, "I think my being big enough to forgive him if he did nothing wrong won't quite be enough."

"Oh, you've both gotten yourself into a pickle,"

Pennington said softly. "But, I think it was old Will Shakespeare who said something trite about the path of love never being smooth or some other such nonsense. So, suffice it to say, eventually it *will* smooth out."

She held out his handkerchief. "Eventually could be a terribly long time. Are you *certain* you aren't interested in women?"

He chuckled, drawing her in for a quick hug and pressed a kiss into her temple. "If I was, Duch, you would be the one I'd be chasing. Blackthorne is a fool, if he really did kiss that harlot. She is a pretty package, but has no substance at all. You are good for him. Be patient with him. We both know he is bullheaded and thick at times."

She pulled back, cocking her head slightly to her left as she wrinkled her nose. "Duch?"

"You don't like it?"

She smiled up at him and shook her head. "No, it's fine."

"Let me talk to him, and perhaps you should as well."

Her spirits sank. "I doubt it would do any good, Pennington. He was so angry and so—so *smug* when he assured me I'd come to regret it. And do you know the worst part?" She looked up at him and let out a slow sigh, her smile fading. "He was right. I *do* regret it. I've pushed him right toward that awful woman, and there isn't a bloody thing I can do about it now.."

"Well, never say die and all that." Pennington stepped back. "And all isn't lost, and I'm certain there are a few more tired sayings I could throw out, but I won't. Instead, why don't you go for your ride and hopefully come this evening, your husband will be more than willing to not only talk, but to find some way to salvage this."

"I'm afraid I won't have time for that ride now. My parents are leaving on the four o'clock train to London and I should see them off. They're going back to the States and won't be back for a long time, if ever."

As she spoke, a sense of sadness settled over her. She'd looked forward to their departure, when she and Ioan would have more time alone to come to know one another better, had looked so forward to sharing their adventures on the Continent. She hoped to be able to grow more comfortable with the dowager duchess, to see her as family as well.

Then again, she had no idea her entire world would fall apart in the span of twenty minutes and now, she wanted her parents to stay. If nothing else, at least she would have allies. Once they left, she was on her own.

"I will come calling tomorrow to see how you're doing." Pennington caught her by the elbow to guide her back toward the horses. "If everything is as it should be, simply tell Marmaduke neither of you wishes to be disturbed."

"And if he should tell you I've thrown myself off the conservatory roof, you'll know otherwise."

He chuckled, shaking his head. "There is no need for dramatics, Your Grace, lest you wish me to call you Sarah instead of Duch."

"Sarah?"

"Bernhardt? I assumed you've heard of her."

Although she had no idea who Sarah Bernhardt was, she nodded just the same. "Oh, of course. I merely confused her with someone else."

"Perhaps she will tour England again and if so,

Blackthorne might be willing to take you to London to take in a performance."

"I think I would like that."

"Good. Go and bid your parents farewell and hopefully, I *won't* see you tomorrow."

CHAPTER TWENTY-FOUR

Ioan couldn't concentrate. No matter how many times he scanned the column of numbers, the math evaded him. Somewhere, he'd misplaced five hundred pounds, and he needed to find it. Quickly. Although he had enough in his accounts now, thanks to the Montgomery family, having spent the last year watching every last shilling left him trained well enough to find missing money as soon as humanly possible. Old habits and all.

"Your Grace?"

Biting back an oath, he lifted his head to look at Marmaduke, standing in the doorway of his study. "What is it?"

"Lord Pennington is here."

He threw down his pen and sat back in his chair. "Show him in and have a tray of something sent up. I don't give a damn if it's biscuits or pastries, just something to nibble on."

"Yes, Your Grace. And tea as well?"

Ioan shook his head. Tea wasn't nearly strong enough. "Thank you, but no."

Marmaduke bobbed his head. "Of course, Your Grace."

The study doors closed without a sound, only to be opened a few minutes later by Pennington, who stepped into the study and closed the door behind him. "Am I interrupting?"

"Not anything that cannot wait. My duchess has taken it upon herself to redecorate and replenish her wardrobe, and I'm going mad, looking for a wayward five hundred pounds. Perhaps she forgot to have a bill sent to my attention."

A confused look skittered across Pennington's face. "Don't you have a man to do that for you?"

"I do, but I needed the distraction. However"—he flipped the ledger closed and shoved the leather-bound book away—"I think I'll let him tear his hair out instead of me ripping out mine."

"Probably a wise idea." Without waiting for an offer, Pennington moved to the piecrust table. Three decanters stood there, only one remained full. He plucked the stopper from the bottle, and crystal clinked against crystal as he tipped it to pour a small amount into a glass.

"Help yourself," Ioan said, not troubling to keep the dryness from his voice. "What brings you here?"

"I bumped into your duchess earlier, and I don't mind telling you, she looked quite upset. Didn't you assure her you were *not* with Nora?

"I've not had the chance." Ioan fought off a wince even as his gut kinked in irritation. His head still ached, and before he'd had the chance to try to corner Sophie, she'd left to accompany her parents to the train station.

No matter how he tried, things kept happening to prevent his confronting her. Time found a way of slipping by him, and when he did find himself with his bride, some*one* always happened upon them as well, and he wanted no audience when he apologized to her. It was as if the universe was determined to keep them apart.

As much as he regretted the ice between them, he couldn't stop thinking about the night in the chair. Each of the seven nights since that one, he stood outside the door to what had been *his* chambers, determined to throw open the door, and find some way to convince her she'd been wrong. Night after night, he'd stand there, remembering his promise that they would make love every damn night until they conceived a child. Night after night, he wanted only to sweep her into his arms and love her the way he had on their wedding night. Night after night, the narrow bed in his too-quiet, too-drafty dressing room was where he slept.

Damn it all, he was such a bloody fool.

Pennington swirled the whiskey in his glass. "I loaned her my handkerchief to dry her bloodshot eyes, all the while acting as if I had no idea what she spoke of."

"What are you getting at?"

Pennington settled in the leather chair on the far side of Ioan's desk, the glass coming to rest on the chair's arm. "Correct me if I'm wrong, but aren't you and your bride supposed to preparing for your wedding trip now? Traveling around Europe? Tearing the sheets off every bed between here and Rome in sweaty passionate hopes of conceiving your all-important heir?"

"We weren't to leave until after her mother and father returned to America, after the holiday."

"Which they are this afternoon, or so I'm told. Although, I thought they originally planned to be here longer?"

"They did, but plans change and besides, what do you care, Pennington?"

"What happened?"

The doors opened and Marmaduke came in bearing a small tray with the biscuits Ioan had requested. He set it on the piecrust table. "Is there anything else I might fetch for you, Your Grace?"

Ioan shook his head. "We're fine, thank you."

"Of course."

Ioan waited until after the butler left to answer Pennington. He tapped his pen against the blotter on his desk. He'd known Pennington for too long, knew him too well, to be fooled by his seeming innocence of what upset Sophie. "I'm sure my wife has already told you, so stop playing games, Pennington and tell me what you're about?"

"What I'm about—have you gone completely mad, Blackthorne? Have you gone completely and utterly stark, raving mad?"

"It's entirely possible."

"Lady Nora?"

He groaned softly and let his head fall back against the chair. "Not you, too, Pennington. I *told* you what happened."

"So, why does she believe otherwise? I mean, unless you and Nora—"

"Never." Ioan jerked his head up hard enough to send a hot sting shooting along the side of his neck. He ignored it as he added, "Not with a stolen cock, Pennington. I did nothing. *She* kissed me."

"And you didn't kiss her back? And you've done nothing with her at all, despite bering given Sophie's blessing?"

"I told you. I want nothing to do with Nora. I just need to find some way to convince Sophie as well."

"So tell her what you've told me, you dolt!"

Pennington plucked a chocolate biscuit from the platter. "It really isn't quite so difficult, you know?"

"I've tried!" Ioan's voice reverberated about the room. "Bloody hell, I know exactly what she thinks and why, and I've given her no reason to accept my explanation from the start. I was perfectly content to let it be made clear this marriage was for one reason and one reason alone. Her fortune."

Pennington lifted the glass to his lips to throw back a mouthful of whiskey. Lowering the glass, he said, "And now?"

"I was wrong. Sophie's fascinating, Pennington. She's warm and witty, and she's interested in me—*me*, not my bloody title, not this rundown monstrosity of an estate. And she's amazingly gifted, plays the piano, did you know that?"

"Ah, so she does play. I thought you simply used it to seduce her that one afternoon.."

Ioan didn't smile. Didn't so much as grin as the memory sent heat streaking through him. "She doesn't play it well, but she just enjoys it and it shows."

"Doesn't play well, but is amazingly gifted?" Pennington's eyes narrowed. "How is that even possible."

"No, she's a temptress, my friend, and I know that doesn't mean anything to you, but for me? She could be the only woman I've ever been with and that would be fine. I told you about the night—"

"In the chair, yes, I'm afraid you did." Pennington sat back in his chair and stared as if he'd never seen Ioan before. "I've not slept since, I'm afraid. I did *not* need the details, you know."

"She's amazing, Pennington. Simply amazing."

"So *tell* her that."

"She knows I need an heir, and she'd think I was simply buttering her up. It won't go over well at all."

"So, let your own needs go by the wayside for one night, for two, for however long it takes to convince her, you fool jackass." Pennington leaned forward to set his glass on the desk. "Take care of *her*. Make her sing your praises, so to speak, and if she so much as *looks* at your cock, remind her it's about her and get back to the business of making her shiver and shudder against you."

Ioan sighed softly. In theory, it sounded so wonderfully simply. In practice, however... well, it might not be so simple at all. "Well, I might, if she was even speaking to me. Which she's not, by the by."

"Because she thinks you've acquired a mistress, you oaf."

"Yes, Pennington. I am painfully aware of that." His chair squeaked as he rose, then skirted the desk to pour himself a drink. "She *told* me to take Nora as my mistress, that I'd be free to rendezvous with her whenever the mood struck."

"After your duchess conceives, I'm assuming."

Ioan nodded as he poured bourbon into his glass. "She thinks I've betrayed her, yet she knows I need that bloody heir as well, and she's still willing to fulfill that duty."

"So convince her of the truth." Pennington shrugged. "Seems simple enough."

"If I knew how, I would. In the blink of an eye. But, I haven't been able to do that just yet, you know. And in all honesty, I just seem to have a special talent more making a bad situation worse at every turn."

"True. If you can make it worse, you probably will."

At Ioan's glare, Pennington held up a hand. "Forget I said that, won't you? It was stupid."

"I won't correct you."

Pennington drew in a deep breath. "Why not simply try talking to her? One never knows. Besides, perhaps she's looking for you to break the chill. And perhaps," Pennington wiggled his eyebrows, "she enjoys the baby-making as much as you do, only she certainly cannot come right out and *tell* you so now, could she?"

"Well, I certainly hope so!" He shook his head. "But, me being me, I tried that. I tried simply talking to her and managed to bungle *that* as well. And thank you for reminding me of what I'm missing by avoiding my wife's bed."

"Don't snap at me. I've not been with a woman, remember."

Ioan sighed softy, holding the glass in one hand, tracing its rim with another. "Perhaps you're better off."

"Sneaking about? Being made to feel as if I'm doing something dirty and immoral and criminal because the world sees it as dirty and immoral and criminal?" Pennington's smile faded. "I think not. Sometimes I wish I hadn't been born different."

He set down his glass and stood. "Your duchess is special, Blackthorne. Don't let this be the end if you can still salvage it. Nora Etheridge is hardly worth losing a lady such as Sophie. Nora's a whore and has been since we were thirteen years old and she first let Sir Richard touch her bubbies."

"Those were hardly breasts, those little nubs."

"True, but she liked it."

"Be that as it may." Ioan met his gaze and set the glass down untouched. "I was a fool to explode at Sophie the way I did. And to simply walk away the way I did. And for everything else I've done since. I've never regretted anything more."

"So *tell* her that." Pennington clapped him lightly on the shoulder. "Arrange a nice, quiet dinner and a nice quiet evening and talk it out."

"Mother is coming to dinner tonight," Ioan groaned. "There'll be no putting her off, I'm afraid."

"Tell her you plan on conceiving your heir this evening. That should do it."

"You've met my mother, Pennington. Think about what you've just said."

Pennington moved to the doorway. "Just make certain you tell Sophie what you've told me. She'll listen. Promise."

Pennington didn't wait for him to respond, but showed himself out and with a sigh, Ioan moved back to his chair. He swiveled it about to gaze out the window overlooking Blackthorne Hall's rolling back lawns. The gardens were in the distance, naked and barren, but come the spring, he'd be treated to a lush burst of brilliant pinks and lavenders, reds and yellows, in flowers of all sorts, most of which were cultivated right in the Blackthorne greenhouses. He looked forward to lazy strolls through there, with Sophie on his arm, as they caught up with each other's days. He looked forward to picnics out where the leafy beech and elms provided them plenty of shade from the sun-splashed meadows.

He tilted his head back, letting his eyes close as he imagined Sophie lying on a blanket beneath him, her glorious chestnut hair spread beneath her, her lips plump and rosy from his kisses. There, away from prying eyes, they could make love in the copse. When their efforts bore fruit, he imagined lying quietly with her, his head on her breast as he whispered to his unborn child. A child he would later chase through those trees as if it was the greatest game ever invented.

In all the times he thought about taking Nora as his wife, not one of these scenarios ever went through his mind. Nora was not the mothering sort. She would hand off any children to nursemaids and governesses while she spent her time whirling through London society, behaving as a childless woman might. He couldn't see her sitting up all night at a child's sickbed, or comforting one from a nightmare. No, she would again pass that off onto someone else so that her own sleep wouldn't be disturbed.

Somehow, he didn't think Sophie would push any mothering off onto anyone. He simply couldn't see it.

He sat up abruptly and crossed to the bell pull in the corner alongside the bookshelves, then he paced as he awaited Marmaduke.

"Yes, Your Grace?"

"Send word to the dowager duchess that I will have to reschedule our dinner for this evening, and let Mrs. Frayne know I would like a quiet supper served for the duchess and I in our chambers."

"Your Grace?"

"You heard me right, Marmaduke. And the duchess and I are not to be disturbed for any reason. Is that clear?"

"Of course, Your Grace."

"Thank you."

He waited for the butler to leave, then turned back to the window with a smile. Pennington was right. He had to talk to Sophie and clear the air. And what better way to grab her attention than to make this evening all about her?

****

Snow had begun to fall halfway home from the rail station, and Sophie couldn't help but smile as she watched the flakes swirl this way and that. It helped take her mind off how much she didn't truly want to go back to Blackthorne Hall and how much she missed her father. She wouldn't miss her mother's constant criticism or her unabashed social climbing, but she would definitely miss her father's quiet comfort. Where she'd once looked forward to having more time alone with Ioan, she now dreaded it.

As the coach rocked to the top of the drive and she saw the servants had all gathered out front to welcome her, she bit back a sigh. So much ceremony for the smallest of things. She'd never understand how something as silly as a trip to the rail station called for every man and woman employed at Blackthorne to hurry outside and stand silently when she returned.

Yet, there they were, straight-backed and somber faced, standing in order of rank. A footman tugged open the door and said, "Welcome home, Your Grace."

"Thank you, Michael."

He smiled as she stepped down and Mrs. Hopkins came over to say, "Welcome home, Your Grace. His Grace has asked that you go to your rooms as soon as you can. He wishes a word with you."

Although her stomach did a slow, painful roll, Sophie nodded. "Of course, Mrs. Hopkins. But he does remember the dowager will be joining us, doesn't he?"

"I'm afraid he's rescheduled that."

"Oh, he has, has he? I see." She glanced up at the rows of windows high overhead, although she still wasn't entirely certain which ones were the ones to their rooms. Not that it mattered, but it gave her a moment to gather her thoughts and *not* blurt out what she thought of her husband's high-handedness to the servants. "Did he say why?"

"I'm afraid not, Your Grace."

"Of course he didn't. Very well."

As she turned to go inside, the housekeeper fell into step with her. "Did your parents get off without any trouble?"

"They did, thank you. They'll spend tonight in London and then tomorrow, their ship leaves for New York."

"And how are you doing?"

She managed a soft laugh. "I've been better, but I will be fine in time, Mrs. Hopkins. Thank you for asking."

"Of course."

At the foot of the staircase, the housekeeper paused. "Is there anything you need?"

"I don't know. I should probably see what His Grace has already called for in my absence."

"Of course. Very well then, if you'll excuse me."

Sophie nodded and as the housekeeper took herself off, Sophie could only stare up the staircase. What could Ioan possibly need to speak with her about, when he'd gone out of his way over the past week to avoid speaking with her? What was this about?

Her stomach did a slow curdle. Perhaps tonight he would insist they try to conceive. Perhaps in the chair again?

Her mouth dry, she mounted the stairs and plodded up to the gallery. He waited, but she couldn't make her feet move any faster. Dread filled her, but she wasn't certain if it was because she hoped he wanted to make love or because she hoped he didn't. Either way, it was the longest walk of her life, and when she reached their room, her hand hovered above the crystal handle.

The soft *swish* of movement came from behind the door. Ioan was in there. She just didn't know why.

"Only one way to find out."

She opened the door, stepped inside, and froze.

Candles flickered all around, casting dancing shadows and bathing everything in a soft, golden light. Ioan sat at the small table in the far corner, and he rose when he saw her. "I was starting to wonder if your parents had missed their train, that perhaps you were staying in London with them until the morning."

She managed to close the door behind her. "No. They were fine." She looked up at him. "What is this? What is going on?"

He smiled as he crossed to her. "I thought it was time we talked, Duchess."

"Talked?"

"Talked."

Pennington's words echoed within her head. Had he been to speak with Ioan? She didn't know how to ask without just coming out and asking, which she didn't want to do. "Duke, I—"

To her surprise, he caught her face in his hands. His thumbs swept lightly along her cheekbones. Back. Forth. Her eyelids grew heavy, her heart seemed to beat harder against her ribs, and a deep sigh worked its way up from the soles of her staid walking boots. She held it at bay, even as he tilted her head back and his lips came down upon hers.

She caught him by the wrists to draw his hands from her, she had to break the kiss before her head began to spin. If that happened, she'd never be able to turn him away and she honestly didn't know if she could lay with him again, knowing he'd leave her to go to Nora.

Nora.

An icy chill washed over her even as the tip of his tongue slid between her lips, slid silkily along hers. No. She couldn't give him that power over her again.

She jerked back. "Please, stop…"

"Sophie," his voice was soft and tender, "I don't wish to stop."

"But I do." She pulled out of his grasp. "What is this? You don't speak to me for almost a week and when you do, it's because *you've* decided we should do this? Do I not have a say?"

"Of course you do. I'm certainly not about to force myself on you. I've already told you that wasn't an option."

"Oh, well, thank the Maker for that."

Darkness flashed through his green eyes, but was gone as fast as it came. "Sophie, I don't wish to fight with you. I've never wished to fight with you."

"And yet, you—" She sighed softly, casting her gaze to the floor as her thoughts fell all over one another into a jumbled pile.

"And yet I what?"

"Ioan…"

"I've arranged for us to have a quiet supper up here, and we should talk. I mean, *really* talk. You and I have proven we are both very good at hurt and anger, and not so good with admitting our mistakes or when we're wrong." He held up a hand. "And I am taking the first step in admitting to behaving like an ogre and letting you think things that were—"

A sharp knock cut him off and he sighed softly as he said, "Come in."

One of the footmen came in with a tray laden with covered dishes, and a second footman came in bearing wine. They set the table, and then smiled, each saying, "Enjoy, Your Grace."

Ioan waited for them to leave, then moved to draw a chair out. "Please, sit and let me do some sufficient groveling."

She skirted him to sink into the chair, her belly twisting into such apprehensive knots, she wasn't at all certain she'd be able to eat anything.

Wine, however, was a must, and when Ioan poured it into her goblet, it took all the will she possessed to keep from simply throwing it back.

He sat across from her. "I owe you an apology, Duchess."

She froze, the goblet halfway to her lips. Was he about to apologize for Nora? For betraying her and breaking his vows? Was he going to ask for a second chance?

Would she offer him one?

"An apology?" she replied, fighting to keep her voice as unconcerned as she could manage.

He nodded. "I allowed you to think something that was untrue." He lifted his own goblet for a sip, and lowering it, said, "I have no mistresses, Sophie. I have not slept with another woman since you arrived at Blackthorne Hall. Nor will I."

She wanted to believe him, but considering how her instincts seemed so damned determined to be wrong at every turn, to do so seemed so foolish.

And yet, there was no mistaking the sincerity in his voice, or in his eyes as he held her gaze. He reached across the table to cover her hand with his and let his thumb graze along hers. "There is only you, Duchess. Only you."

She stared down at their hands as he tightened his fingers over hers. "Are… if… Why? Why would you let me think such a thing?"

"Because I am a horse's ass at times. Proud. Stubborn. Determined to never be wrong. Perhaps I'm not a horse's ass, but instead an utter jackass."

Sophie looked up then and holding his gaze, replied, "You certainly are."

He didn't say anything at first. The air thickened around them as they just stared at one another.

Then he smiled. "I wish I could argue it, but… I certainly am. But…" His chair creaked as he rose, and her heart tripled its pace when he came around to her and caught her hand to draw her up beside him. "I will also make it up to you."

He loomed over her, his eyes glittered in the candlelight, and caught her face in his hands. Tilting her head back, he whispered, "I *will* make it up to you," before his lips came down upon hers.

They were soft and gentle and despite her mistrust of her own instincts, she melted as they moved against hers. Without thinking, she let her hands come to rest on his forearms, her fingers curling into the solid muscle roping them as she parted her lips and his tongue swept along hers.

His thumbs grazed her cheeks, his kiss slow and deep and filled with a longing she'd come to know so well. She savored every moment of it, and when he drew back, it was to wrap her in his arms and pull her closer still.

His lips brushed her ear and he murmured, "Turn around."

"I beg your pardon."

"Turn around." As he spoke, he turned her and she bit down hard on her bottom lip as he brushed her hair aside and swept a kiss along the slope of her shoulder.

Oh, this feels nice…

He nipped her gently, then soothed the love bite with the tip of his tongue. Her eyelids grew heavy once more and this time, she let them slide shut.

He eased an arm about her waist.

Kissed the nape of her neck.

Tiny fingers of desire uncurled within the pit of her belly. She melted against him, reached over one shoulder to slide her hand about his neck, to let her fingers creep up into his jumble of dark curls. The arm about her waist eased and that hand slid up.

With each kiss, each caress, the ache in her heart subsided a bit more. She didn't know his true motive, and yet, she had the feeling she did indeed know at the same time. Was this his way of trying to right things with her? His way of saying something for which he had no words? This was not simply a means to an end. Each touch, each stroke, had more than that behind it. She felt it in each kiss, each caress. There was most assuredly something else behind each touch.

His breath came warm upon her skin, his lips a whisper against her. His arms tightened about her as if he feared she'd fight him for freedom, to escape.

No, nothing could be further from the truth. As

angry as she'd been, she'd also missed him, missed what she'd hoped had begun to bloom between them.

Maybe—just maybe— it wasn't too late for them.

"Oh…" It emerged as a breathless cry as he cupped her breast to give it a gentle squeeze. He did it again, nipping the slope of her shoulder once more. Without thinking, she rocked her hips back. She couldn't help it. Instinct trumped all else.

He groaned softly into her neck at the contact. The firm ridge of his erection pressed into her and she had the wildest urge to reach behind her and trace the length of him. To tug open his trousers, slide her hand inside to curl about him, and just caress him. Dear God, she'd missed him.

But his hand on her breast eased and tugged her bodice to ease her breast free. When he did, he caught her nipple to roll it slowly between his thumb and forefinger. Heat filled her. Her nipple tightened into a hard bead, one he tormented in the most sensual way possible. How could she possibly deny herself anything that felt this good?

She reached for him, but to her dismay, he angled his hips away from her. "No, love," he breathed, his voice low and husky. "Not this time."

"What?"

He didn't answer, but eased his arm free, and a moment later, the back of her gown fell open. A gentle push and he eased the bodice from her shoulders. Over her hips. To land in a dark green puddle at her feet. Her corset was next. He caught the ribbon of her chemise to tug. The garment opened, and he swept it from her.

He slid his hands up, cupped them at the same time, and rolled both nipples as she bit down hard on her bottom lip to hold back her breathless cry. Deep inside her core, knots tightened. Sensual knots. Desire. Arousal. Pain. Pleasure. The dampness between her legs came swiftly. Her body was such a traitor, readying itself for him, and at the moment, she didn't give a damn.

"So beautiful," he whispered, turning her toward him. He stepped back, his gaze growing greedy as it swept down. His pupils dilated. His smile grew lupine. "I am a lucky man, indeed."

"What are you talking about?"

"You, love," he whispered, stepping back up to her. "Only you."

He offered up a smile that made her heart skip a beat and his eyes glittered like cut emeralds. With that, he bent and captured a beaded nipple between his lips. She shoved her fingers into his hair, her eyes closing as the tip of his tongue swirled about the aching bud, as he drew it deep into his mouth and teased her into a nearly mindless want. She arched toward him, toward the amazing sensations he sent spiraling through her.

Ioan kissed his way down over her belly, sinking to his knees before her. She gazed down in wonder at the sight of the powerful Duke of Blackthorne on his knees before her, gazing up at her as if in awe of her. He looked up, definite wonder in his voice as he murmured, "The most beautiful woman in all of England. On two continents, even. And she is mine."

He held her gaze, his eyes heavy-lidded and seductive, an equally seductive smile on his lips. She'd never seen a man as handsome, as sinfully desirable, as the one before her now.

"What are you up to?" she asked, trailing her forefinger along his cheek.

"I'm going to prove to you, love, there is no one else but you." He leaned in to nuzzle the fluff of chestnut curls between her thighs. Then...

She wanted to melt against him as the tip of his tongue speared those curls. Forget heat, fire tore through her as he swirled his tongue about the nub of her pleasure. With each teasing stroke, he brought her closer to the edge. Closer to nirvana. She arched to meet him, her fingers sinking into his hair once more. He nipped and suckled, licked and flicked, and when she shattered, he didn't let up. Her climax, hot and spicy-sweet, burned through her, left her moaning his name as she fought to prolong the utter bliss of release. It tingled through her, pulsed with each beat of her heart, filled her and washed over her at the same time, and just when she thought it couldn't get any sweeter, he proved her wrong.

"Ioan!" Her hoarse cry echoed about the room, and tears blinded her as the sweetest pleasure she'd ever known engulfed her. Swept her out onto an erotic sea of ecstasy that made her knees weak and her breath almost impossible to catch.

She tugged the handfuls of hair in her grasp. "Please," she said, and she didn't care if she begged, she needed him badly enough to do just that. "Let me..."

He rose, catching her by the wrist. "I am not finished with you, darling."

"I don't care." She pulled free, popped the button on his trousers, found him hot and hard and smooth. He rocked to meet her, his breath coming in harsh gasps as she stroked him faster and faster.

"Wait..." He caught her wrist to stop her. "No..."

"Why?"

He smiled, bringing that hand to his lips. "I don't

want you think I'm keeping my promise to make you regret anything, darling."

For the first time in what felt like a lifetime, she smiled. "I want you. I don't care what the reason is you want me back, Duke, but I want you."

"That's what I mean." He kissing her fingertips. "I don't want us to do this only to create a child. I want to explore with you, Sophie. I want to make you scream my name and claw at my back, and I want to taste you from head to toe and love you until you go mad from it."

Her heart skipped a beat, but in the least painless way possible. "Your Grace…?"

"If we conceive a child tonight, I don't want it to be the last time we share a bed, Sophie. I have no desire to seek out mistresses. I've never wanted that. I've never done that. Not when you are all I need, love. And you *are* all I need, Duchess. Our fortune—*your* fortune— could be gone tomorrow morning, and I would still only need you in my arms to make everything right with my world. And I know how trite that sounds, but I know of no other way to tell you."

"Ioan." She pressed her fingertips against his lips to quiet him. "Before you swoon."

He smiled, kissing those fingertips. Then, he caught her around the waist and lifted her to meet his eyes, his "*Vixen,*" a throaty whisper as his mouth came down upon hers.

He spirited her to the bed, pressed her down into the thick mattress, seized the breath from her lungs as he kissed her more deeply, more thoroughly, than ever before. She melted against him, wound her arms about his midsection, dragged her fingernails down along the smooth planes of his muscled back. He shivered against her, but didn't break their kiss, and as the fire filled her once more, he thrust against her.

She slid her hands down, along the firm curve of his backside. Her hands tightened of their own volition, pulled him into her, and he moaned softly into her mouth, his tongue plunging deep to tangle with hers.

Ioan rolled, bringing her atop him, his hands sweeping down to cradle *her* bottom now. His touch was so light, so teasing, it sent shivers along her spine and made her belly twist into those delightful knots. She gripped the hem of his dove gray silk shirt to tug it upward, and this time, he offered no resistance as she wrestled it over his head. Her hair, pulled free by his fervent hands, spilled around them, and she drew back to find him smiling at her, his eyes glittering in the semi-darkness like faceted jewels.

Scooping a handful of hair away from her face, a hint of self-consciousness swept through her as his gaze roamed over her. Her first instinct was to fold her arms over her chest, to hide herself from that greedy gaze, but then she realized how much darker his eyes seemed. A sense of triumphant power surged through her blood even as she whispered, "Why do you stare?"

"Because you take my breath away," came his whispered response.

She smiled and bent toward him. Their lips met in a fiery kiss. His hands clamped about her hips to pull her firm against him. He thrust. She rocked into him. They sighed as one.

Sophie reached between them, down into the vee of her thighs, and caught the waist of his trousers. He lifted his hips and with one hand, helped her to tug them from his hips. They slid free easily, barely made a sound as she shoved them over the side of the bed, into the shadows of the floor.

A sense of wicked daring scorched her, and without breaking eye contact, she pressed a kiss into his belly, just above his navel. His eyes darkened, his gaze intent as she moved lower. She nuzzled the dark curls between his legs. He reached for her, let his fingertips graze along her cheek,

A deep breath, and she shifted to close her lips about him.

"Sophie…" His voice rose into the darkness, a low, whispery moan as he shoved his fingers into her hair. He twisted. He arched to meet her. He shivered as she explored that part of him with all of the sensual slowness she could muster. He was smooth. Hot. Sleek. And when she slid a curious hand between his thighs to cup him, he sucked in a sharp breath and exhaled with a, "Oh, Sophie, love… yes… do that again…"

She swirled her tongue along him, let her fingers explore him, used his sighs and his thrusts as her guide. His breath came ragged and low, his body shuddering as he managed to grit, "Oh, darling, please… don't stop…"

His fingers tightened in her hair, twisted as he tensed beneath her. She didn't stop, bracing herself for the inevitable.

"Sophie!" His voice echoed all around them as he went over the edge. He shuddered, arched hard, and she accepted him, caressing him as he sank back against the bed. She drew back, pressing a kiss into the front of his thigh as he fought for air and trembled beneath her.

His eyes were closed, his breathing harsh, but as she rested her cheek against his hip, he whispered, "Oh, love… that—that was amaz—amazing…"

"So, I did it right, then?"

He nodded, a sleepy smile curving his lips. "You did it perfectly, darling. Come here."

She slid back along the length of his body, and he wrapped his arms about her. Her head came to rest on his chest, and as she traced the tip of her forefinger through the dark hair sprinkled above his left nipple, he whispered, "You didn't mind swallowing that?"

"No." Her finger went still. She hadn't thought about how he might react to what she'd done. Perhaps she's made a terrible mistake. Her heartbeat echoed in her ears as she forced herself to ask, "Does that disgust you?"

"Not at all." He stroked her back with one hand, then brought that hand up to her head to smooth along her hair. "It's rather something, to know you'd accept that part of me without hesitation."

"Well, it isn't as if I had time to think it over," she said without thinking.

He let out a drowsy chuckle. "I'll fire a warning shot next time."

Sophie lifted her head to find him regarding her with sleepy eyes. "I didn't mean it the way it came out."

"I know, love."

She sank back against him, the silence settling about them peaceful and warm. There was something to be said for just lying in his arms, with his hand moving ever so gently along her hair and his heart beating softly beneath her ear. For the first time in what felt like forever, she was genuinely happy. Sleepy, but happy.

"Ioan?"

"What?"

"I'm sorry I doubted you."

"No. You've no need to be sorry, darling. I'm sorry I gave you reason to doubt. I should have known she was up to something nefarious, and I should have made damn certain Regan was there the entire time." He pressed a kiss into the top of her head. "But you needn't worry about her, or any other lady who sets foot inside this house. They all pale in comparison to the feisty American girl who agreed to take me as her husband."

She chuckled, lifting her head once more. "Why would you say it that way? I think I did quite well in landing a duke, you know."

The linens rustled as he rolled to pin her beneath him. "I insist that I've gotten the better end of the bargain."

She pursed her lips as if thinking it over, then she nodded. "I agree, Duke. You *did* get the better end of the bargain."

He held her gaze, then smiled. "I am very much going to enjoy being married to you, Duchess."

"And I to you." The words *I love you* hovered on the tip of her tongue, but before she could utter them, he dipped toward her and snatched the breath from her lungs once more.

CHAPTER TWENTY-FIVE

He couldn't recall a time when he so enjoyed holding a woman in his arms, when he never wanted her to leave his bed. As Sophie's breath came soft across his bare chest, Ioan didn't care if the sun ever rose again. In fact, he rather hoped it wouldn't, for then this amazing night would never draw to a close.

His wife was a brazen, sensual woman who treated his body to sensations he'd never felt before. She teased him, explored him with her hands, her lips, her tongue. And when she'd taken him in her mouth from start to finish, he thanked the Lord for making him a man and for bringing his beautiful Sophie into his life.

She stirred, lifting her head to squint up at him. "Is everything all right?"

"It's fine, love," he murmured, smoothing her hair away from her face. "Why do you ask?"

"Well, you're still awake."

He smiled. "I'm watching you sleep, darling. Did you know you snore?"

Her eyes widened. "Do I?"

"Yes, but they are tiny snores and rather cute, so you needn't worry."

"It's not very nice of you to point it out, though."

"Perhaps not, but they are."

"You're terrible."

He laughed, tightening his hold on her. "And I am

all yours."

"How fortunate for me," came her dry reply and she rolled away from him to give him her back.

What a sight it was. In the darkness, her pale skin reminded him of alabaster—smooth and unblemished. The coverlet only came up to her hips, the curve of her waist beckoned him closer. He couldn't resist, inching over to press his lips into the warm skin over her left shoulder blade.

Soft. Creamy. A hint of lavender clung to her skin as heady as any perfume. He moved down, along the valley of her spine, up over the curve of her left buttock. He drew the coverlet down as he moved, kissing along the back of her thigh. The entire time, she remained still. Only a slight hitch of breath gave any indication of how she felt.

He kissed his way down.

Her knee.

Her calf.

He moved back up along the opposite leg, pausing long enough to gently nip her right buttock.

She jumped. "Duke!"

"Did I bite too hard, love?"

"No." She settled back against the pillow and he thought he heard her sigh. "It's fine. I was just caught off-guard."

"My apologies." He nipped her again. "How was that?"

"You are terrible."

"And you are delicious." He moved up, over her hip, back up toward her shoulders. As he moved, he flatted himself against her, bracing his weight mostly on his left arm, while with his right hand, he brushed the outer slope of her breast. She shifted ever so slightly and he smiled as he found her nipple. Soft.

But not for long.

Her breathing grew deep as he gently plucked that soft nipple. It beaded slowly beneath his touch. Another sigh rose from her.

He cupped the firm mound.

Her back arched.

He nipped the nape of her neck.

"Ioan…"

He released her breast. Slid his hand along her body, beneath her, into the soft curls that were now dry.

But not for long.

He didn't miss her sharp intake of breath as he parted those curls to stroke her to life. He found that bud that made her shiver and gasp, the one that became so satiny smooth beneath his tongue. He circled it. Caressed over it. Teased it mercilessly.

Her body responded. She grew damp, his fingers moving through that silken wetness toward her core. He slid a finger inside her. She arched to meet him.

He slid it back out.

In.

Out.

She moved with him, her hips rising to nestle his cock against the cleft of her backside. His blood warmed, spilling that heat through him. Fire sparked in his groin once more. Christ, what this woman did to him…

He lifted her hips, positioned himself, and slid inside her, going deep as he breathed, "Sophie…"

She was hot and tight around him, greedily holding him inside her as if afraid he'd disappear otherwise. He moved, the sensations rippling along where they joined to fill him entirely.

Another thrust. And another. He found his rhythm, his thrusts leisurely at first, but that didn't last as his climax grabbed hold of him. His body spurred him on, the pleasure hot and sweet and threatening to consume him.

She moved with him perfectly, arching her hips to take him deeper still. Dear God... the pleasure was enough to immolate him, but when she squeezed him... She brought him to the very edge of madness and held him there, his body trembling, his jaw tight. He didn't want this to be over yet, didn't want to come until she did, but he wasn't at all certain he could hold out.

He forced his eyes open, gazing down at her. Her hands were on either side of her head, fingers twisted in the sheet beneath them. She tensed all around him, and he had to fight to go still as he managed to growl, "Are you close, darling?"

She shook her head. "Don't wait for me, love."

He pressed a kiss into her back. "The hell I won't."

With that, he slid his hand back between her thighs. He found that nub and tortured it as sensually as he knew how. She shuddered beneath him, her eyes closing, her cheeks flushed, her breath coming quicker and quicker. She grew slicker, he thrust harder, and then—

It happened.

They exploded together, each throbbing into the other. He crushed her against his chest as she quivered and squeezed him, crying out her pleasure as he thrust as hard as he could.

They sank against the bed, both fighting to breathe, and he pressed a kiss into her shoulder as he whispered, "I love you, Duchess..."

Beneath him, Sophie trembled. "Ioan, don't say it because you feel you must."

"I'm not, darling. I swear to the heavens." He lifted himself so she could roll over and as she did, he was again struck by just how damn beautiful she was, with her dark hair streaming over the pillows and her luminous dark eyes wide as she gazed up at him.

"Why?"

"Why? How can you ask me that?" He dipped toward her, brushed her lips with his then said, "The question is why not? You're really quite lovable, Duchess. Surely, you must know that by now. Why, even Pennington sings your praises and he's notoriously picky."

She couldn't hold back her smile. "Lovable? I'm not so certain I would agree with you on that."

His chuckle came soft against her ear. "Are you fishing for compliments, love?"

"What? Oh! No, of course not." She drew back far enough to meet his gaze. "I apolo—"

"Don't you dare," he told her. "But I don't think I'd mind hearing you loved me back. Unless, of course, you've decided I've done far too much damage. I wouldn't fault you if you did, you know. I've thoroughly mucked things up."

"You have," she replied, her eyes and voice serious. His heart sank as she gazed up at him, but then, her eyes softened, a smile played about her lips, and she murmured, "But, I do love you, you know. And I have for some time."

He smiled, then leaned once more to kiss her ever so lightly on the lips. "I was worried I might lose you to Pennington," he replied with a wink.

Her smile faded and he fought off the urge to sigh as she eased her arms about his waist and her fingernails danced along his back. "There is nothing between him and I," she told him softly. "I promise."

He kissed her again. "I know, darling. You aren't the sort he fancies."

"I know. He told me."

"He told you?"

"About Lord Mallen."

He relaxed. She told the truth where Pennington was concerned. "How do you know?"

She hesitated. "He told me. I saw him, earlier. And we got to talking and it came out."

"I'll not give him up as a friend."

To his surprise, she smiled. "Why on earth would you? I think he's a sweet man."

Relief surged through him. He was, as far as he knew, the only one who knew of Pennington's proclivities. Not even Nora knew. "It doesn't color your view of him?"

"I admit," she hedged, her hands going still, "I was taken aback at first. But, it doesn't change who he is, only who he loves. And who am I to question that? I'm only a simple girl from America."

"You are anything *but* a simple girl. Trust me on that. But, how is it he told you? It's hardly a thing one would blurt out."

To his surprise, her cheeks reddened. "I confessed I wished he'd taken an interest in Lady Nora."

Ioan stared at her for a long moment. "Sophie, I told you—"

"Yes, I know that, but still... he's so very handsome and so very charming and I thought if he tried, he could win her away and I wouldn't have to worry so much."

With a low sigh, he shifted off her, stretching out alongside her. "I've told you, you needn't worry about her at all."

"How do I *not* worry? She threw herself at you the day after our wedding. You'd just been married, and that didn't give her pause. Why should I think anything else would, either?"

He didn't know what to tell her. Nora was headstrong, and when she had her sight set on someone or something, she didn't rest until she snatched it. He'd seen it happen too many times to assure Sophie it wouldn't happen again. All he could do was reassure his wife she had nothing to fear. Ever.

He rolled onto his belly, bunching the pillow beneath his head as he turned to look at Sophie. "She can try all she wishes," he finally said, "but it will only be a waste of her time. I cannot promise you she won't try again, darling. What I *can* promise is that I will never reciprocate."

She went quiet, then murmured, "May I ask you something?"

"Of course, love. Ask me anything your heart desires."

"Did you not want to look at me, is that why you kept me facedown?"

Remembering their conversation the last time this position came up, he rose and leaned to brush her lips with a kiss. "Not at all, Sophie. I thought it would feel good for you. A different angle. More depth. You certainly seemed to enjoy it."

A winsome smile tugged at her lips. "I did."

"And just wait, love," he told her, "for there are far

more positions I fully intend to explore with you."

"There are?"

"Oh, yes. And trust me, you *will* thank me."

Her eyes darkened in the soft light, and even in the semi-darkness, her flush was visible. "Perhaps we might try it in the chair again?"

A jolt shot through him. "You enjoyed that?"

"It's probably wicked of me to admit," she murmured, holding his gaze, "but, yes."

He bit back a groan at the image of her astride him, facing the mirror, to put her on such erotic display to him, burned through him. "As did I, Duchess." He drew her close for a slow, lingering kiss. Breaking it, he whispered, "And we most certainly *can* definitely do it in the chair again. Whenever you wish."

CHAPTER TWENTY-SIX

The tree in the gallery looked as if it would scrape the vaulted ceiling, and Sophie smiled as she craned her neck to take it all in. "Did you cut the largest one in the forest?"

"I did no such thing. I didn't cut it at all," Ioan told her, easing his arm about her waist to pull her against his chest. "Are you ready for the influx tonight? This is your debut as hostess, Duchess."

"Of course I am." She spun in his arms to face him and eased her arms about his waist. He smelled of snow and frosty air, his dark hair more tousled than ever. "So, who *did* cut this tree down?"

"I had help. Pennington thought the Duchess of Blackthorne should have the grandest tree in Berkshire for her first Christmas here, and I agree. It took us and Mr. Harrington to cut it and bring it to the house. Marmaduke almost fainted when he saw it."

"Is it still snowing?"

"It is, love. Would you care to see?"

"Yes, actually. I would."

"Well, then come with me." He tucked her arm through his and escorted her out through the front doors. Once outside, he swept off his coat to drape about her shoulders. "I don't want you to catch a chill, darling."

She smiled at him. The last few weeks had been the most wonderful weeks of her life. Every night, Ioan swept her into bed, where he loved her until she thought she'd go mad from it. And he hadn't lied about the positions—he found new and wonderful ways to make her tremble and rake her fingernails along his arms, or his back, or whatever part of him she could reach. In return, she tried to treat him to the same sensual delights, using her imagination and hitting more than she missed. But, the misses usually ended with them laughing and finding a way to turn it into a hit, so night after night, she drifted off, wrapped in his arms, secure in his love and happier than she'd ever thought she could be. More than once, she found herself astride him in the chair, sometimes facing the mirror, sometimes not. But, each time left her trembling in his arms, her head spinning from the fiery pleasure he sent through her,

But tonight would be the true test. Lady Nora Etheridge was on the guest list. Although Ioan had been perfectly willing to cross her off, Sophie wouldn't hear of it. She wasn't about to go out of her way to avoid Nora. Rather, she wanted to drive home to Nora how she would never again kiss Ioan St. John. Not if she wanted to remain healthy and avoid being socially shunned.

Their first Christmas together. How she looked forward to it. It would be odd, not being in New York, with her mother and father and their servants all around, but according to their last letter, they had arrived home safely, the trouble with Samuel was rectified, and they would spend the holidays with him and his wife, Charlotte, in Connecticut. As fond as she was of her brother and his wife, she'd much rather be spending the holiday exactly where she was. She'd sent her love and gifts, and sent a package to Joy as well, including an invitation to Blackthorne Hall for that summer.

Hopefully, Joy would be able to spend the season with them. It would make her ever-growing happiness just about perfect if she could.

The dowager stumped out to stand beside Sophie. "Did something happen out here?"

"No, Mother," Ioan replied, easing his arms about Sophie to tug her against his chest. "We are simply enjoying the snow."

"I do hope it doesn't keep our guests away," Sophie said, holding out one hand, palm up, to catch flakes on her outstretched palm.

"Nonsense," the dowager sniffed. "No one ever backs out of a party at Blackthorne because of a silly thing such as snow."

Ioan gave her a gentle squeeze. "Worry not, love," he told her, pressing a kiss into the top of her head. "Mother is right about that."

The thunder of horse hooves sounded well before Lord Pennington rounded the bend to come up the drive, and Sophie smiled as he drew his mount to a halt. "Good day, all! Lovely weather, isn't it?"

He swung down from his saddle, the reins resting in one hand, and crossed over to them. "Did something happen out here?"

"No." The dowager rapped her cane against the stone. "Nothing has happened. We are but enjoying the snow."

"Perhaps later we can arrange for a snowball fight," Pennington chuckled, leaning over to brush Sophie's cheek with a kiss. "The English winter suits you, Duch," he said. "You glow."

"Why thank you, my lord."

"My *lord*? *Duch*?" The dowager turned to Sophie.

"He is Pennington to you and you are *not Duch* to anyone. Indeed!"

"Mother," Sophie said, as she turned to her mother-in-law with a smile, shaking her head, "only his lordship may address me as Duch and he knows it. And"—she turned her smile to Pennington, winking as she added— "he is *not* to do it in the presence of anyone other than the three of us."

"I wouldn't dream of it," he said, offering up a contrite look. "Forgive me, Duchess Mary. I beg you."

"You are a scamp." The dowager tapped his shin with her cane. "Go take that horse to the stables before it catches a chill. And when you return, remember your manners, Pennington."

He winked and brushed *her* cheek this time. "I do love you, Duchess Mary. Iron Duchess, indeed. You are softer than dandelion fluff, you know." He whistled as he swung back into his saddle and turned the horse in the direction of the stables.

The dowager sighed softly. "He will never change." She cast a glance at both Ioan and Sophie. "You *did* make certain to invite Lord Mallen this evening, didn't you? No one should be alone at Christmastime."

Sophie looked up at Ioan, who merely nodded. "I usually do."

"Good." The dowager gazed off in the direction of the stables. "He should be happy as well."

"I—I don't know what you mean, Mother."

"I mean, I've known about him and Mallen for some time now. And although I would never admit it beyond these walls," the dowager shrugged, "they make quite a lovely couple, if I do say so."

Ioan met Sophie with a shocked look and Sophie

said, "Wait… you know?"

"Of course I do," the dowager said over one shoulder as she headed back inside. "I've known since he was a boy and flirted tirelessly with Ioan. I do believe the last one to see it was Pennington himself."

And with that, she made her way into the house and Sophie shook her head as she looked up at Ioan. "She is an endless wonder, you know."

He still stared after his mother, but nodded. "That she is. Just when I think I know her…"

****

Despite the snow, all who were invited showed up at Blackthorne Hall, and Sophie greeted each of her guests with a warm smile, her arm tucked through Ioan's. Her fingers tightened about his forearm, however, as she stopped to welcome Lady Nora Etheridge.

"How lovely to see you," Sophie said, keeping her voice as neutral as she could.

"Good evening, Duchess," Nora's smile wavered ever so slightly as she glanced at Ioan, "Duke, the decorations look lovely."

"Thank you. I daresay, my wife outdid herself this year. I've never seen Blackthorne so festive."

"I had some help," Sophie told him, giving his arm a squeeze.

"Yes, well, Blackthorne Hall looks lovely. And thank you so much for the invitation. I wasn't at all certain I would receive one."

"Because you kissed my husband?" Sophie asked, fighting the urge to smile at the sudden look of terror that crossed Nora's face. Surely Nora didn't think she'd get off easily, did she? If so, she was sorely mistaken.

"I never did apologize for that," Nora began, "and

I—"

"Please," Sophie cut in, her smile still firmly in place, "don't bother with an apology we both know is a lie. And keep this in mind, if you so much as think to do it again," she added, her voice as warm and friendly as she could muster, "I will toss you out of here by the scruff of your neck and then I will *ruin* you but good. Am I clear?"

A fiery blush stretched across Nora's slanted cheekbones, and murder shone in her eyes even as she replied, "Quite."

"Good. Now, if you will excuse us"—Sophie gazed up at Ioan, who looked more than a little amused at Nora's reaction to her threat—"Lord Pennington has returned from the stables."

She gave a gentle tug on Ioan's arm and as they stepped away from Nora, he leaned close to whisper, "You are terrible, love."

"I meant every word of it," she told him. "I haven't forgotten, nor have I forgiven. I want her to see with her own eyes she stands no chance."

Ioan dropped his arm to slip it about her waist. A gentle tug, and he pulled her into the empty second library, where he then proceeded to wrap her in his arms, bend her back, and kiss her until she thought she'd swoon from it.

"What was that for?" she breathed when he finally let her stand upright.

"Because I love you, you bloodthirsty Yank."

"Bloodthirsty? I didn't threaten to do anything more than toss her bodily from our home and see to it every door in London is slammed in her face."

"I know. And hearing you say it arouses the hell out

me."

"Ioan, *everything* arouses you these days."

"That is not true. Only everything about you and you can hardly fault me for that, now, can you?" He trailed his fingers along her back, so lightly, she only barely felt them. "In fact, if I didn't think someone would barge in on us, I'd pull you down onto one of those sofas and let you have your way with me right now."

"And if I didn't think someone would barge in on us, I'd absolutely take you up on your offer." She wound her arms about his neck. "But, since we are both probably right about that, we should probably wait until everyone takes their leave."

"I suppose. Although, I must confess, I rather like the idea of trying to do it without getting caught. Doing something wicked can be such fun as well."

She rather liked the idea as well. It was so wickedly daring and so unlike anything she would ever do normally. But this was nether the time nor the place, no matter how enticing.

"Another time."

His hands skimmed down over her backside, cupped her cheeks, and gave a gentle squeeze. "I'm going to hold you to that, Duchess."

"I expect no less." She pushed up onto her toes to brush his lips with hers. "Now, before anyone misses us, we should go back out."

But he seemed to be in no hurry to return to the party. Instead, he just drew her closer and whispered, "I love you, Duchess."

Hearing those words would never grow old. They would never not cause that delicious flutter in her belly. Only now, as she gazed up at him, his dark hair looking as if she'd run her fingers through it during a passionate moment, his green eyes soft and tender, the fluttering in her belly had nothing to do with his words and everything to do with the words she was about to say.

"We love you, too, Duke," she murmured, waiting to see the question in his eyes.

He didn't disappoint. "We?"

"Your son and I," she replied. "Or perhaps your daughter. We won't know until the summer, but the future Lord or Lady Blackthorne—or whichever they will be called—will arrive with the warmer weather."

"Wait..." He stepped back. "You're... you're pregnant?"

She nodded. "I am. By almost six weeks, if my math is correct. But, I haven't told anyone aside from you."

"And do you wish me to keep it a secret?"

"Not if you don't wish to," she shook her head. "I just thought you should know before anyone else."

He smiled, tugging her close, wrapping his arms about her, and lifted her to meet his eyes. "We are having a baby, darling."

She couldn't help but return his smile. His eyes sparkled more than she ever thought a man's eyes could could and he seemed genuinely tickled by the notion of their having a child. Somehow, she didn't think it was simply because he had his heir. "Yes, I know."

"And I am going to drive you mad with fussing over you, just so you're forewarned."

"Duke, I wouldn't expect anything less of you."

"And you won't put up a fight when I do it?"

"Now, let's not go that far."

His laugh echoed through the empty room. "And if I tell you I plan to spoil you both rotten?"

She gazed down at him, into those brilliant green eyes, and whispered, "Joy was right, you know."

"What was she right about?"

"When she found out I was coming here to marry a duke, she told me, *some girls have all the luck*. And do you know something? She was right. Some girls do have all of the luck. And I am the luckiest of them all."

"Is that so?"

"It is."

He drew her down to brush her lips with his. "You are not the only lucky one, darling. Not by half. Now, let's go and dance and sip champagne and enjoy this evening, and once everyone leaves, I will lock our bedroom door and show you how lucky we both are."

"I like the sound of that." She smiled as he set her down, and as she slipped her arm through his, she gazed up at him. "But, I do have one question."

"What's that, love?"

"Do either of these doors lock?"

"I believe so, why?" He grinned as she squeezed his upper arm.

"I think I should like to try it on a sofa."

"Your wish is my command, darling."